DEMON REIGN

DEBBIE CASSIDY

CONTENTS

A Brief Glossary

The demon realm is a big place, so I thought I'd give you a little breakdown of the setup, a little reminder to refer back to if you get confused. I hope it helps.

There were nine demon realms accessible via nine monoports, but only three remain active.

Libidine: ruled by Prince Merihem and linked to the Shadow Court, which is ruled by Duke Umbrane.

Iram: ruled by Prince Levistus and linked to the Court of Flame. The Court of Flame is ruled by Duke Ignatius.

Superbia: ruled by Prince Ramiel and linked to the Ivory Court. Duke Zepar rules the Ivory Court.

Morningstar : a neutral ground ruled by Satan.
Satan: a title which Beelzebub held and now is to be passed down to one of his heirs.

Now on to the creature classifications.

Pure Daimon: belong to the abyss. There is a lot more around these beings, but I don't want to put spoilers here.

Pure Demon: live in the demon realm or the courts. Some are elevated to Devil because they trade using contracts rather than trading in favors and goods (e.*g.* zuni, imps, and Erinyes).

Fallen: celestials who were exiled from heaven and now reside in the demon realm. They rule it. There are several generations of them, including the princes who are original fallen from the first generation.

Abyssbloods: born of demon and daimon unions (e.g., incubi and succubi).

Nephalem: creatures born of fallen and demon or fallen and abyssblood unions. Satan spawn are Nephalem as Beelzebub was a fallen.

Nephilim: creatures born of fallen and human union—they were wiped out a long time ago.

Demon Blood: demon and human union.

We also have **djinn** and **conji** (mage-like beings) who entered the demon realm from another world. They do not fall into any of the above categories.

Previously on Demons of Morningstar

Our heroine Nyx is stabbed by Dhuma, a daimon who was being held prisoner by Prince Merihem. Dhuma was one of the daimon queen's mates. The injury sends Nyx to an in-between place for high daimon. Yep. Nyx finds out she's part high daimon. And with the help of three guardians, she makes it out of the in-between and to a doorway that allows her to go back to her body.

But the princes aren't happy about her existence because high daimon and fallen can't procreate, and she's an anomaly. So they put cuffs on her to mute her power and say there'll be a trial to determine what to do with her.

Dhuma explains that he knew what she was and that was why he stabbed her—to activate her power. He'd hoped she was the daimon queen reborn. But she isn't. Still, he pledges his allegiance to her as he knows she is of the same bloodline—a royal bloodline—and goes back to Morningstar with her.

Orina is worried about Nyx and tries to find out what's happened to her. She finds out that Nyx is Satan spawn and has been roped into the ascension trials and reaches out to the Order to try to get her access to Morningstar's keep. She also contacts Quinn, their best friend, to let her know that Nyx might be in trouble.

The news of Nyx's heritage means that there is a target on her back, so Ignatius and Zepar agree to take turns keeping her safe with invites to the Ivory Court and the Court of Flame.

Sev finds out that Erinea is working with Umbrane and that she's managed to secure votes from the nobles to have Nyx executed.

Artimus, Sev, Ignatius, and Loke plot and plan on how to save Nyx by getting her out of the demon realm and tell her that an exit will be available for her once she returns from the Court of Ivory.

A strange breach linked to the fawda is detected in the Court of Flame while she's there with Ignatius, and while at the Court of Ivory, there's an attack on her life, which Zepar saves her from.

Umbrane thwarts Nyx's escape plan, and the trial goes ahead. Despite her efforts and the testimony of her siblings, the princes decide to execute Nyx. They have a special weapon—a celestial sword, modified to kill high daimon. But before Levistus can kill her, Sin shows up, and it's revealed that he's Lucifer and that he has already claimed Nyx as his electus (mate).

The final trial takes place where the siblings are tasked with retrieving a key from one of the barred demon realms. Although they succeed, they end up trapped by lava. But before it can take them, they all vanish into thin air.

All caught up? Goodie.

Now let's see what happens next...

ONE

ARTIMUS

I learned restraint as a youth. Being locked away to detox after my blood and sex spree was an exercise in control. The agony of those long days and even longer nights was sufficient to teach my mind and body the value of moderation. But now hunger is a constant simmer in my veins, and the beast waits beneath my skin, looking for a lapse, for one moment of weakness, to spring free from its prison and devour.

Nyx has been missing for almost forty-eight hours, and I'm beginning to lose my grip on my emotions.

My skin itches, and my throat aches, desperate for the hot, coppery flood of blood. I assuage it with the fiery sear of whiskey. It burns, momentarily blocking out the voice in the back of my mind that urges me to smash the Atrium to smithereens and tear out Erinea's throat.

How can she look so fucking calm?

My gaze flits to Zepar, standing in a corner of the room

with his mother, Odette, her head bowed as she whispers to him.

His hands are clenched into fists, and his wings are visible, signs the fallen is just as distressed as me. Even Umbrane looks anxious, sitting there with his long, pale fingers curled around a half-empty glass of whiskey, dark brows low over his eyes.

I wish Ignatius and Sev were here. I'm sure The Duke of Flame would be here if he knew the spawn were missing. He probably hasn't received my message yet. And Sev...I've sent him and Dhuma out to search the nearby villages for the spawn.

It's a long shot, and I doubt they'll find the spawn in a tavern drinking ale, but it gives them something to do, and I, of all people, can attest to how important it is to be doing something, *anything* right now. The task also serves to keep the nightmare away from Umbrane and the princes. With Nyx and the spawn missing, I wouldn't put it past Umbrane to demand the princes give Sev back to him.

Every moment is another moment that Nyx is in danger, and I'm stuck here. Impotent. Waiting for news, for someone else to *do* something.

I want to be in the demon realm, scouring the Scarlett Canyon for Nyx and her siblings, but instead I'm here, cloistered in this fucking room on Ramiel's orders.

"They'll find her," Zepar says. "They have to."

I look up to find him watching me. Am I that easy to read right now? I relax the grip on my glass a little—any tighter and it'll shatter.

"This makes no sense," Erinea says. "How could they just...vanish? None of them have conji power."

"But the high daimon, Nyx, might have some ability,"

Odette says. "We have no idea what she's truly capable of yet."

"You've bound her powers with muting cuffs, Mother," Zepar snaps. "Or have you forgotten that?"

"Maybe the cuffs failed," Umbrane says. "If Nyx did this...she would have brought her siblings back to Morningstar."

"Providing she even did it," Erinea says. Her eyes fly wide, and her mouth makes an 'o.' "Maybe she didn't do it on purpose. Maybe it just...happened in the heat of the moment."

"Maybe she didn't do it at all," Zepar growls. "*Maybe* we need to be contemplating the possibility that there are other forces at play here. Have you forgotten the assassination attempts on the siblings? How many spawn have we already lost?"

He's right. "Not to mention Satan's murder. There's a killer out there, a movement that wants power."

The fawda are out there—a movement hellbent on taking over the demon realms. They don't belong in this world but somehow followed the djinn into the demon realm and are, only now, making a play for power. They used Nyx's sibling Veena to murder several of the spawn, tried to kill Nyx twice, and possessed an original fallen, but we have no idea who's in charge or where their base is.

The only clue we have is the breach in the Court of Flame that Ignatius and his djinn are monitoring.

We need to consider the possibility that the fawda might be involved in the spawns' disappearance. The original fallen know about the fawda. They know because we saved Prince Merihem from a fawda plot, freeing him from the marid possessing his body. Odette and Zepar know everything too. They were there when Ignatius tricked the marid into vacating Merihem's body, and Umbrane...For all we know, he's working *with* the fawda. He was responsible for our carriage being diverted into the Old Forest. Sev overheard him speaking to someone about it.

Part of me wants to tell Ramiel and the other originals about his duplicity, but with Sev as our only witness, it's unlikely they'll believe me. There's no love lost between Umbrane and Sev, and the princes know it. It would be Umbrane's word against Sev's.

I study Umbrane over the rim of my glass, looking for a sign that he's complicit in the disappearance of the spawn, but either he's a fabulous actor or he's genuinely as flummoxed as we are. His custodia and betrothed, Veena, is also missing.

No, I don't think he's involved. This time.

I top up my glass and drain the contents, cursing my metabolism for not allowing me to get intoxicated.

Zepar makes a sound of exasperation, then stalks over to the drinks tray and pours himself one too.

"Zepar, my boy, you must keep a clear head," Odette croons. "Your father might need to call on you to assist in the search."

He has his back to his mother, so she doesn't see the look that crosses his face, but I do. The corners of his mouth tighten, and his eyes flash with annoyance. He's holding on to his temper by a thread, but when he speaks, his tone is cool and unaffected.

"When has Prince Ramiel ever asked for anyone's help? He demands. He orders. He does not ask."

Odette looks like she's about to argue but then presses her lips together, sighing through her nose.

There are family politics here, but I can't bring myself to care. "I need to get out of here."

"You can't," Erinea says. "Prince Ramiel was clear that we have to stay here."

"And why do you think that is?" Umbrane says bitterly. "They suspect that one of us may be responsible."

Erinea pales. "No..."

I've come to the same conclusion, and I'm surprised Erinea hasn't. Odette and Zepar don't seem surprised either.

"Ramiel knows I'm loyal to him," Odette says with a smirk.

In other words, she's the guard dog in our midst.

I pull out a chair and am about to park my ass when the air ripples.

Prince Ramiel and Prince Levistus stride into the Atrium through the southern exit, bringing the scent of winter and the chill of frost with them.

Ramiel nods at Odette, who hurries to the drinks tray and pours two glasses of whiskey, which she hands to Ramiel. He passes one to Levistus and downs the other.

Levistus pulls out a seat and drops into it before taking a leisurely gulp of his drink. He runs his hands through his golden locks, and they slick back, wet from the melting frost clinging to them.

"Any news from Merihem or Sin?" Ramiel asks Odette.

"They're not back yet," she says.

Ramiel sucks on his bottom lip and shakes his head. "We scoured the frozen lands beyond the Scarlett Canyon as far as the Solum Flumen. There's no sign of the spawn. Our conji aren't able to pick up any signatures either."

The Solum Flumen is one of the demon realm's five main rivers, and it's several miles away from the monoport to Fertilis. There was no doubt that they'd searched thoroughly.

"Are you certain the lava didn't take them?" Odette asks tentatively.

Ramiel shoots a sneer her way. "Are you suggesting I should doubt the evidence of my own eyes?"

"I would never—"

"Then why ask such an inane question?"

"Don't speak to her that way," Zepar says.

Ramiel's eyes narrow and fix on his son. Tension saturates the air, thrumming against my skin. "Excuse me?"

Zepar's jaw flexes.

Back down, you fool.

But he doesn't.

Instead, he takes a step forward. "You heard me."

Odette crosses the room and slaps Zepar hard across the face. "Don't." She glares at him, but I catch the edge of desperation in her eyes and recognize the slap for what it truly is.

Protective instinct for her son.

Zepar swallows and slowly, stiffly, inclines his head. "My apologies."

Ramiel exhales through his nose. "Accepted. It is a trying time, and—"

The stench of burning flesh and feathers fills the room.

Heat blasts my back, and perspiration breaks out across my brow.

Erinea gags, then slaps her hand over her mouth, her eyes wide with horror and fixed on the entrance behind me.

Sin stands in the doorway, skin smoldering and bubbling in places as it heals from several burns. Ash falls to the ground behind him where his feathers have been eaten away by fire, and his hands are charred to the bone in places, but he doesn't let go of the figure cradled in his arms.

Nyx?

My heart lifts then plummets, because the figure is burned to a crisp and gasping its last breath.

Two

The figure in Sin's arms isn't Nyx.

The relief is a hot flood of adrenaline that leaves my limbs trembling.

"Merihem!" Ramiel rushes forward.

Levistus's chair clatters to the ground as he joins his brothers.

Yes, the burned, gasping creature in Sin's arms isn't Nyx, but that means she's still out there somewhere.

Still out there, or even...No, I can't think it. I won't.

Sin crosses the room with his cargo, and Ramiel and Levistus step back to give him space as he lays Merihem on the huge conference table. The original fallen opens his eyes, startling white against the blackened, burned skin of his face.

"Well, that wasn't fun." His voice is a painful wheeze.

"Hush, you reckless fool," Sin growls.

Merihem's chuckle morphs into a dry, rasping cough.

"Water!" Ramiel orders.

Odette hands him a glass.

Sin steps away from the table as Ramiel gently lifts Merihem's head to feed him the water.

"What happened?" Levistus demands.

"Merihem decided to fly too close to the lava, that's what happened," Sin replies.

"I thought I saw—" Merihem breaks off to cough. "Saw something."

There's a soft crackling sound, and Sin's wings flare slightly. He's healing quickly. The charred patches of skin on his face are almost gone.

"You'll heal," Sin says. "Eventually."

"Yet you seem to have healed already," Levistus points out, his tone bitter.

Sin gives him a flat look, and Levistus averts his gaze. Well, that's a first. Levistus isn't one to back down from anything or anyone, and yet here he is, dropping his gaze after one look from Sin.

There's no doubt in my mind who's in charge now.

"He'll heal," Sin says again. "In a few days, he'll be as good as new, but it'll be painful."

"Odette?" Ramiel turns to the conji.

She bobs her head. "I'll make a healing tincture to speed up the process and numb the pain." She sweeps from the room.

Merihem closes his eyes on a shuddering sigh.

"What now?" Ramiel looks to Sin. "Where do we search now?"

"Maybe we need to consider the possibility that they're dead," Erinea says flatly.

Sin's lip curls. "I don't recall asking your opinion, Eryines."

Erinea presses her lips together, but I can tell from the

fire in her eyes that she's about to say more. Challenge him maybe?

I have no love for the woman, but I can't stand by and watch her commit suicide. "Shut up and sit down, Erinea."

She stares at me in shock because I've never spoken to her this way. But damn does it feel good.

Sin slides a glance my way, the corner of his mouth lifting. Yes, he knows what I've just done. "She's alive," he says to me. "I can feel it through our mate bond; she is my electus, after all. And if she's alive, then so are the others, because there is no way she'd let it be otherwise."

The relief his words bring leave me lightheaded.

"So, I ask again," Ramiel says. "What now? We've searched the whole of Morningstar and every court. The human and Mageri government report no magical disturbances in their territory." He stands and rakes a hand through his hair. "We've searched everywhere."

"Have we?" Sin arches a brow.

It takes a moment, but then the answer hits me. Ice grips my nape. "You can't mean—"

"The abyss? Yes," Sin says.

"It can't be," Ramiel says. "The wards. The lock..." But he doesn't sound so sure.

"She's a high daimon," Levistus says. "A fallen, high daimon abomination."

Sin's smile is almost smug. "Yes, who knows what my little electus is capable of."

He's proud of her. Proud that she may have somehow gotten herself trapped in the abyss. "Then we need to go after them."

Sin slow blinks at me. "We can't."

"Why not? They're the spawn. We need them alive. We

can send in a small team and shut down the wards as soon as they pass through."

"That would be a good plan," Sin says, "*if* we had the key to the wards."

"What do you mean, you don't have the key?" Zepar asks. "Where is it? Who has it?"

Sin slow blinks again. "The key was hidden in Fertilis, but now...Now it's with the spawn."

Nyx and her siblings have the key to the abyss. And they might be trapped inside.

"Do they know what the key is for?" Zepar asks.

Sin shakes his head. "No."

Zepar turns away, hands on his hips, shaking his head. "Fuck..."

"I can't believe there's nothing we can do," Erinea says. "Morningstar needs a Satan. We *need* the spawn back, or all the power..." She trails off, realizing that she may be saying too much.

"There is nothing to do now but wait," Sin says. "Wait and trust that the spawn will figure out where they are and what they have in their possession. We must trust they'll find the exit back to the demon realm."

"And if they don't?" Zepar demands. "Come on, you're telling me you guys didn't build some kind of failsafe? A way to override that key?"

"There is no way to override it," Ramiel snaps, irritation beating off him in waves. "If the spawn are in the abyss, then they're on their own."

But it's worse than that.

If the spawn are in the abyss, then they're all in mortal danger.

THREE

NYX

"Is there anyone out there?" Veena's voice trembled with fear. "Nyx?"

I scanned the empty street beyond the grimy, cracked window of the building we were bunked in. It smelled mildly of cheese and something musty and gross, but my olfactory system was adjusting, and soon I wouldn't notice the iffy smells.

"It's clear. They've gone." *They* being the strange hound-like creatures that had chased us for almost a mile.

I ducked away from the window and sat on the dusty wooden floor of what once must have been a store. The place was mostly stripped bare, but there were a few boxes in the back that I'd look through as soon as my heart stopped trying to crack open my ribcage.

"You all right?" Keelan asked.

He'd folded his huge frame into a crouch by the shelving unit opposite me. His face was smudged with dirt, and he had a cut on his brow. He looked as exhausted as I was.

I gave him a weary smile. "I'm good."

"Why haven't they come for us?" Veena asked in a small voice. "I don't understand…"

Tristeene put an arm around her, but my zuni sibling didn't relax against her. She was too wired. We all were.

Guilt twisted in my chest. "I'm sorry."

"Stop that!" Tristeene said. "This is *not* your fault."

But it was wholly my fault. "I brought us here."

I wasn't sure how, but I'd felt the burst of desperate power that had shattered the cuffs on my wrists when I'd wished to take us home, back to our quarters. But something had gone wrong, and the power inside me had brought us here.

I'd been thinking about why for several hours now, and I'd concluded that maybe my power was linked to my ancestry. My blood. So it brought me to my ancestral home. The abyss. It was the only theory that made sense.

I'd tried to zap us out of here. Tried over and over but with no luck. We were stuck.

"You saved us from being swallowed by lava," Mallini pointed out. "Trust me, this is better than that." She leaned her head back on the unit behind her and closed her eyes. "Let's keep things in perspective."

My Erinyes sibling was a warrior. A fighter who dealt in logic and knew when to shut down emotion. We were similar like that and in so many other little ways, which was probably why we'd clashed so hard in the early days, and although I took on board her words now, I couldn't dispel my doubts completely.

The lava would have been a quick death, but the abyss housed the sickness—a taint that wouldn't just corrupt our bodies but also our souls. I'd seen the lost spirits of daimon when I'd been in daimon limbo. They'd been desperate to find their way to peace but were locked out because of the sickness that tainted them.

So yeah, I wasn't sure I'd done anyone a favor. In fact, I was beginning to worry I may simply have delayed the inevitable.

We'd been here for almost two days, and no one had come for us. Despite my best efforts, I was beginning to lose hope of a rescue.

The tall, dark towers of the city were visible in the distance. I remembered them from the paintings Ignatius had shown me. They were linked by walkways high up in the air. High up enough to create a lockdown and stop the sick getting in. If anyone was still alive and unaffected by the sickness here, then they'd be holed up in one of those towers. I was sure of it because that's what I'd do. Take myself above it all and build traps to keep out the infected.

The others agreed with my theory. They trusted me, but the past few hours of running, hiding, and waiting for the fallen to come save us was wearing on me. Was I wrong? Would anyone figure out where we were and come for us?

"They can't possibly know where we are," Mallini said matter-of-factly. "This place is locked down."

I guess I wasn't the only one with doubts.

"They probably think we're dead," Tristeene added.

My heart sank. We needed to avoid this line of thought because it would fuck with our morale.

"I don't believe that." Gus toyed with the leather strap hanging around his neck. It held a piece of iron alongside the key we'd found in Fertilis. I'd been afraid we'd lose it, so I'd given it to him to keep hold of. "They might think *we're* dead," he continued, "but Sin will know Nyx isn't."

I met his gaze sharply. "What do you mean?"

He glanced at my chest. "The mark. The one he put on you."

I touched the spot through my shirt. "The electus thing?"

Gus's warm blue eyes filled with confidence. "You're his mate. He'll know you're alive, and he won't stop looking."

Sin had a plan for me. I wasn't sure what, but the fact that he'd been in my life all these months, the fact he'd marked me, protected me, told me he needed me for something proved I mattered to him. Sure, I'd briefly confused his interest with emotional attachment, but I was over that now. Sin dealt in deals and trade, and my gut told me I had yet to pay up.

"He'll come for us?" Veena perked up a little.

"He'll come for Nyx," Mallini corrected, her tone a little bitter.

Veena deflated with a soft moan, and Tristeene gave Mallini a reproachful glance, but there was a tension in the set of her mouth that told me she was thinking the same as Mallini.

I couldn't have that. I couldn't let our unit fall apart now. "We're a package deal. It's all of us or none of us. I'm not going *anywhere* without my family."

Mallini's throat bobbed. "No. I don't suppose you will." She gave me a tiny kitten grin. "You stubborn bitch."

"You're one to talk."

The tension in the room ebbed, and Veena finally snuggled up against Tristeene.

I wanted to ask Mallini how she could even think I'd leave them behind, leave her behind, after she'd been ready to sacrifice her life to save us. She'd shut us inside the tunnels in Fertilis, making sure we were hidden and safe, then used herself as a decoy to protect us from the creatures hunting us.

We'd thought she was dead, but the crazy bitch made it out. Made it back to us, only to have *me* bring us here to the abyss. A place the fallen had sealed to prevent an awful sickness getting free.

"At least this place is dry," Tristeene said. "And there might be something to eat in those boxes." She made to get up, but Gus waved her down.

"I'll check." He hopped to his feet and hurried across the room. His small imp frame meant he wouldn't be seen easily through the windows. Perks of being an imp.

"I'll help." Keelan followed him but did so in a stealth crouch.

Yeah, there was no hiding his large Minorax frame.

They began rummaging through the boxes, and I pulled myself up. Maybe there were some blankets or something around here. It got cold when the sun went down. We'd learned that the hard way last night when we'd been forced to pile together for warmth in a drafty shed. Veena had snuggled close, claiming that I was the warmest sibling in the bunch.

The paintings Ignatius had shown me of the daimon realm hadn't included the small towns and villages we were traveling through now. This world reminded me of a cross between Morningstar and the human world. Would the city be that different?

There was a room at the back of the store, and enough dying sunlight spilling in from two rectangular windows high on the wall opposite for me to scope out the space.

We'd investigated a few buildings over the last few hours, and they'd all been broken and dusty inside. Wood, moldy fabric, and décor I'd expect to find in the Fringe. But this room was different. It had dark wood floors and was devoid of any furnishings. Completely unremarkable, except for the metallic wall to my left.

There were seams cutting into it, rectangles and squares of various sizes.

"What is it?" Mallini said from behind me.

"I don't know."

I crossed to the metallic wall and pressed my fingers to the metal near one of the seams.

There was a click, and that part of the wall began to slide out.

I backed up as the ledge glided out. Metal legs flipped out from beneath it to brace on the ground and turn it into a table.

Mallini arched a brow. "Slick." She pressed another part of the wall, and a counter appeared. We spent the next couple of minutes opening out the wall to reveal a kitchen area.

"Well, that's high tech," Gus said from behind us.

"Yeah." I crossed my arms and watched Mallini fiddle with buttons and knobs, but even though the mechanics were operational, there was no electrical power to turn anything on. "We might find more evidence of high-tech equipment the closer we get to the city."

"It's a shame none of this works, though," Mallini said with a huff. "I don't remember ever being this thirsty."

We'd avoided drinking from a stream we'd passed because of all the debris floating in it. Luckily, it had rained a little at night, and Gus managed to collect enough rainwater for us all to have a little this morning.

The image of a tall glass of cold water floated in my

mind. Funny the things we took for granted when they were accessible.

"Wait a moment." Gus joined Mallini by the kitchen counter. "You missed one." He pointed at a small rectangle high up against the ceiling. Out of reach for him and Mallini.

Not for Keelan, though. He pressed the metal, and a panel with strange symbols on it slid out.

"Oooh." Gus's eyes lit up. "It's ancient demonic. I studied it."

Tristeene and Veena appeared at the entrance to the room. "We wondered what was taking you all so long," Veena said. Her eyes went wide at the sight of the kitchen. "It's so shiny."

"Since when do they teach ancient demonic in Morningstar?" Mallini asked Gus.

Gus looked sheepish. "No. I, er...I studied it for fun."

"And now it'll be invaluable," Keelan said. "What does it say?"

Gus frowned up at the symbols. "It says...spin for... energy...? No wait...Turn for power!" He beamed up at Keelan. "It's the on switch."

"Yes!" Mallini fist pumped the air.

"Which dial?" Keelan asked Gus.

"The blue one."

Keelan reached up and turned it.

Nothing happened for long seconds, then a low hum filled the air, and lights came on above us.

Mallini touched the tap. A gurgle rattled the pipes buried in the walls, and then water gushed into the sink.

I joined in the collective cheer. We'd needed this small win. This boost in morale.

"We need glasses," Gus said.

"Fuck that." Mallini drank from the tap for long seconds before stepping back. "It's good. So good."

We took it in turns, quenching our thirst, and for a few moments, I believed we'd be okay. We'd sleep, recharge, and make it to the city tomorrow. We'd find survivors, and if not, we'd find a secure location in the city and wait until Sin came for us. Because there was no doubt in my mind that he would.

He had to.

"We should bunk in here," Tristeene said. "It's warmer."

Gus touched the floor. "It's the floor. It's heated."

Veena lay down and sighed. "It feels so good."

Underfloor heating. Nice. "Okay, we'll sleep in here tonight." We had heat and water. Maybe tomorrow we'd find food and—

My hackles rose. Danger.

The sun was setting rapidly. We hadn't secured the entrance.

Crap.

I shot to the door and peered into the shop floor gloom. There were shelves blocking my view, so I ventured forward on the balls of my feet to peer around them and down the aisle that would give me a clear view of the entrance.

The exit was gone.

No. Not gone but blocked by a huge hulking figure.

"Nyx?" Keelan's voice was a low rumble of inquiry. "Fuck."

Yeah, he saw it too.

There was something in the shop with us.

Something huge and hulking.

It turned its head, and I caught the gleam of red eyes, noting its sharp muzzle and pointed ears.

It froze. Its crimson gaze fixed on me.

Keelan grabbed my shoulder to haul me back as it broke into a sprint toward the light spilling from the kitchen.

Toward me.

But it was too late.

There was no outrunning this thing.

FOUR

IGNATIUS

There is a ball of anxiety in my belly. The extra breach that my conji have discovered in the Court of Flame could mean an impending invasion.

It's a sliver.

A crack.

But it could be the start of something bigger.

"What are your instructions?" Hrath asks.

Instructions. Yes. I'm here to resolve this issue and give my people direction, but my mind drifts, and I struggle to focus. "Monitor it along with the other."

The silver-skinned conji who's been standing silent up until now speaks. "Your Grace, may I make a suggestion?"

"Go ahead."

"I suggest we send a spy through the main breach."

"It's too dangerous. Like we discussed before, the fawda could have guards stationed on the other side."

"Or they may not," the conji says. "They may be

confident in their treachery, believing us unaware of their doorway into our lands."

"Or they might not be fawda at all," Hrath points out. "We won't know until we send someone." He shoots me a sidelong glance. "Someone who can move like the wind. Someone they won't see."

Is he suggesting... "No."

His brows come down in annoyance. "No?"

I grit my teeth and drop my gaze to the conji. "Excuse us a moment, Pelar." Pelar inclines his head and moves away to give us privacy, and I turn to Hrath. "It's too risky."

"It's less of a risk for me than anyone else," he counters. "Why don't you tell me the real reason?"

I glare at the knowing smirk on his face. It isn't often that Hrath is playful. And now definitely isn't the time for playfulness. This is a serious matter; still, I find my tense shoulders relaxing.

"I can't lose you, Hrath."

"You won't."

"You can't make such promises when walking into unknown danger."

Hrath sighs. "You know that Pelar is right. This is the best course of action, and I'm the most suitable candidate. I swear to you, I'll merely observe and return with information. I won't interact with anyone."

"Hrath, if they're fawda..."

"Sylphs did not join the fawda." He lifts his chin. "We fought against Shaitan, not for him. No one will see me."

"I know. I..."

"Have no valid objection," Hrath finishes. "But you are the duke, and if you forbid it, then I won't go."

"Forbid?" It's my turn to smile knowingly at him. "When have I ever forbidden you from doing anything, old friend?"

"Then I have your blessing?"

"Yes. But let's wait a little and—" The knots of anxiety in my belly tighten.

"Ignatius? What's wrong?" Hrath asks.

I shake my head, trying to latch on to the cause of my growing disquiet. "I'm not..." And it hits me. "Nyx. I can't feel Nyx."

SEV

I can't help but wish the hallway housing the spawn quarters was longer. Pacing it leaves me unsatisfied. Dhuma leans against the wall by the window with his arms crossed while the gauzy curtains billow either side of him, in and out, like heavy breaths.

Chase is an alert, watchful sentry by Nyx's chamber door.

We're in limbo.

Waiting.

My skin is hot and itchy, but the wards around the keep stop the icy air from getting in. I should go back outside, but what if Artimus shows up with news about Nyx and the others?

I hate this.

I hate being relegated to the sidelines like I don't matter. Like I'm nothing to her when I know different.

Sin may have claimed her as electus, but he doesn't have her heart, not yet. He has no right to shut me out. She's my... A low growl vibrates my chest because there is no name for what we are to each other. No mate bond, no electus mark.

Nothing but a debt which can be broken once paid in blood.

I need more.

I need a name for what we are.

Once she returns, I'll claim it. I'll claim my place at her side, and they'll never push me aside ever again.

"I feel your ire, friend," Dhuma says. "Inaction grates on my nerves."

We've scoured the surrounding villages, while knowing there's little chance of finding the spawn there. But at least we were doing something. But now...Now we're cloistered in our quarters waiting for word from the princes and the Seneschal. Waiting. Waiting. Fucking waiting.

The only thing keeping me sane is the bond that still thrums inside my chest.

It sings as long as she lives, but there's fear too. Fear of the silence that might come if it stops.

"I'm going to the Atrium." I stride toward the exit, but the Minorax on guard shakes his head slowly as I approach.

I could fight him. Knock him out. I'm fast, a shadow if I need to be, but I like him. We've had conversations. His name is Jarmi, and he has two spawn that he adores. He's following orders.

I don't want to hurt him.

I back down, spin on my heel, and punch the wall. My bones crack, and pain shoots up my arm, but I heal in a few seconds.

The wall, however, doesn't.

"Did that help?" Dhuma asks.

I offer him a grunt in return.

Chase pads over to me and nudges my thigh before looking up at me with huge brown eyes that tell me not to worry. That Nyx can take care of herself. That she's not alone. She has her siblings, and they'll find their way home, wherever they may be.

The rage rushes out of me, and I stroke his head. "Thank you."

"You have a bond with the hound that reminds me of the bond between the demibeasts and maras of the abyss."

I look up at him in surprise. "Demibeasts worked with maras?"

"Certain units were raised with their own demibeasts. They developed a bond, became brothers in a sense."

"Not the demibeasts that Umbrane keeps. He has them trained to kill."

"He needs to die."

"I agree." The duke is a thorn that will forever prick at my psyche. He raised me to kill. To revel in inflicting and receiving pain. He almost broke me, but Nyx saved me.

She gave me hope, and now I would die for her.

The doors to the quarters open, and Artimus enters. His dark hair is mussed, and his sapphire eyes are filled with shadows.

Something has happened.

"What is it?" Dhuma asks. "You have news."

"It's not good," Artimus says. "Sin believes that Nyx and the spawn may be in the abyss."

"What?" Dhuma and I say in unison.

He presses his lips together and exhales through his nose. "It's the only place we haven't looked."

"But the wards..." Dhuma's brow furrows. "How could they get past..." His brows flick up. "Nyx's power. She must have come into a power that allowed her to bypass the wards."

"It's the only explanation," Artimus says.

They know where she is. "Have they gone to get her?"

"They can't. They don't have the key to bypass the wards."

"Then where is it?" Dhuma demands.

Artimus shakes his head as if he can't believe what he's about to say. "The spawn have it."

"How? How could they have the key?"

"It was part of the trial. They were sent to fetch it."

"So if they have the key, they can use it to get out. I don't see the problem."

Artimus shakes his head. "They don't know what the key does."

I can't believe what I'm hearing. "So what now? How do we get them out?"

"We don't," Artimus says.

Dhuma steps forward, eyes narrowing. "They're expecting the spawn to find their way to the hub, aren't they?"

Artimus's jaw flexes. "Yes."

I look up to Dhuma. "What's the hub?"

"The location of the gate in and out of the abyss," Dhuma says. "All I know is that they built it somewhere that would be inaccessible to the infected." He rubs his chin. "But the spawn wouldn't have entered the abyss via the hub. If they've slipped past the wards, they could be anywhere in the abyss, any distance from the hub, with no idea where they should head." His chest heaves and fuels my panic.

"We have to hope they figure it out," Artimus says.

"And if they don't?" Dhuma asks.

Artimus's throat bobs. "Then the power of Morningstar will be lost forever."

But I don't give a shit about the power. All I care about is Nyx.

Chase chuffs softly, and I meet his gaze, hearing the

words that he can't say. Nyx clawed her way back from death. There's no way that the abyss is going to keep her.

I place my hand on his head. "Where's the entrance to the hub on this side?"

Artimus shrugs. "The princes won't say."

"Then maybe it's time we make them tell us," Zepar says from the doorway.

How long has he been standing there?

Artimus turns slowly to face him. "Do you think you can convince Ramiel to share the location with us?"

Zepar's smile is a jagged, wicked thing. "Fuck asking. I say we demand it."

Well, this is going to be interesting.

FIVE

NYX

The beast rushed us, wide, muscled shoulders flexing as it ran. I'd seen this breed of creature before, fought it in the arena to save Sev's life. It was a demibeast, but twice the size of the ones I'd gone head-to-head with.

Keelan stepped in front of me with a roar, head down, ready to tangle with the monster. He was a Minorax warrior with a proud heritage and a general for a mother, but he was no match for this demibeast.

"Keelan, no!" I made a grab for him just as the demibeast skidded to a halt.

Oh fuck, were we in a stare-off with a demibeast? Yes, yes, we were. Its nostrils flared as it sniffed the air, then the crimson hue in its eyes dimmed.

It backed off and turned away.

My grip on Keelan tightened. What was happening here?

The demibeast stopped a few feet from the exit, and my

skin broke out in goosebumps that had nothing to do with the beast or the fact that my siblings had come up behind us.

This was something else.

Keelan stepped back, taking me with him. "Something's out there," he said in a hushed tone.

The demibeast drew back into the store, its body low, its movements stealthy. It sensed it too. This creature wasn't sick. It wasn't in a frenzy, and it had refrained from attacking us, but now...Now its body expanded and bristled with lethal intent.

Something was coming.

The patter of feet and the sound of ragged breathing registered.

The demibeast threw back its head and howled, and a moment later the windows shattered inward, letting in hunched figures.

The infected were here.

THE DEMIBEAST ATTACKED, snarling and snapping at the creatures. Tearing off limbs and chunks of flesh.

It was the perfect distraction for us to make our escape, but the fight blocked the exit.

"There's a side exit," Mallini said. "If we could get to that and bust it open—"

"Move!" Keelan ushered us toward it.

Mallini led the way, with Gus and Veena going next, followed by Tristeene.

I faltered, looking back at the demibeast surrounded by lost and fighting for its life.

Yes, this was the perfect distraction, but if we used it, that beast would die.

"Don't even think about it," Keelan growled.

I pulled my pretty silver dagger from my boot. A gift from Ignatius and adept at silencing shiqq. Would it have the same effect on these fuckers?

"You can't," Keelan said. "The infection."

The demibeast howled in pain, and my head whipped around to find it trying to shake off the scrawny figure who had its teeth buried in the beast's flank. The infected thing held firm despite its wasted-away state.

This ravenous male had once been a daimon or a demon, but now its sole purpose was chaos and destruction. My mind flashed to the night in the Old Forest when I'd been attacked by the feral Erinyes. They'd had the same wild, emaciated look about them, as if nothing they consumed would ever sustain them.

"It's too late," Keelan said. "The demibeast is probably infected now too."

"Then we need to kill it. Before it joins them and comes after us. It has our scent, remember?"

"No. We run and find a better spot to hunt from."

The demibeast roared and threw off the infected before whipping its body toward the exit and sprinting out into the night. The infected followed, enraptured by the beast, their hunger for its flesh stopping them from investigating farther into the building.

Keelan sagged. "That was close."

"What the heck, guys?" Mallini joined us in a crouch. "Door, remember?"

"They've gone," Keelan said.

She peered around the aisle. "Thank the earth."

"We can't stay here, though." I stood and headed for the

side exit. "If the demibeast is infected, it could come back and bring the others with him."

"Yeah, we need to go," Mallini agreed.

"We'll stay downwind," Keelan said.

We hurried to the others, who were huddled by the door.

Veena looked past us. "What's happening? It's gone quiet."

"It's all right," Keelan said. "They've gone, but we need to go too, just in case they come back."

He rattled the door, then slammed it open with a shoulder nudge. Yeah, having a tank as a sibling was a bonus.

Cold air rushed over my skin. Dammit, we could have had a nice, warm night's sleep, but now we'd probably end up on the move all night, stopping for small rests in drafty spots unless we could find another building with power.

Power... "Oh shit."

"What?" Tristeene asked.

"You don't think turning on the power attracted the infected, do you?"

"The lights..." Gus said. "Maybe...Or the hum of power..."

"No way of knowing," Keelan said. "We'll play it safe from now on."

I wasn't about to argue with that. "Let's put some distance between us and the store."

We jogged down the street, sticking to the shadows, alert for any sign of the demibeast or the infected. The world was silent and icy. I could tell by how my breath misted, but I was beginning to suspect I wasn't feeling the chill as acutely as the others.

My cuffs were off. My true nature was now free. Maybe daimons ran hotter?

"We need to find shelter," Tristeene said through gritted teeth. "I'm used to the cold, but this...this is ridiculous."

We'd been jogging for almost ten minutes, and we'd gone a good distance. "We should stop for a bit. Warm up, then continue."

We turned onto a domestic street lined with abandoned homes. An iron fence ran down the street creating a border between the houses and the pavement.

One house stood out from the rest because the windows and doors were still intact. "Let's check this one out."

I veered toward it. It had to be safe inside because if the infected had gotten in, the place would be smashed, right?

Keelan and Tristeene ran ahead to scope it out, but I was distracted by the chattering of Veena's teeth. "Come here." I scooped her up and hugged her.

Her small frame shivered in my arms for a moment before she relaxed against me with a sigh. "So warm, Nyx."

I kissed the top of her head.

Mallini held her hand out to Gus. "Get up into my plumes. They'll keep you warm."

Gus didn't argue with her. His ochre skin tone had lost its depth, and his tiny, feathered wings were folded tight against his back, shriveled from the cold.

It was best to keep the smaller siblings tucked up warm against us.

Keelan and Tristeene were almost at the house when I caught movement on the roof.

Scrawny, shadowy figures ran along the tops of the buildings.

Infected. "Watch out!"

The infected leapt off the roof toward my siblings.

Tristeene screamed.

Keelan spun away from the house and ran toward us, scooping Tristeene up and throwing her over his shoulder enroute.

But the infected were too close. They were about to—

A demibeast appeared around the side of the house. It slammed into Keelan, shunting him out of danger's path and taking the brunt of the infected daimons' attack. But the move knocked Tristeene out of Keelan's grip. She arced through the air, propelled by the force of the impact. Her scream of shock was cut short when her body landed on the iron fence with a sickening, wet thud.

My limbs froze, my brain struggling to compute what I was seeing because that couldn't be an iron spike jutting out of my sister's torso.

It couldn't.

But Veena's bloodcurdling scream confirmed that it was.

SIX

Tristeene was bleeding to death.

We'd pulled her off the fence. She should be healing. Why wasn't she healing? "Tristeene, stay with me." Her eyelids fluttered closed. "Tristeene, look at me!"

"Hold it. Hold and put pressure," Keelan instructed Veena, who was busy pressing his shirt to Tristeene's wound.

Beyond the fence, two demibeasts tore into the infected, turning the night into a cacophony of screams. But the battle didn't matter. The danger didn't matter. All that mattered was Tristeene.

"It's not helping." Veena's voice shook. "Keelan..." Blood soaked through the fabric and stained her hands. "We have to get her out of here."

Keelan scooped Tristeene up. She screamed shrilly, then passed out from the pain.

We ran for long minutes until we could no longer hear the fight between demibeast and infected. Only then did we pick a building and duck inside.

It looked like it may have been a workshop. Strange tools lined shelves, gathering dust, and the air smelled musty, but at least it was relatively warm and dry.

Gus found a tarp and dragged it over. We laid Tristeene on it. Her torso was soaked with blood, the wound still gaping. It was bad. *Mortal wound* kind of bad. My stomach clenched in fear as I flashed back to the Old Forest and Keelan's injuries. He'd survived because he was Minorax, built to endure, to take a hit and keep coming. But Tristeene was a succubus, and…

She was a succubus! "We need blood."

"Yes!" Gus's stunning blue eyes lit up. "Yes, blood will help her heal."

"She can feed off me," Keelan said.

"No," Gus said. "She needs powerful blood." He looked at me. "High daimon blood will have the best effect."

"So be it." I gently tapped Tristeene's cheek. "Wake up. It's suppertime."

Veena snort-laughed then covered her mouth in horror.

"It's all right," Mallini said. "We're all in shock. It's okay."

Tristeene groaned and opened her eyes.

"Hey." I stroked her hair back off her clammy forehead. "You're going to be okay. You've just got to feed off me."

Her pupils grew large and dark. "Nyx…I can't…I've lost too much blood…I could…could lose control and take too much."

She was thinking about my welfare, even now, when she was bleeding to death. "I'm tougher than I look. And Keelan is here to stop you if you go bloodlust crazy."

She shook her head. "It's too—"

"Do you want to die?" Mallini said bluntly. "Because if you don't feed, that's exactly what will happen."

Tristeene squeezed her eyes closed, her pale heart-shaped face etched with pain.

"Dammit, Tristeene." I pinched her jaw. "Look at me." She opened her eyes and met mine with a look of torment. "Please, just feed. We need you."

She swallowed and nodded. "I...I won't be able to make it painless."

A succubus bite came with endorphins to make it pleasurable for the person being fed on. It could be sexual and intimate, and I could totally do without it. "I'm good with the pain, thanks."

Mallini gave a dry chuckle. "Yeah, because otherwise things are going to get weird."

Tristeene's laugh morphed into a wet cough, and her eyes rolled back, eyelids fluttering.

"Hey!" I slapped her sharply. "No passing out."

She groaned. "So tired."

"I know. But not for long. Help me get her up."

Keelan gently lifted Tristeene into a sitting position, and she let out a wet scream.

I slapped my hand over her mouth, catching her tears. "Hush, hush...Okay. It'll be okay." She moaned against my palm, red-rimmed eyes spilling more tears. I blinked back the heat gathering behind my eyes. "We're going to fix this." She nodded, letting me know she was good. I removed my hand. "You need the jugular?"

"Yes." Her voice was a thick whisper.

I swept my hair aside and gently, cupping the back of her head, brought her close.

She was too weak to hold herself upright, so Keelan braced her.

"Come on, Tristeene, bite me."

Her icy lips brushed my skin. This was going to hurt.

Badly. I gritted my teeth, ready for the pain. It came sudden and sharp, slicing into me like a razor. I bit back a cry and squeezed my eyes shut, hands fisting, toes curling as I breathed through the agony of fire ants flooding my bloodstream. Each pull of her mouth evoked a fresh wave of needles in my blood. And each draw got stronger, more eager, until she was holding on to me and digging her fingers into my flesh.

It was suddenly harder to breathe.

"Enough..." My voice sounded far away.

"Enough!" Keelan snapped. "Tristeene, stop."

But Tristeene's grip tightened, and her fangs sank deeper. Numbness spread across my neck and across my collarbones.

"Stop," Veena said. "Let her go."

My body jostled as my siblings tried to pry Tristeene off me, but she held on like a limpet.

I no longer had the breath to protest or the energy to push her off. I was a juice box in her grip, being squeezed and drained.

Drained.

Fuck, I was going to die.

"Pull her off. Squeeze her jaw!" Mallini said. "Make her let go."

The sound of tearing flesh was loud in my ear, and I was suddenly free. I hit the ground on my side. Moths fluttered inside my chest, and my head was filled with bees, while my throat throbbed in a steady, deadly, beat.

My throat...Had she ripped open my throat?

There was pressure on my neck, warm and insistent as someone tried to hold me together.

"Tristeene, close the damn punctures," Mallini ordered.

"I'm sorry. I...I'm sorry," Tristeene said.

"Stop babbling and fix it!" Mallini growled.

"I can't. I can't. The damage is...It's too much..."

Well, that sucked. When had it gotten so cold?

Blissfully floaty and cold.

My cheek stung.

"Don't you dare check out on us," Mallini growled. "Heal, dammit. Heal."

"You can heal," Gus said. "You're a Satan spawn. You're high daimon."

"She's too weak to heal," Keelan said, his voice a low tremble.

He was right. I could barely keep my eyes open.

"What do we do?" Veena said. "What do we do?"

They were drifting away from me. Or maybe I was drifting away from them. I tried to fight. I needed to stay with them. There was still so much to do, but the pull of oblivion was too strong. Darkness swallowed my vision.

GUS

My heart stops then starts again, fast and furious in my chest. She's dying.

She's dying, and there's nothing we can do to stop it.

"What did I do? Oh earth, what did I do?" Tristeene tugs at her hair, tears streaming down her face.

Nyx's blood has healed her, but it also drove her into momentary bloodlust. She sits on her haunches, mouth all bloody, fangs still visible. Still in feed mode but gripped with remorse.

Nyx lies between us, her body still and silent, the only evidence of life the continued blood gushing from her neck.

She's bleeding out.

She'll be dead in seconds.

We can't lose her. *I* can't lose her. My eyes burn with the threat of tears. Impotent, useless tears, because for the first time in a long time, I'm at a loss for a solution. All the libraries, all the books, won't help me save my sister.

My sister...My friend. The linchpin of our ragtag crew.

"Nyx, no." Veena grabs Nyx's hand as if she can stop her soul from leaving her body by mere force of will.

"She'll come back, though, right?" Mallini says. "She's a high daimon...Right?"

She's high daimon, but she's also fallen, and Dhuma explained that three lives aren't always guaranteed, not even for a high daimon, and in Nyx's case...who knows?

"Gus!" Veena looks up at me imploringly. "She'll come back...right?"

I swallow the lump in my throat. "I don't know." I lift my chin. "We should...should say goodbye just in case."

Keelan makes a soft sound of distress.

Mallini begins to cry.

Tristeene is silent and still, her dark eyes fixed on Nyx as if she can will her to heal just by staring at her.

We're waiting for her to die.

The pump of blood slows.

Not long now. My heart hurts, and my vision blurs hot and angry.

"No." Veena shakes her head, vehemently dislodging tears. "No. I *won't* let her go." She squeezes Nyx's hand. "Stay. You *have* to stay with me." Her voice cracks. "Please. Don't go. I won't let you." Her voice hardens with determination.

Nyx has been more than a sister to Veena. She's stepped

into a maternal role, giving Veena the comfort and love she's been craving all her life. Her death will take a piece of us all, but Veena...It will destroy my tiny sibling.

I reach for her, intending to pull her into my arms, to provide some comfort, but freeze as the air grows heavy. Awareness sweeps across my skin, leaving goosebumps in its wake.

Something is happening.

"What the..." Keelan says.

Glowing silver lines have appeared on Nyx's hand. They spiral out from where Veena grips her and spread up Nyx's wrist.

A nugget of knowledge worms its way up from the deep recesses of the archive that is my mind.

"Look," Mallini says. "Look at her skin."

Nyx's eyelids twitch.

"Did you see that?" Tristeene says. "Veena, what are you doing?"

"I...I'm not doing anything." A huge yawn stretches her jaw, and the answer surges up to slap me in the face.

"It's not Veena. It's Nyx. She's siphoning."

"What?" Keelan looks confused, but Tristeene's eyes fly wide with comprehension.

She knows what I'm talking about, but I explain quickly for the others. "It's a lesser-known ability because it was wiped out with the Nephilim. It's the ability to draw energy or power from someone else. Nyx is doing it unconsciously."

Veena's eyelids droop, and I grab hold of her. "I've got you. Let me help." I press my hand to Nyx's arm, then look up at the others. "Come on. Touch her!"

"If the walls had ears right now," Mallini drawls.

I can allow myself to crack a smile because there's hope

now. Silver swirls spread across Nyx's skin from where I touch her.

Mallini takes her other hand, and Keelan places his on her brow.

The wound on Nyx's neck begins to knit and heal. It's working. She's going to be okay. We can help her regenerate. Help her body to produce more blood to replace what she's lost.

It's going to be all right.

Long minutes pass, and the silver swirls cover every inch of exposed skin before melting away.

It's done.

But Nyx doesn't open her eyes.

"Why isn't she waking up?" Veena asks.

I shake my head, dumbfounded. "I don't know."

SEVEN

NYX

What was this vast dark space? There were tiny specs of light in the distance. Where was this? Where was I?

I shouldn't be here.

I'd been doing something important, but I couldn't remember what that was. Still, I needed to get back to...Back to where?

A silver shape appeared in the distance. It was moving toward me. Another two shapes joined the first and took on humanoid forms. But any illusion of humanity was ruined by their inky black eyes and too-wide mouths.

My pulse thrummed as they circled me, making sounds.

Were they speaking to me?

Did they expect me to answer?

I opened my mouth to tell them I didn't understand them, but some primal instinct, a primitive alarm inside the back of my mind, warned me to hold my tongue.

I couldn't let them know that I was different from them.

They drifted closer, and my skin tightened. I kicked, trying to get away from them. They babbled louder, moving closer and reaching for me.

Panic ballooned in my chest. If they touched me, laid their hands on me...it would be the end. I didn't know how I knew it. I just did. I kicked harder and managed to move away a little, but not far enough, not quickly enough.

Terror dug claws into me.

They were going to get me.

A golden light shot between us, blazing brightly before settling into the figure of a woman.

The silver creatures reared back, mouths stretching wide enough to take up their whole face.

The golden figure babbled at them, and they turned and whizzed away.

My scalp prickled. I knew this figure. Knew that I was safe with her.

Relief flooded me as Tiana, the guardian from the daimon afterlife, turned to face me. "Hello again, Nyx."

I'd have hugged her if I could figure out how to make this body work properly. "Your timing is impeccable."

"But your sense of preservation needs work." She placed her hands on her hips, brows snapping lower over her eyes. "What are you doing here, hmmm?"

"I...I can't remember."

She rolled her eyes. "Of course you can't. The tethered are always confused in this part of the astral plane."

"Astral plane? Is that where we are?"

"A small part of it, yes."

"And what were those things?"

"Inhabitants of this place. Creatures looking for a ride to the mortal plane. Nasty things if they latch on to you."

"But they were scared of you."

"Let's just say I've made a name here. Come. We must get you back to your body."

"I'm dreaming, aren't I?"

"You could call it that." She grasped my hand and pulled me into a rainbow. Colors rushed by, but we continued to float.

I resisted the urge to touch the flowing colors. "Are we moving?"

"No. The astral plane is shifting."

I didn't have the energy to wrap my brain around that one. "I'm sorry that you died." It came out blunter than I intended, but she laughed.

"Oh, child, death is simply the end of a chapter in our existence. It was my time to move on, and I hold no grudge. But you have much yet to do. Your chapter has many pages to go."

Wait a second... "Am I dying?"

She winced. "You were, but now you're not. Because it isn't time. Not yet."

The fact that I couldn't remember what had happened to me to bring me here was—

Memories flooded my mind. The abyss. The infected. Tristeene getting hurt then... "I have to get back!"

"Ah, see, your memories have been restored, which means that we're almost there..." The rushing rainbow slowed into a gentle wave. "You probably won't remember this, at least not consciously, but the next time you leave your body, avoid the..." She said something that was more of a sound than a word, but it penetrated my mind and settled there. "You'll be fine. Now go." She placed both hands on my shoulders. "Go and forge your path."

"My path..." Someone else had said that to me recently...

She grinned. "I can't wait to see who wins."

"Wins? What do you—"

She shoved me, and the rainbow dropped me back into darkness.

I BOLTED AWAKE, and hands grabbed my shoulders.

"It's okay. You're okay," Mallini said.

Veena threw herself into my arms, and I hugged her on instinct. "What happened?"

"You almost died." Mallini's tone was accusatory. "Don't you *ever* do that again."

"I'm sorry," Tristeene said. "I lost control. I'm so sorry."

I held my hand out to her, and she took it. "It's all right. I knew the risk. But it's okay. You stopped."

She blinked sharply, and her mouth turned down. "No. I didn't. Not in time."

"What?" My siblings exchanged glances. "What happened?"

"I tore out your throat," Tristeene said softly.

My hand went to my neck, crusted with dried blood but intact and healed. Yes...I remembered now. The numbness. The cold.

"You were too drained to heal," Veena said.

"Then how..."

"You siphoned energy from us," Gus said. "You drew enough power from us to heal yourself."

"I can't do that."

"You can now," Keelan said.

"It must be your high daimon power," Gus said. "Dhuma told me that most high daimon have an affinity for an element or some other minor ability. Yours must be siphoning."

"It used to be a Nephilim trait," Mallini said, a wicked gleam in her eyes. "The princes are gonna love this."

"What if they lock her up again because of it?" Veena looked horrified.

Mallini's smile fell. "Shit."

"No, they won't touch her now that she's Sin's electus," Gus pointed out.

I was done with the princes, their trials, and their rules. If they thought they were shackling me and getting me to jump through hoops again, then they were sadly mistaken. I was done. We all were.

It was time to pick a Satan and finish this twisted game. "We'll worry about that when we get home. Right now, we need to focus on making it through the night."

Mallini got up and crossed to the window. "It's quiet out there. I think the demibeasts may have taken out the infected."

"But the question is, why?" Keelan said.

I had a theory. "I think the demibeasts could be working with the survivors here in the abyss."

"I agree," Keelan said.

"They didn't attack us," Gus added. "Because we weren't infected. It's like they're trained to only go for the infected."

"He had a bite in his flank," Veena said. "I saw it before..." She glanced at Tristeene. "Before you got hurt. But it wasn't sick."

"Yet," Gus added. "Wasn't sick *yet*. Who knows how long the incubation period of the infection is?"

"Or maybe...Maybe the demibeasts are immune," Tristeene said softly.

"It's a possibility," Gus agreed.

The workshop was clean, dry, and warm. "We should stay here and get some rest. Move out at first light."

"There are more tarps in the box," Gus said. "We can use them to sleep on and cover us too."

Keelan rose to his feet. "I'll get them."

The tarps were thick and soft from use. Perfect for creating a nest for us to snuggle into.

"I'm not tired," Tristeene said. "I'll take first watch." She gave me a sheepish look. "Your blood is potent."

I shot her a smile. "Glad I could help."

Gus shook his head with a sigh. "Remember the days when we weren't constantly in mortal peril?"

Veena giggled.

We settled into our nest.

"Wake me when you start to flag," Mallini said to Tristeene.

I curled up with Veena and Gus on either side of me and closed my eyes, but I couldn't have been asleep long before Tristeene's urgent voice pulled me back to consciousness.

"Nyx, Keelan, wake up."

My eyes snapped open to the pale smudge of her face hovering above me. "We're not alone in here. I don't know how...but..."

I sat up slowly, skin pricking with the awareness of several presences in the room with us. Hiding in the shadows. Watching. If they were infected, they would have attacked us already, right?

Keelan sat up too, and our eyes met in the gloom.

He senses it too.

There was no running from this.

I lifted my chin and spoke into the dark. "Who are you and what do you want?"

The shadows shifted, and several figures stepped out of the gloom, silver spear tips aimed at us.

They had us surrounded.

EIGHT

IGNATIUS

I was supposed to be gone a day, but I've been gone almost two. The journey to the second breach took up most of the first day, then setting up the perimeter to watch it took the rest.

I should have come back sooner.

Should have checked up on Nyx. Should have monitored our tenuous connection. When had it died? How many hours had it been since I'd felt her? I'd been so caught up in business, I'd failed to recognize the change. I assumed she'd be safe. Assumed this final trial was a formality. But what if I'm wrong?

I rush to the spawn quarters first, but they're empty, and the Minorax guarding the space confirms the spawn aren't back from their final trial yet.

Panic squeezes my insides.

Nyx is Lucifer's electus. He won't allow any harm to come to her. In fact, he must have felt her absence too. He's probably already acted.

"The Seneschal and Duke Zepar were here a moment ago," the Minorax tells me. "They just left with the nightmare and the daimon."

I bolt out of the quarters and into the hallway beyond and catch sight of Artimus just as he's about to round the corner.

"Artimus!"

He stops and looks back. "Ignatius. I'm glad you got my message."

"What message? I didn't get any message."

The others appear from around the corner to join us.

Artimus frowns. "I sent it yesterday."

"I've been away from court."

"But you heard...right?"

"Heard? No. What's happened? Why aren't the spawn back?" I touch my chest lightly. "Artimus...I can't feel Nyx any longer."

"I feel her," Sev says. "She's alive."

A bitter tang claws at the back of my throat. He feels her, and yet my connection is muted. How can his blood debt bond be stronger than my soul bond?

I should have solidified it. I should have consummated our bond before leaving. "Where is she? Where's Nyx?"

Artimus sighs. "Come, I'll explain everything on the way."

"Where are we going?"

"To demand some real answers," Zepar says.

Nyx is in the abyss.

The knowledge is a cold pressure in my chest, and my

pulse pounds so hard in my veins that I'm surprised the others can't hear it.

A Minorax stands guard at the entrance to the Atrium. He looks uncertain as we approach. Minorax belong to my court, but right now, this one is working on orders from Prince Levistus. He's young. It's probably his first rotation in Morningstar.

Artimus takes the lead. "We need to speak with the princes."

"The princes are not to be disturbed," he says.

"You tell Prince Ramiel his son wants to speak with him," Zepar bites out. "Now!"

Panic bleeds into his eyes. "I'm...I'm not supposed to enter the Atrium." The unease is evident in his expression.

Artimus makes a sound of exasperation.

Fuck it. "Get out of my way, guard."

He almost obliges but checks himself in time. "I cannot." He lifts his chin defiantly.

I've got to give him credit for not backing down. I'm aware of the effect I have on the residents of my court. But right now, I need him to cave. Right now, I need to know where they've hidden the portal to the abyss on this side of the wards. It was something the fallen didn't share with the efreet. Something they kept to themselves.

"Do you understand the penalty for disobeying your duke?"

He blinks sharply, and his throat bobs. "Will it be as harsh as the one for disobeying a prince?"

I narrow my eyes. "Oh, it'll be worse, because it won't be exacted against you. It'll be exacted against those you love." I don't care how cold that sounds. All I care about is Nyx. "Now move before I move you."

Zepar is right behind me, backing me up. I can feel the

threat beating off his skin. We need the guard to abandon his post, to disobey an order, because attacking him isn't an option. It breaks the Morningstar Accords. But if he moves of his own volition, then we're free to enter without any breach.

I understand how cruel this is to the guard, understand that it could cost him his position here, but I can't bring myself to care. Instead, his defiance spawns rage, and my skin heats, white-hot flames skimming up and down my arms.

His eyes go wide, and he opens his mouth to speak.

"What's going on here?" The voice is feminine, and I'm momentarily thrown before realizing it's coming from behind me.

"Ah, Mother." Zepar's tone is derisive. "Perfect timing. We need inside the Atrium."

Odette arches a brow. "Do you? And why might that be?"

"We need to speak to the princes," Artimus says.

She adjusts a linen cloth over the wicker basket she's carrying. "The princes are busy, and you know that." She gives Artimus then Zepar pointed looks. "I highly doubt they have the time for an audience."

Zepar's smile is all teeth. "Humor us."

Odette shrugs. "Very well. Wait here." She takes a step forward, then stops with a small laugh. "Although, what else can you do but wait?"

She slips past the guard into the Atrium, leaving a fizz of magic in her wake.

We move away from the guard, who sags in relief.

"It's Merihem," Artimus says. "He's in a bad way."

A prince is hurt? "What happened?"

"He got too close to the lava when searching for the spawn. The burns will take some time to heal."

"I have a conji who might be able to help."

"Tell my mother that if you want your head ripped off," Zepar says. "To think that any conji could be more powerful than her."

"Healing is a specialist art," Dhuma says. "Odette is not the most adept at it." He lifts his chin. "I will suggest it. Merihem is my friend, and I will not see him suffer needlessly."

Odette reappears. "The princes will see the Seneschal, the dukes, and the daimon." She smirks at Sev and Chase. "You two will wait out here."

Chase lets out a low, menacing growl, and Sev's silver eyes flare with indignation.

"That hound and that nightmare are two of the most important beings to Nyx," Zepar says tightly. "I doubt the princes want to alienate them, especially considering that Nyx may end up being our next Satan."

Odette shrugs. "I'm merely relaying the message."

"In that case, step aside. Sev and Chase are with me."

The surprise on Sev's face echoes mine.

Zepar isn't one to share anything or anyone, and yet he's willing to give Sev a seat at the table. Not to mention the tone he's using with Odette. So far, I've only seen him act deferentially to her.

Maybe the fallen isn't the stuck-up cold-hearted bastard I've come to believe he is.

Odette doesn't step aside. She lifts her delicate chin and locks gazes with her son. "Do not forget who you're speaking to, boy."

Zepar's jaw ticks, and his eye twitches. "How could I, Mother? You won't let me."

I catch Artimus's smile before he hides it.

Odette turns on her heel and leads the way into the

Atrium. I follow Zepar into a room that smells like herbs, sulfur, and charred flesh, and my heart sinks at the sight of the blackened figure laid out on the large conference table.

"He's no longer in any pain," Levistus says from his spot by the table. "He'll sleep and heal now."

Ramiel is busy pouring a drink, and there's no sign of Sin. The prince turns to us with a cold, hard look on his face. "What is so important that you tried to strong-arm our guard into letting you in?"

"We need to know where the hub from the abyss leads," Zepar says. "Where's the doorway on this side?"

"You want to know, hmmm?" Ramiel says. "And what in the earth gives you the right to want anything?"

Zepar bristles, and I catch the impression of wings twitching at his back. "Maybe I don't have a right, but Ignatius and Sev do. They're important to Nyx, and I'm sure you want to keep your strongest contender for the throne happy."

Ramiel presses his lips together. "There are contracts in place. We can't share the location with you, even if we wished to."

"So what? You expect us to sit around and do nothing?" Zepar asks incredulously.

"Do you have faith in your custodia?" he asks him. Then to me, "And you? Do you have faith in your twin flame?"

"I have faith in her. But I can no longer say I have faith in any of you."

My words are received with stunned silence. Even Artimus looks shocked, but I'm done playing lesser to these fallen.

"Excuse me?" Levistus says. "We are your princes."

"Only because my kind allowed you to be. But no longer. My people are not weak by any means. Our power is not to be looked down on. The only reason you're able to place yourself above us is because the seed of our power is out of reach in the abyss, beyond the wards *you* put up. You gave us no time to retrieve it, and in doing so, you were able to call yourselves our masters."

"Ignatius, watch your tone," Levistus says.

"Maybe you should watch yours." Dhuma comes to stand beside me, his larger frame a solid backup. "*You* are no prince of mine." He looks down at Merihem's sleeping form. "My debts were paid long ago. I stayed for friendship. But make no mistake, I bow to no fallen."

Sin steps into view across the room. His hair is damp and swept back off his horns, and he's dressed casually in a white shirt, open at the neck, and loose black pants. His feet are bare. He looks like he's preparing to relax in his chambers, not prepping to save the Satan spawn.

"What's this? A mutiny?" His tone is amiable, but his eyes are sharp with anger. "Are you here to test us?" He strolls to the drinks cabinet and pours himself a glass. "Well?" His gaze fixes on Dhuma.

The corner of Dhuma's lip lifts. "You may be changed, Sin, but you're still no match for me on the battlefield."

Sin shrugs. "Maybe not. But we aren't on a battlefield right now, are we?" His tone hardens. "You're in Morningstar. In our domain. A guest, until we decide otherwise." He takes a gulp of his drink, and any illusion of geniality vanishes. "Don't make me decide otherwise."

I can read the discord play across Dhuma's face. The need to bite back, to challenge. But he's no fool. It's been decades since we spoke, centuries since we dined and laughed together. He was my mentor's family and was a constant peripheral in my life, so I know this daimon does not make rash decisions. He knows when to hold his peace and when to strike.

He crosses his arms now and stares straight at Sin. "You forget that this world does not belong to you. You are just as much of a guest in it as I."

Sin smiles. "Yes. You're right. Which is why we must work together to retrieve the spawn because without Morningstar and without the power in the throne, we will all be weakened, and the threat that looms in the wings will have its advantage."

He's referring to the fawda. We'll need the Morningstar power to fight them. "All we're asking for is some action."

"And I ask for patience," Sin replies. "My chosen conji are monitoring the gateway on this side. When the spawn reach the hub and communicate with us, we will act to retrieve them." He refills his glass. "Now go. I'll send word when we have news."

My heart sinks because there's nothing more to do here. No more arguments to be made.

We exit the Atrium.

"He said when," Sev says. "*When* they reach the hub, not if."

"Yes, he's confident in the spawns' abilities," Artimus says.

"Then we must be too," Zepar says.

"We can wait in my quarters," Artimus says.

But something niggles at my mind. It gnaws away at me until we're almost at Artimus's room, and then it hits me.

I grab Artimus's arm. "I thought you said we couldn't get to the spawn because we didn't have the key."

"That's right," Artimus said.

"That's what the princes told us," Zepar says.

"Then why did Sin just say that as soon as the spawn got

to the hub and *communicated* with them, then they'd *retrieve* them?"

Sev curses softly. "More lies. More deception."

"No," Dhuma says. "It means there *is* a way out of the abyss, but they must find it and knock until someone on this side answers."

"It also means that the key alone won't be enough," Zepar says.

It means that the spawn not only have to find the hub but figure out how to send a distress signal. We were forced to run and leave so many efreet, abyssbloods, and daimon behind. I can only hope that some survived the sickness, that there's a colony there, someone who remembers the past and can help the spawn. But even as I hope, my stomach sinks, because I recall the chaos. The death. The endless battle and the virulence of the infection.

So instead, I close my eyes and send out a prayer to the seed of our power to keep my *qalbi* safe and to bring her home to me.

NINE

NYX

S pear tips glinted in the strip of moonlight that lay between us and the shadowy figures. They reached for us, ready to stab. The creatures wielding them, however, remained in the shadows.

Finally, one of them stepped into the light. The silvery rays revealed a wiry frame kitted in a black form-fitting bodysuit that covered him head to toe, sitting high on his neck so that only his face was uncovered. Even his hands were sheathed in gloves. He studied us with eyes like silver coins set against dark blue skin.

There was something about him...

"Who are you?" he demanded, throwing my question of a moment ago back at me.

His tone was sharp and authoritative as if he was used to being obeyed and getting answers. A leader then? Not infected.

A survivor.

Good. This was exactly what we needed. "My name is Nyx, and these are my siblings."

He studied us skeptically, probably noting the lack of familial appearance.

I gave him a tight smile. "We share a father. Beelzebub."

He blinked sharply. "That can't...But that would mean..." His eyes narrowed in suspicion. "You came from the outside." Excited murmurs broke out around us. "You were sent for us."

"There's another way out?" one of his comrades asked.

"We need to secure it now," a second one said.

Mallini leaned closer to me and whispered, "What are they saying?"

She couldn't understand them. Which meant they must be speaking daimonword, and so was I. Activating my high daimon genes had given me the ability to understand a range of languages and speak them, switching instinctively between them depending who I was speaking to at the time, but the problem was I had no idea that the languages were different unless someone else pointed it out.

The shadowy figures continued to whisper among themselves, the tone getting more and more excited until...

"Silence," the leader ordered. "Lower your spears."

They obliged immediately.

I gave him a small nod of thanks. "Do you speak demon tongue?"

He frowned. "A little, why? You speak daimonword perfectly well."

"But my siblings don't. The universal language outside of the abyss is demon tongue."

Confusion flitted across his face. "Demon tongue?"

"Yes."

His nostrils flared. "Very well." His gaze swept over the

others. "My name is Lynal. I'm the leader of the marasguard."

Marasguard? He was a morpheses like Sev. They all were.

"You survived the sickness," Gus said. "Are there more of you?"

Lynal had obviously switched to demon tongue. His smile was grim as he responded to Gus. "Yes. We survived, and we completed the task set for us. We gathered the uninfected, cleared the city of the sick, and maintained the barriers. We did everything to save our home and make it habitable again. But she didn't come back for us."

She? "Who are you talking about? Who didn't come back for you?"

His frown deepened. "The daimon queen, of course."

Wait a second…"The daimon queen asked you to stay in the abyss?"

"Yes."

My siblings and I exchanged glances. As far as we'd learned from Dhuma, Soreena had perished closing the breach to Inferis—the place they called the pit. Had she given them orders before leaving?

"Did she give the order herself?" Gus asked. "In person?"

Lynal's eye twitched. "Why is that important?"

Oh boy. "Trust me, it's vital."

"No, we received a missive signed in her hand and sealed with the royal seal."

Fuck.

"What aren't you telling us?" he demanded. "Speak!"

"Lynal…Soreena…The queen is dead. She died helping Lucifer close the breach."

His expression paled. "No…That can't be."

"Let me guess," Mallini said. "The missive came after the breach was closed, right?"

Had the princes done this? Faked orders from the daimon queen to get the maras to stay back and clean up the mess? All this time, the maras had believed they were doing their queen's bidding and that she'd return to them once the work was done. But instead, the princes had locked them away and forgotten about them.

"Maybe the note was meant to be delivered regardless of what happened," Tristeene said. "Your queen's final wish. It makes sense for her to want her home to survive, and who better to entrust this world to but her guard?"

I slid a glance her way. She sounded sincere, but I knew her well enough to know that she didn't believe her own words. She was smoothing this situation over. Taking away any reason for them to vent on us. After all, we were the spawn of one of the princes who'd betrayed them, and if they realized that, then...

Yes, Tristeene was making a wise move, and the rest of my siblings must have realized it too because they were silent, letting her have the floor.

"I think your queen would have been very proud of you," Tristeene said with a soft smile.

Lynal's frown relaxed, but there was pain in his eyes. "All this time and she's been gone. We did not know. We did not grieve, and we did not hold a ceremony for her passing."

"Our queen would have left instructions with her surviving consort and the princes," one of the other maras said. "Why have they not answered our call for exit?"

"Maybe the hub is broken as we suspected," Lynal said. "It explains why they've sent you to retrieve us."

They'd mentioned this hub before. "What's the hub?"

"The tower that contains a gateway directly into the

demon realm," he said. "It was built when the Chaos War began and used by our people to escape from the abyss after the wards were put in place. The gate was locked from the outside, but instructions were left on how to send messages to the twin hub in the demon realm. We've sent many but received no response. It must be broken. But now you're here..."

He thought we were here to save them. To get them out, and they were all looking at us with hope. As if we were their salvation.

I was going to have to kill that hope. "We're not here to get you out. We're trapped, just like you."

His mouth thinned in disbelief. "You expect me to believe that? The wards around the abyss are impregnable. They were designed that way for a reason. No known creature can get out. No known creature can get in."

"No known creature?" Gus said, shooting me a look and a nod.

They needed to know what I was. "I'm that wild card. The *no known creature.*"

He canted his head and narrowed his eyes. "Explain."

"I'm Beelzebub's spawn, but I'm also high daimon." There was no need to go into detail about my bloodline, especially since no one understood how it could be possible, especially as no daimon, except Dhuma, had made it out of the abyss alive.

"This isn't possible," Lynal said. "Fallen and high daimon cannot produce offspring."

"Tell that to the evidence," Mallini drawled.

I filled them in on my death and how I'd come back, which confirmed my nature. Then I told them about Beelzebub's death and how as Satan, his demise had resulted in trials to pick an heir. "The last trial ended up with us being surrounded by lava. I wanted us to be safe, to get home somehow, and the next thing I knew, we were here. I don't know how I did it. And I don't know how to use the power to get back. Believe me, I've tried."

His shoulders sagged, and the light in his eyes dimmed. "In that case, you're fortunate our demibeast patrol found you. Although we've managed to herd most of the infected to the northern regions, these parts are still riddled with them. They're drawn to the city. Probably by instinct. It was, after all, home to many of them." His eyes narrowed as if he was thinking something through. "It seems that you're important to the princes. These trials to choose an heir to this Morningstar place prove that. I doubt they'll leave you trapped here."

He didn't know the half of it. Didn't know about the power inside the throne that needed a conduit.

Needed one of us.

"We'll keep you safe in the city," he said. "And when they finally come for you..." He gave me that grim smile again. "Well, then we'll have our answers and our way home too."

His words should have eased the knots in my belly; after all, he was offering us sanctuary and protection. But instead, the knots tightened, because this moment here felt very much like we were being taken hostage.

TEN

The abyss didn't feel half as terrifying when surrounded by marasguard and flanked by four demibeasts. In fact, with the sun high and the chirp of birds filling the silence with life, the abyss felt almost like home.

It helped that we'd left the abandoned settlement far behind and were on a wide road that led into the city. The road itself was made of dusty orange bricks riddled with nicks and grooves from years of bearing travelers.

Turned out, the demibeasts were immune to the infection, and so was the wildlife. The sickness didn't affect them, making them perfect scouts, hunters, and guards for the maras.

The thick suits the maras wore protected them from an infected's bite. Lynal explained that the infection needed an open wound to spread. The infected had wicked sharp teeth and strong jaws so were able to pierce a maras' thick skin. The lightly armored material provided a much-needed extra layer of protection.

I fell back to walk beside Keelan in companionable silence, leaving Lynal chatting to Gus.

Veena strolled beside one of the demibeasts, chatting softly to a marasguard with silvery skin and deep navy hair. I caught a little of their conversation, mainly her questions about what the demibeasts ate and how they were taken care of. The guard's answers sounded awkward and stilted to my ear, but that was probably due to the fact he was speaking demon tongue, which wasn't his first language.

"So do you train them?" Veena asked.

"I have trained Ulla," he said. "She is mine, and I have one other. They work with me, but it is not easy to command them when...um...if there are many sick."

"When there are too many infected?" Veena provided.

"Yes. If too many, then the demibeasts will maybe only want to survive."

"What do you mean?"

"They forget training and run," he said.

"They'd just leave you?" Veena sounded worried.

He shrugged. "It is primal instinct to want to live."

"But I thought they were immune to infection."

"Yes, but not to being ripped up."

"Oh...I see."

"It is hard to train them because they are descendants of infernal hounds."

My ears perked up because I'd heard of these hounds before from Dhuma. They were creatures from Inferis. Apex predators.

The guard continued. "The story says, long ago royal blood saved the brood mother of the infernal hounds. Then the royal blood was offered protection for his bloodline."

A Knightwood had saved the brood mother. That's what Dhuma had said.

"So the demibeasts are a type of infernal hound?" Veena asked.

"They have the blood. Yes. They say the queen kept them close and asked us to work with and nurture them."

A memory, a connection, bloomed at the back of my mind, struggling to rise to the surface.

"What kind of transport do you have here?" Gus's question, posed to Lynal, disrupted my train of thought, drawing my attention to my imp sibling.

"We only travel by foot now," Lynal replied. "But once upon a time, we used electrically powered vehicles. There are wind farms to the east. But we were forced to shut them down a long time ago."

"Why?"

"The electricity seems to attract the infected. We're not sure why."

"Well, that explains why turning on the power at that store got us noticed," Mallini said, joining in on the conversation.

"Yes, some dwellings have generators," Lynal said. "We shut down all that we could, and now we use fossil fuels to power the city. We've reverted to our primitive ways to survive."

"How many survivors are there?" Keelan asked.

The corner of Lynal's mouth tipped up. "Enough to matter."

Intriguing.

The conversation ebbed, and we continued in silence. Fields of corn swayed far to our right, and a meadow stretched out to our left. The sky above was a bruised purple laced with streaks of orange, and the city spires rose into it, tall and powerful, even from this distance. What would they look like up close?

My stomach bubbled with excitement to see the place I'd only been able to visit in paintings. A part of me came from here. My mother had been a high daimon. Would someone here know her? The possibility that I'd find out who she'd been was slim. The one person who could have answered that was dead, but there was nothing wrong with hoping.

We stopped for a rest on the edge of the road, and the marasguard shared their supplies with us. Bars made of raisins and nuts, packed full of protein. Great for an energy boost. Lynal passed around a canteen of water for my siblings and me to share.

When it was time to set off again, the maras that Veena has been speaking to carefully lifted her up onto his demibeast, Ulla. Veena smiled down at him, and his eyes lit up. It looked like my sister had charmed this male.

An hour later, the city walls loomed over us, rising so high that I couldn't see the top.

"The wall runs around the whole of the city," Lynal said. "There are several walled sectors beyond this one, each with mechanical gates that can be closed if need be. A wall also surrounds the royal towers."

"It works well in case of threat or invasion," Gus explained. "They can shut down parts of the city and protect the citizens."

"Correct," Lynal said with an indulgent smile. "The feature was invaluable in the Chaos War. It's what saved many of us." He looked back at the road we'd traveled, and his mouth turned down. "Still, so many of our people perished."

We were close to the iron wall now, and the seam to a small door was visible. Lynal banged a fist against it, and a hatch opened, revealing a pair of eyes. The hatch closed, and the door swung open.

Several marasguard trooped through.

"How will the demibeasts get in?" Veena asked her guard buddy. "This door is too small."

"There is a way farther down the wall for them," the guard explained while helping her off the creature. "It leads to the courtyard inside."

Veena patted the demibeast's cheek gently. "I'll see you later, Ulla."

The beast snorted and closed its eyes as if reveling in her touch before following the marasguard along the wall to wherever the other entrance was.

"Shall we?" Lynal swept a hand toward the doors.

I hesitated. Once we were inside, there'd be no escape without them letting us out. And that shouldn't be an issue, but the idea of being caged, however large the cage, didn't sit well with me.

"Nyx?" Keelan frowned down at me. "If you have second thoughts..."

My siblings crowded around me, feeding off my doubt, suddenly unsure. The only way home lay inside the walls of the city. Lynal said the hub was broken, but maybe we could find a way to fix it. See something they'd missed? Gus was super smart with all things mystical, and if they weren't using electrical means of communication, then the hub must be employing mystical means. Even if we failed, I was sure Sin would come for me, and the city was the safest place to wait for him.

"Nyx?" Keelan jolted me out of my thoughts. "Are you going in?"

Lynal waited at the door, but he didn't say anything to

encourage me to follow him. Instead, he waited for me to make a final decision.

We were his hope of getting out of the abyss. Of restoring contact with the demon realm, and there were more of them than us, so, if he wanted to, he could simply force us inside. But he didn't do that.

Instead, he waited. Patiently. Almost wearily.

They didn't deserve what had happened to them. They didn't deserve to be abandoned like this. If my being here could help them find a voice with the princes, then so be it.

I nodded. "Yeah. Yeah, we're going in."

ELEVEN

The area beyond the gates was a huge courtyard occupied by maras and a few smaller demibeasts held in pens. Younglings, no doubt.

Small campfires were spaced out across the courtyard, and the smell of cooking meat saturated the air. There was a small smithy with a workshop beside it, and the clank and grind of weapons being forged and sharpened created a symphony of its own.

This place was filled with life, and after the beautiful but barren landscape outside the walls, it was a sight for sore eyes.

Several maras stopped to look at us curiously as we were led past them toward a second iron gate, and I noticed the females for the first time. They were smaller than the males, but with the same tough skin. Some had tails; others didn't. Their breasts were covered in the same thick hide as their legs. It covered their nipples, making it look as if they were wearing bindings.

These females were warriors just like the males. You could see it in their eyes.

"Where are Jysten and the demibeasts?" Veena asked Lynal. "He said there was another way in?"

Jysten? So that was her friend's name.

"To the left there." Lynal pointed past the smithy and workshop to a wide passage leading to an arch and a stable area. A set of wide outer gates lay beyond. A maras was already dragging them open.

Veena hurried forward, eager to see her friend again. I caught sight of Jysten with Ulla close behind him. He raised a hand in greeting and made to step forward, then stopped abruptly to look over his shoulder.

A bellow ripped the air behind him, and a demibeast roared in response.

"Close the gates!" Jysten yelled. "Infec—"

Something slammed into him, knocking him out of view.

"Jysten!" Veena made a break for the gates, but Keelan plucked her off her feet before she could get too far.

She bucked and fought him. "No!"

Chaos erupted around us as the marasguards surged toward the gates because they were too heavy to close in time to avoid—

Snarls and growls rose above the pounding of feet and the thunder of blood in my ears.

"Get inside the city!" Lynal shoved me toward the second gate we'd been heading toward. "Go!"

But the infected were already through the gap in the outer gates, already tearing at the unarmoured maras with teeth and talon.

It was too late to run.

Maras fought to stop the infected and force them back out of the gate, but there were too many of them.

Combat was inevitable.

"Weapons ready!" My voice was almost buried under the cacophony of sound, but my siblings heard me.

Keelan swung a sobbing Veena onto his back. "Hold on!" He ducked his head and drew his blade.

Mallini was ready with a blade in each hand, and Tristeene and Gus both had small daggers. I palmed the silver blade Ignatius had gifted me and braced for impact as the infected surged toward us.

Crimson eyes flashed, and hungry maws snapped.

"Get back!" Lynal ordered us. "Get inside. Please! You're our only hope now." He shoved an iron key into my hand as even more infected spilled into the courtyard. The maras had abandoned trying to close the gates, their energy taken up by the battle.

"Go, please!" he said again.

Keelan's shoulders heaved as he locked gazes with me, conflict blazing in his eyes. He was a warrior, and running from a fight wasn't in his blood, but this was a fight we couldn't win, and we all knew that. Bravado was pointless.

We backed up, turned, and ran for the inner gates.

We hit the door, and I searched for the keyhole.

"No!" Veena cried. "The demibeasts are leaving. There are too many infected. Jysten said...He said..."

"Get the door open!" Keelan ordered.

But in that moment, the memory that had been knocking at the back of my mind ever since Jysten had mentioned that the demibeasts were descendants of the infernal rushed to the surface. I was back in the arena with Sev, facing off against three demibeast.

One had bitten me.

It bit me, and then it had backed off because...Because of my Knightwood blood!

The same blood the demibeasts' ancestors were sworn to protect.

There was hope. There was a chance.

I shoved the iron key at Keelan and ran back toward the chaos.

"Nyx!"

There was no time to explain. Only to act. I ran toward the retreating demibeasts and sliced open my arm, waving it in the air. The pain barely registered past the heat of adrenaline coursing through me.

"Hey! Hey you!" I sliced at the other arm, then at the first one again because the wound was already closing. "Come on! You owe me!"

But it was the infected, not the demibeasts, that turned to me. Their bloodred eyes lit up, nostrils flaring as they caught a whiff of my blood.

Had I fucked up? Come to the wrong conclusion? Maybe my Knightwood blood wasn't strong enough to get the demibeasts' attention.

The infected abandoned their attack on the maras and rushed me.

Oh shit.

"Nyx, run!" my siblings screamed in unison.

Yeah, definitely time to—

A gust of air hit me in the face as a wall of fang and fur landed between me and the infected.

"Nyx!" Mallini rushed to my side. "What the fuck?"

"Get behind me!" My bellow raked the inside of my throat and made my ears ring. "Get behind me now!" The order was for anyone and everyone.

I caught Lynal's open-mouthed stare, but then he snapped to attention. "Do it!" he ordered.

The uninjured maras wove between the feuding beasts and infected to get behind me and run toward the inner gate.

"Ulla!" Veena cried.

The huge beast glanced at Veena before leaping deep into the fray. Snapping and swiping, pouncing, and tearing at the creatures.

"Jysten!" Veena shouted.

I spotted the maras a moment later as he burst out of the throng and rushed toward us. He was grimy and bruised but with no visible open wounds.

With the wall of demibeasts to cover us, we ran for the inner gate. A few of the infected broke through, but the armored maras cut them down. Tristeene grabbed my hand as we ran. Keelan was already at the gates, pulling them open, and we weren't too far behind when Tristeene yanked her hand out of my grip.

She was no longer running beside me. She was on the ground a couple of meters behind me, trying to kick off the infected who had a grip on her ankle.

Hell no. I ran toward her and kicked the infected in the face. "Get off!" It held firm, but in the next moment it was gone, torn off her by a demibeast.

I hauled Tristeene to her feet, and we made the final dash to the gate, rushing through and onto a gravel road to join our siblings. I sagged on my feet, my heart pounding in my throat.

We'd made it.

We'd actually fucking made it.

Tristeene squeezed my hand before letting go.

"Close the gates! Summon more guards!" someone yelled.

More orders were flung back and forth.

We moved farther up the road to give the maras room to secure the gates. Grassland spanned either side of the road. A few benches dotted the grass, and there were trees farther back. It was all neatly trimmed and organized. It looked like a park.

"How did you know what to do?" Mallini asked me. "How did you know your blood would call the demibeasts back?"

"I overheard Veena talking to Jysten. The demibeasts are descended from infernal hounds from Inferis. The hounds are bound to protect the Knightwood bloodline."

"Smart," Gus said with a grin. "But then I'd expect nothing less from my sister," he said proudly.

Keelan pressed a hand to my shoulder. "I'm glad it worked, but Nyx, you could have been killed. What if the demibeasts hadn't turned back in time?"

"I know. I just—"

Tristeene made a strange sound and swooned.

Mallini grabbed hold of her. "You okay?"

She pressed a hand to her temple. "Just...dizzy and..." She looked down at her boots. "My ankle hurts." She sounded confused.

I glanced down at her booted foot. "Did you sprain it when you fell?"

"Sit." Mallini led her to a bench, and we all followed.

"Let me see," Gus said.

Tristeene kicked out her leg, and Gus crouched to examine it. "Does it hurt when I do this?" He squeezed her ankle through the boot.

She sucked in a sharp breath. "It burns."

Gus pulled his hand back, and Veena let out a shocked cry. "You have blood on your hand."

"It's not mine," Gus said. "Wait." He ran his fingers along the back of Tristeene's boot. "It's ripped. You must have cut yourself."

Tristeene's eyelids looked heavy. "It feels odd."

Ice pricked at my nape. "Take her boot off."

Gus pulled off the soft leather to reveal a thick sock. He peeled it back to reveal a scratch. The skin around it was red, swollen, and angry looking.

"It isn't healing." Gus looked up at Tristeene with confusion.

No...

"Is everything all right?" Lynal's attention dropped to Tristeene's ankle, and his face paled.

I sidestepped, trying to hide Tristeene from view. "It's nothing. Just a scratch."

"How?" Lynal demanded.

I opened my mouth, the lie heavy on my tongue, but Tristeene beat me to it.

"One of them grabbed my ankle. I think...I think its talon must have cut through my boot."

I gritted my teeth. "You're fine. It's just a scratch."

"It isn't healing," Gus repeated in dawning comprehension.

"A scratch is all it takes," Lynal said. "I'm sorry."

"No." Veena moved toward Tristeene, but Keelan pulled her back.

"You can't," he said, his voice thick. "Tristeene is infected."

TWELVE

As if by unspoken command, a couple of maras appeared behind Lynal.

I placed myself between them and my sister. "Touch her, and I swear I'll sic your own demibeasts on you."

Lynal's eyes narrowed. "What you did out there only a Knightwood could do."

"That's right. I'm a Knightwood."

He balked then studied me with a hard, assessing gaze that lasted for several seconds. "It's been a long time since I saw a Knightwood female. But I cannot deny that you have the Knightwood bone structure and eyes." He pressed his lips in a thin disapproving line. "You should not have kept the truth from me."

"Yeah, well, now you know. You guys work for *my* bloodline." I was reaching here but fuck it. Whatever it took to buy some time.

"The Knightwood family is royal, but we answer only to the queen's direct bloodline, and that ended with our queen."

I crossed my arms. "Maybe, but your demibeasts answer to me."

His jaw ticked. I was obviously trying his patience, but I didn't give a shit. "You've seen what the infected can do," he said. "She must be exiled. We cannot put the city at risk."

"Nyx—" Keelan sounded broken. "If she's infected…"

"*If.*" I glared at him. "*If* she's infected, then we'll deal with it. But right now, we don't know for sure if she'll…turn." I looked to Lynal. "I'm asking for a little time. Just to be sure. Please." Fuck it, I wasn't above begging for this. "She deserves a little time."

Lynal chewed on his cheeks. "We have cells for potential infected."

Relief expanded in my chest. "We'll take it."

He nodded. "Very well, but if you choose to go this route, and she turns while inside these walls, there will be no exile, only *immediate* execution."

"I wouldn't have it any other way," Tristeene said from behind me. "If I become one of those things, then please…kill me."

I swallowed the lump in my throat. "I promise. If that happens, I'll kill you myself."

She smiled up at me, her eyes shimmering with unshed tears. "I know I can count on you. Thank you."

She was thanking me for promising to kill her. This was so fucked up. Over a scratch. A tiny scratch. She'd be fine.

She had to be.

"Get the shackles and the bit," Lynal said.

Tristeene made a soft sound of distress, and I opened my mouth to argue, but he held up a hand.

"This part is *not* negotiable. The cells are in Central City, which is two hours away."

And she could turn in that time. Yeah, I understood that.

The bounty hunter in me appreciated the threat she posed, but the sister in me didn't care.

"It's okay," Tristeene said. "Do it."

I kept my gaze locked with hers while they slipped the muzzle over her head and a hollow pit opened inside me, because if she turned...If she became one of the infected, I was afraid I wouldn't have the strength to end her, despite what I'd just promised.

I BARELY TOOK in the landscape on the way to inner city. My attention was on Tristeene, watching for any inkling that she was about to turn, but she showed no sign. Even muzzled and shackled, my sister held a regal air. Armored maras clutching spears flanked her, but she kept her eyes on the road ahead.

Nausea clawed at my belly with every minute that passed. Would she turn? Would she become a monster now?

"I can do it, if need be," Keelan said softly from beside me.

He was offering to kill Tristeene if she turned. I gritted my teeth and shook my head. "I promised. But it won't come to that. She'll be fine."

"Nyx..."

"Keelan, please..."

He sighed. "Hope is a powerful thing, Nyx, but it can also distort reality and cause pain."

He was right. Of course he was right, because the possibility that Tristeene would escape infection when all others had failed to do so were slim to nonexistent, but I needed to believe it was possible.

We continued in silence down the gravel road with the vast parkland either side of us. Low, flat buildings were visible in the distance.

"Another wall," Mallini said.

It cut across the road we were on, barring entry. It wasn't as high as the main outer wall, but it was tipped with iron spikes, and there was a lookout with a maras stationed in it.

He spotted us and shouted down to open the gates.

The doors swung open, and Lynal led our procession into a gray flagstone space, twelve-foot wide before it hit another wall. This second wall had narrow windows cut into it and beyond that...

I stepped forward, my eyes adjusting to the vibrant colors of the market square beyond. Yellow cobbled streets and red brick buildings, stalls with bright blue and green canopies, and daimon...So many daimon milling around in groups, chatting or shopping at the food stalls. The square was filled with life, and the distinctive smell of baking bread saturated the air.

"We won't be taking the topside route," Lynal said. "Not with your potentially infected sibling in tow. We don't want to cause a panic."

Yes, taking a shackled, muzzled person through the streets wasn't a good idea. The maras may have agreed to allow Tristeene to stay until she turned, but I doubt the public would.

"This way." Lynal led us to an iron door built into the ground. There was a complex lock on it, which he twisted this way and that until the hatch opened, revealing a set of stone steps. "This is an emergency route into the Central City. Only a handful of maras know the code."

"What if one of those maras is turned?" Gus asked. "Won't they be able to access it?"

"We've had a lot of time to study the infected," Lynal said. "They have very little higher brain function. They're driven by hunger and primal aspects. Even if a maras who knew the codes *was* turned, he wouldn't recall the code. To add to that, we have protocols in place, and no maras would enter the city if he'd been injured by an infected." His gaze slid to Tristeene. "The cells were used in the early days before the city was cleared of the infected." He climbed down the steps. "Jysten, Garth, you stay with us. The rest of you are dismissed."

The maras he'd dismissed broke away, and Jysten and Garth flanked Tristeene.

We followed Lynal into the gloom, where he lit a lantern to guide the way.

The tunnel went deep, and once we were at the bottom of the steps, we walked for what felt like forever before Lynal brought us to a halt at another iron door with another lock. He passed me the lantern, then worked on the lock until the door popped open.

He ushered us through into a wider passage, then closed the door behind us.

"Final door." Lynal knocked with a series of taps that sounded like a code.

Long seconds passed before the door was finally opened. Light spilled into the passage, and it took a moment for my eyes to adjust to what lay beyond.

Wall sconces lit up a large stone room lined with iron cells.

A dungeon?

"What is this?" The man holding the door open was a head taller than Lynal. "Who are these creatures?"

"Guests," Lynal said to him. "From the demon realm."

I caught the flicker of surprise in his eyes before he

masked it. "So they finally sent someone to investigate. Did you locate the entry point?"

"There is none," Lynal said. "And they weren't sent." He filled him in on what I'd told him about the trials and how I'd somehow transported us here. There was a reverence in the way he spoke to this guy that made my scalp prick. "So we're sure the princes will come for them," Lynal finished.

The monolith of muscle and sinew finally transferred his attention to us, glaring with suspicious violet eyes that narrowed when his gaze landed on Tristeene. "An infected? You brought it into the inner city?" he said incredulously.

"No." I stepped into his line of sight. "She's not infected yet. Not until she turns."

He lifted his chin with a cruel smirk. "You fool. It's simply a matter of time." His hand went to the blade at his waist. "I'll make it quick and painless."

My lip curled. "Forget it, big guy. No one touches her but me."

He arched a brow. "You're not in charge here, and I don't give a fuck who you are or what you are. My duty is to the safety of my people, and your sibling is a threat."

"Listen, asshole, I made a promise to my sister that if she turned, I'd be the one to end her. I won't break my word."

"Not my problem," he said.

I turned to Lynal. "Who the fuck is this guy?"

Lynal's smile was wry. "Nyx, meet Trystin Knightwood."

"Knightwood?" I stared up at the huge, arrogant male.

"Yes," Trystin said. "And when it comes to Central City, I'm the asshole in charge."

Oh fuck.

Thirteen

"Lynal made a deal with you," Trystin said. "So I'll honor it. But let me make one thing clear: inner city is *my* domain, and if you want to stay, then you'll follow my rules. I will *not* tolerate insubordination."

He was a Knightwood. My bloodline. Were we related? Lynal hadn't mentioned it. Why? I'd take my lead from the maras and keep my heritage quiet for now.

Questions could wait. Tristeene had to come first. "Look, we're not here to rock the boat. We want to help."

"Help?" he snorted. "Help should have come decades ago when we asked for it."

"Trystin..." Lynal shook his head. "This is a blessing. The princes will come for them, and we'll finally have a chance to evacuate."

Trystin sighed and nodded. "Fine. Lock her up." He jerked his chin toward Tristeene. "The rest of you, come with me."

"We're staying with Tristeene," Veena piped up.

He looked down at her in surprise.

"That's right," Mallini added.

An emotion I couldn't define crossed his features, but then he nodded.

"I'd like to see the hub," Gus said. "If that's okay?"

"I'll come with you," Keelan said.

Trystin snorted. "And what makes you think I'll permit such a—"

"They are Beelzebub's spawn," Lynal pointed out. "Future heirs to a throne in the demon realms..."

Trystin's jaw ticked, then he plastered a smile on his face. "Very well. Jysten will show you the hub."

Jysten shared a look with Veena before leading Keelan and Gus out of the room. Garth escorted Tristeene to a cell, removed her shackles, and held the door open for her. She looked back at us, her eyes filled with shadows.

I nodded encouragingly, and she stepped into the cell. The door clanged shut, and she reached up to take off her muzzle.

"You can sit there." Lynal pointed to a bench across from Tristeene's cell.

My sister dropped the muzzle and took a seat inside her prison, massaging her delicate jaw. The rest of us headed for the bench. The next hour or two was going to be tense.

TRISTEENE WAS FAST ASLEEP, curled up on the narrow cot in her cell, her breathing even and steady. How could I not hope for the best? She seemed fine.

The wound on her ankle had healed too.

All good signs.

"I don't like him," Veena said, peeking across the room at Trystin. "He's mean."

"He's up his own ass," Mallini added.

Trystin was talking to Lynal in a low voice. He was a Knightwood. Family on my mother's side. There was part of me that wanted to ask questions and get to know him. To know who the Knightwoods had been, but the other part wanted to punch him in the face. Lynal still hadn't introduced me as a high daimon or a Knightwood, so I'd keep quiet for now.

"If being a Knightwood put him in charge, surely you can take over," Veena said. "You're a Knightwood with fallen blood."

"It doesn't work that way," Mallini said. "The people know and trust Trystin. He's been here from the start."

"I don't want to be in charge. I just want Tristeene to be okay and for us to go home. Besides, Lynal hasn't mentioned I'm a Knightwood yet, which tells me that maybe it's best to keep that information to ourselves for now."

"Good point," Mallini said.

We fell into our own thoughts for a few minutes, and Veena was the first to break the silence by voicing hers.

"Do you really believe that Soreena sent that letter to the maras asking them to stay and build a haven?" she asked. "Wouldn't she have wanted her people to be safely away from here?"

I'd been thinking the same thing, but then, I didn't know Soreena the way her people did. The way the maras did. "They believe it. They knew her best. Maybe she loved the abyss and believed it could be saved, that something could be salvaged."

"I suppose if everyone had evacuated, then the infected would have run rampant and procreated, swelling their numbers." Mallini sighed. "Or they may have died out without food."

She meant people to eat. "They're dying out now because of the maras' efforts."

"True," Mallini said. "I guess we'll never know."

Trystin strode out of the room, and Lynal wandered over. "You must be hungry. I'll see about getting some food brought down for you all." He glanced over at Tristeene. "She's held out longer than expected," he said.

"Would an infected have turned by now?" Veena asked.

Lynal chewed his lip. "Anywhere between two to four hours. It's been three hours now, so there's still time."

My heart lifted. "So another hour?"

"Two to be sure."

"Maybe she's immune like the demibeasts?"

"It would be a first, but we must consider it." He gave me a small smile. "I do hope so. After all the death today, it would be good to see a life spared."

My heart sank. Of course, he'd lost many maras today, and I'd been so focused on Tristeene that I hadn't even considered his loss. "I'm sorry, Lynal. So sorry about your loss today."

He nodded. "Thank you. But your actions saved many lives. So I'm grateful. We all are."

"Even Trystin?" Veena asked.

He looked away. "It's best we don't mention the demibeast incident to him."

I'd been right. He'd deliberately not mentioned that I was a Knightwood. But I needed to know why. "Why not?"

"Trystin is possessive of his position, and it makes him competitive."

"Oh..." Mallini's lips broke in a sly smile. "He can't do it, can he?"

Wait a second... "Trystin can't command them?"

"No. He's a Knightwood by marriage, not blood. The

Knightwood name is taken by anyone who marries into it. But poor Ione, his wife, passed away several decades ago, and Trystin stepped into her shoes as leader. Over time, the people have forgotten that he isn't a blood Knightwood, and this...incident with the demibeasts might remind them. He won't like that."

"It's a bit late for that," Mallini said. "The maras all know."

"And we know how to keep our mouths shut," Lynal said.

So Trystin would be less than accommodating if he knew about my ability because he would see it as a threat to his position. "We get it, Lynal."

"I'm glad you do." He headed for the exit. "We'll keep this to ourselves until your princes arrive. It can be addressed then." I was about to ask him what he meant by *addressing* it, but he was already walking away. "I'll be back soon. Garth will stay and watch over you."

There was nothing left to do now but wait.

GUS

It's gray and silver inside the walls of the inner city, and there are too many steps. Jysten says there were lifts once and hovering boards that would take you easily to the tops of any tower. But now everyone uses stairs. The upper levels are rarely visited, but the hub is located at the pinnacle of the central tower. What Jysten calls the queen's tower.

"It was her throne room," he says as we climb the steps.

"But no one goes there now. Not for many years since Trystin decided the hub was no longer working."

"How do you know it ever worked?" The question is out before I can stop it, and Jysten falters in his climb.

"Messages were sent at the beginning," he says. "Ione Knightwood was in charge then. Second cousin to Soreena. She sent the missives. Though if they told her the fate of our queen, she did not relay it to us."

"Maybe she wanted to keep morale up," Keelan says.

"Possibly," Jysten agrees. "Regardless, by the time we had the infected under control, the messages were no longer being replied to. Ione passed away soon after. Trystin was brokenhearted, but he picked up the mantle of leader and continued her work. He attempted to send messages, but after no reply, he decreed that the hub was broken."

"Trystin was Ione's mate?" Keelan asks.

"Yes."

I glance out the window at the bridges high above that connect the towers. So many towers. And far below is nothing but mist, as if the world has faded away.

"Who lived in the Central City?" Keelan asks. "Just the royals?"

"No. Many nobles, and maras, efreet, and other dignitaries. Central City was home to us all. They say it was peaceful." He paused to look back at us. "But I was born after the Chaos War, so I don't know. Is it peaceful in the demon realm?"

Keelan snorts. "Peace is relative."

Jysten frowns. "That is also true. We call what we have now peace. The threat is under control..." He frowns. "At least we believed it to be so. I can't understand how the infected got so close without us knowing. Our patrols have been regular and thorough." He shakes his head. "Now our numbers are down, and the people will be frightened again."

Frightened people are easier to control.

I'm not sure why that thought pops into my mind, but now it's there, I can't shake it.

We step off onto a platform and then take a narrow flight of steps to another floor. There are no windows to look out of here, and a sense of claustrophobia sets in.

I'm about to ask how much farther when the passage opens out onto an entranceway and a set of vaulted doors.

"Here we are," Jysten says.

There are no guards. No locks on this door. Strange, considering how important this place is supposed to be.

Jysten pushes the doors open and steps back to allow us into the vast chamber beyond. The ceiling is so high I can barely see the rafters. This is the pinnacle, a hall with many windows looking out at the purple sky, and in the center of the room is a circular control panel with huge black and pink crystals jutting up out of it. I can feel the buzz of energy from here. And they say this hub is broken?

Wait...this looks familiar. "Can I examine it?"

Jysten shrugs. "I don't see why not. It's not like you can break it any more than it is. Broken is broken."

Excitement fizzes beneath my skin as I get closer because I've seen a machine like this before. Not in the flesh, but in an obscure journal buried in the archives at Morningstar, filled with sketches and notes. A journal belonging to someone named H. Harmony Jownes. Sure enough, there are initials etched into a plaque affixed to the machine.

H.H.J.

This is the machine he designed.

And I know exactly how it's supposed to work.

Fourteen

NYX

Lynal offered to take us to guest chambers to wash and change, but none of us wanted to stray too far from Tristeene. Instead, we used the guards' shower in the corridor outside the dungeons. Lynal managed to find me and Mallini some clean clothes. He didn't have anything in Veena's size but promised to get something customized immediately.

It felt good to have the last two days washed off my body. I'd gone nose blind while out on the road, but now that I smelled of jasmine soap, my olfactory system was back on track, and I could practically see the fumes rising off my clothes.

Back in the dungeons, there was nothing to do but wait for Tristeene to wake up.

"So you and Jysten..." Mallini wiggled her eyebrows at Veena.

Veena blushed. "Shut up."

I bit back a smile. "It's okay to like him."

Her expression sobered. "I'm betrothed, remember?"

My heart sank. "Yeah, well, not for long. Once one of us gets that throne, we'll sort that out."

"You can't make my mother change her mind," Veena said. "And that's the only way to end the betrothal." She dropped her chin, allowing her hair to fall forward to hide her face.

This was her defensive posture. Her way of hiding herself from the world.

Mallini and I locked gazes over her head. No words were needed. We knew what needed to be done. We knew exactly how to make someone change their mind, and it wasn't by asking nicely.

But Veena didn't need to know that.

Tristeene groaned softly. She'd rolled in her sleep and had her back to us.

"She's waking up," Mallini said. "Hey, sleepyhead. How you feeling?"

Tristeene groaned again, then propped herself on her elbow.

I stood slowly, my scalp prickling. "Tristeene?"

She made a soft moaning sound and sat up, her back still to us.

Veena grabbed my hand and squeezed. Yeah, she felt it too. The wrongness of this.

Please, please, no. "Tristeene, look at me."

She made a soft choking sound and then threw herself off the narrow cot and onto the floor.

Garth ducked out of the room, probably to go get Lynal.

This couldn't be happening.

I grabbed hold of Veena. "Tristeene?"

Tristeene's shoulders heaved, and she finally stood and

turned to face us. "Nyx..." Her eyes were pitch black, and her pallor was gray. "Nyx, I feel...odd. There's something...I can feel something in the back of my mind. It's watching..."

Gooseflesh broke out across my skin.

"Hello, Tristeene." Lynal joined us. "How are you feeling?"

She frowned at him. "I feel...different."

"She isn't infected," Veena said. "Look at her. She can talk. She's not all crazy."

Lynal pressed his lips together, drew his dagger and walked closer to the cell, leaving about a meter between him and the bars.

"What are you doing?" I stepped forward. "Lynal?"

"A little experiment." He sliced his palm and held it up.

Nothing happened.

She was fine. Still Tristeene and not some infected monster. "See, she's—"

Tristeene's head whipped up. "What?" Her nostrils flared impossibly wide. "There's something wrong." Her mouth widened, teeth sprouting long and sharp.

No...please, no...

She lunged at the bars with a feral growl that turned my blood to ice.

There was no doubt about it. My sister was infected.

GUS

The hub machine is a mystical radio powered by huge crystals that are now inactive. The buzz of power is residual energy, not enough to make it work. But why are the crystals inert?

I think back to the schematics in the journal. I spent long enough studying them, after all. Fascinating stuff.

I run my hands over the symbols etched into the marble that makes up the console. Each corresponds to a letter, and when active, a message can be typed and sent to be received outside the wards.

But why isn't it working?

There should be a panel somewhere...

I crouch and scan the machine for seams, anything that indicates a hidden section.

"What are you doing?" Jysten asks.

"Looking for something." I see it. A small rectangular shape cut into the white marble. "I think I found it." I press it, and it pops open. There should be four small crystals inside, and yes, yes, there they are. Four tiny crystals pushed into oval-shaped slots. There's a hole to one side of the crystals which I don't recall seeing in the schematics. Aside from that, this is exactly how things should be, except...Oh earth, the crystals are in the wrong order. My heart pounds in excitement. I know how to fix this, but hot on the heels of that realization is another: if the hub worked at one time, then it means someone deliberately reordered this panel to *stop* it working.

"Gus? What's wrong?" Keelan asks.

"What are you doing in here?" Trystin strides into the room.

I shove the panel closed and move away quickly to face Trystin. "We wanted to see the hub."

Trystin's jaw ticks. "It's broken."

I nod and frown. "Such a shame."

Broken by design. Broken deliberately, but I'm not sure

it's safe to tell him that. He was married to a Knightwood, to the first leader of this abandoned world. He would have worked with her to send the missives. Understood the machine as she did. And I'm beginning to suspect he might be the one who broke it.

FIFTEEN

NYX

Tristeene frothed at the mouth, black eyes gleaming with malice and hunger, and the teeth...All those teeth in a mouth that no longer fit her face.

My stomach twisted, and I held tight to Veena, smoothing her hair and making soothing sounds, more for my benefit than hers. Because seeing Tristeene, a female so poised and regal, stripped down to this base primal state, made my insides quake with horror and my eyes burn with the threat of tears.

My voice sounded odd and warbly to my ears when I spoke. "Stop it. Just stop."

Lynal stepped away from the cell and wiped his hand on a cloth that Garth passed him. Tristeene sagged like a puppet whose strings had been cut, and her face morphed back to normal.

She gripped the bars with a strangled sob. "That...that wasn't me. Oh earth, that wasn't me." Her dark alien eyes pleaded with me to believe her. "Nyx, I swear I didn't mean to..."

"The blood," Mallini said. "It made you lose control."

"I'm sorry," Lynal said. "But we had a deal."

Tristeene stared at me in horror. "No. I'm still me. I'm still here."

This was all wrong. Killing a rabid infected was one thing, but this...Tristeene was still Tristeene. "This isn't a typical infected situation, Lynal, and you know it."

He looked uneasy. "It doesn't change the fact that she's dangerous."

"So are you. So am I. So is a demibeast, under the right circumstances."

"I know what you're trying to illustrate, but *we* have a choice whether to attack. What happened just now illustrates that *she* does not." He sliced his palm again, and Tristeene went nuts. "See?"

Fuck it.

He wiped his palm clean and moved away from the cage. Tristeene reverted to herself, covering her mouth with a trembling hand, eyes wide with horror.

"Stop doing that!" Veena snapped at Lynal. "Leave her alone."

"No, he's right," Tristeene said. "I'm not in control. I should..." Her eyes went blank.

"Tristeene?" Mallini took a step toward the cage. "Tristeene? Can you hear me?"

TRISTEENE

It's dark and stormy. The wind tears at my clothes, and lightning splits the sky. I'm not alone. There are others here with me. People standing around me with their heads tipped back and their eyes closed. Warm earth presses against the soles of my bare feet, pulsing steadily.

Alive.

I don't like this. I want it to stop. I try to lift a foot, but the earth holds on to me.

My chest tightens with panic. No. Get off me. I tug hard and am suddenly free to stagger forward and collide with the body in front of me. The male sways and rights himself. His feet never break contact with the earth because he has no feet. His legs are joined like the trunk of a tree, and his feet are gone, buried deep in the soil, as if he's growing out of the earth.

They're all the same. Every daimon, demon, and abyssblood standing silently in the storm is literally rooted into the earth.

I have to get out of here because there is no doubt in mind that if I stay, I'll become just like them.

The lightning flashes then dies, and silence falls, thick and suffocating. My scalp crawls with awareness. The sensation prey must feel when it is being hunted.

I am prey, and there is an unseen predator here with me.

"What is this?" The voice is androgynous. "I sense you, little one. You resist me." It sounds intrigued by that fact.

Every hair on my body stands to attention.

"The blood has alerted me to your presence, so there is no point in hiding now."

Don't speak. Don't answer. I press my lips together, heart pounding like a hammer against my ribs.

"Come now. You can tell me your name. Best we get acquainted. We will be spending much time together."

The air ripples, and I sense the entity move closer.

"Come out, come out, wherever you are," it sing-songs.

I have to get out of here. Back to my siblings. Back to... Where were we?

"Oh yes, I feel you. Close now."

The abyss!

Back to the abyss.

I have to get out. Now!

NYX

Tristeene sucked in a sharp breath and snapped out of her daze. "Oh earth..." She grabbed the bars to hold her trembling body upright.

Fuck this. I crossed the room and wrapped my fingers around hers so that we were gripping the bars together. "It's okay. You're okay."

She shook her head. "No, it isn't, and I'm not. I went somewhere. I saw..."

"What did you see?" Lynal asked.

Her gaze flicked to him. "People rooted to the earth. So many of them. Like trees. Daimon, demon, and abyssbloods, just rooted to the earth beneath a lightning storm, and then...I heard a voice. It was something...something bad. And it was looking for me." She shuddered. "Nyx...I think...I think I just met the root of the sickness. I think...I think it's alive."

SIXTEEN

Tristeene perched on the edge of her narrow cot watching Lynal pace the flagstones.

"There has to be a reason why the infection is affecting you differently," he said. "You're a succubus, right?"

"Yes, a Nephalem."

"Yes, and we have Nephalem who were infected. It's always the same."

But it was different this time. Because there was something different about Tristeene. But what?

Veena grabbed my hand. "Your blood. Tristeene drank your blood when she got hurt. Could that be why?"

Oh...fuck...

Lynal looked confused, but the expressions on Mallini and Tristeene's faces told me they'd grasped what Veena was saying and why.

"I'm an anomaly, Lynal. My blood is different."

He exhaled sharply. "Of course. And your blood was in her system when she was infected. It could be why this thing, whatever it is, can't get a hold on her."

"But it's trying," Tristeene said. "It's trying to find me.

Right now, it's as if it can't see me properly, but when you bled, you helped it surge to the surface."

"It's an entity," Mallini said. "Alive. Like a queen bee in a hive controlling all the workers."

"Yes!" Tristeene stood up. "Their consciousnesses are in the gray place with the lightning. It has them plugged into the earth. It tried to take me, but I fought it."

"You can't kill Tristeene," Veena said confidently. "We need her. She could be the key to figuring out what this sickness is and stopping it."

Tristeene's throat bobbed. "I can't...I can't go back to that place. What if it finds me?"

She was right. We couldn't risk that. Yet. "No one will do anything until we have more information on this thing. The sickness came from the pit, so we need to speak to someone who is from the pit."

Tristeene's eyes flared in comprehension.

My smile was mirthless. "We need to speak to Sin."

Gus and Keelan returned a few minutes later, escorted by Jysten. We filled them in on Tristeene's experience with the strange entity, then Lynal left, saying he needed to speak to Trystin about all of this.

Garth retreated to guard the main exit from the dungeons, but Jysten hovered close to Veena. The maras had a thing for my sister, for sure.

"How was the hub?" Mallini asked Gus.

Gus looked at Jysten, as if assessing him. "You saw me open that panel, didn't you?"

Jysten frowned. "Yes. So?"

"Have you been around the hub much?"

"It was broken by the time I was born, so not really."

"Good, then I can trust you," Gus said. "Gather close." He led us toward Tristeene's cell. "The hub isn't broken; it's been tampered with to stop it working."

"What?" Jysten looked horrified. "No. That can't be right. Why would anyone do that? Even if we wanted to, we wouldn't know how."

"*You* might not," Gus said. "But Trystin would. Didn't you say he was taught how to use the hub by his wife, Ione?"

"Yes, but—"

"And then she died, and he took her place as leader."

Jysten shook his head. "Wait...are you implying that Trystin caused Ione's death?"

"I'm not implying anything except that he's the only one who knows that machine inside out. If anyone could have tampered with it to stop it operating, then it's him."

"But why?" Veena asked. "Why do that?"

"None of us want to be stuck here. Cut off," Jysten said. "We did our part. The infection is under control. At least it was until today."

Gus's blue eyes were bright with revelation. "I have a theory for that too."

I was beginning to catch on to where he was going with this. "You think Trystin had something to do with the attack, don't you?"

Gus nodded. "He takes the leadership role. Becomes a king in his own right, but then the infection is under control, and he knows that if he contacts the demon realm then the princes will come and take over. He'll be no one again."

"So he broke the machine," Mallini said.

"But why cause the attack?" Jysten asked.

"Lynal said the people were starting to get antsy,"

Mallini said. "Asking why the hub hadn't been fixed. The attack was a reminder that there's still a threat out there. That they still need Trystin."

Jysten exhaled sharply. "That snake. We must tell Lynal."

"Can he be trusted?" Gus asked. "How close is he to Trystin?"

Jysten's lip curled. "My father has no love for the daimon. But he respects the Knightwood name, and he was devoted to Ione Knightwood."

How devoted had he been? Had he been in love with Ione? "Then we need to bring Lynal on board with our plan."

"We have a plan?" Keelan asked.

"Oh yes," Gus said. "Yes, we do."

Seventeen

SIN

I've learned to be patient. My task requires it, but right now, with Nyx in danger, I'm struggling to maintain my composure.

This is a test for me.

A taste of what's to come.

The part of me that was once Lucifer knows how unlikely it is that the spawn will survive the abyss, but the larger part of me that is Sin is confident that Nyx will find a way to get to the hub. What happens after that depends on the fate of the residents of the abyss.

"They haven't returned our messages in decades," Ramiel reminds me. "Either the hub is compromised, or there is no one left to pick up the messages."

"Or maybe they've forgotten how to use it," Levistus says. "Instructions were left with a select few. If they were killed and failed to pass on the knowledge, then..."

Then nothing. "The spawn will figure it out. They have the skills between them to make it work."

"If they get there," Levistus says.

I snort. "All doom and gloom, *hmmm*? What happened to positive manifestation and making it so?"

Levistus gives me a wry smile. "Where have you been all these decades, brother? Hiding under a rock?"

They have no idea. "It seems my spot beneath a rock allowed me to maintain an element of positivity. Something we'll need if we're to keep our world safe from the foes desperate to take it from us."

"You should have come back sooner," Ramiel says. "Why keep us in the dark for so long?"

They have no idea how long I too was in the dark. Floating, healing. "You know why. You know what Beelzebub and I did, and you know what's at stake if our plan fails now. His death almost derailed it."

"And you're certain there's no other way?" Levistus asks.

"I am." Even though I wish there were. Now more than ever, I wish there was another way. One that didn't involve using her. Because despite my firm intentions, despite my efforts to keep a distance, the damn female has found a way to get under my skin.

She can't die.

Not yet, anyway.

EIGHTEEN

NYX

Gus's plan was simple. We access the hub, rearrange the crystals to activate it, and send a message to the princes to come get us. It was up to Lynal to ensure that Trystin stayed away, and according to the marasguard leader, Trystin retired to his quarters at eleven every night.

The coast would be clear then, and Lynal would keep watch to make sure it stayed that way.

Simple.

Except no one warned me about the stairs.

At least my glutes were getting a workout.

Jysten led the way, and Gus was close behind him. Damn, he was smart. If anyone deserved the Morningstar throne, it was him. He had the brains for it, for sure. He'd make an excellent Satan.

Veena was ahead of me slightly, her small frame agile and nimble as she climbed the stairs. Mallini and Keelan were close on my heels, but Tristeene's absence left our troop incomplete.

Lynal refused to let her out of the cage, and I hadn't pushed him. The sickness had a grip on her, and this entity had a connection to her. We had to be careful. Once the princes got here, we'd figure out the best course of action for Tristeene. I was certain that they'd want to keep her alive and figure out a way to find out more about the entity that had so many in its grip.

Thank the earth we were at the top of the stairs. Jysten hurried us across an entranceway and into a chamber with massive crystals jutting up at the center of it.

Gus hurried over to the circular panel that sat beneath the crystals. I followed to watch him work. He popped open a small panel and quickly rearranged the tiny crystals inside it.

There was a soft whirring sound, and the hairs on my body stood to attention with static.

"I feel it," Veena said.

"Me too." Mallini rubbed her arms. "Tingly."

Oh shit. Her plumes were all puffed up and sticking up around her head. I bit back a smile.

Veena giggled. "Your plumes…"

Mallini reached up to feel them and let out a curse.

Keelan chuckled. "It'll be an asset in battle," he said. "It makes you seem bigger and therefore more intimidating."

Mallini gave him a kitten grin. "Thanks."

Gus was busy tapping at the glowing symbols on the panel now.

"What are you doing?" Jysten asked.

"Sending a message."

I stepped closer, watching his fingers fly across the symbols. "What did you say?"

"Spawn at the hub. Traitor in the abyss. Please send help." He stared at the smooth unmarked part of the panel and waited.

"Gus, what now?"

"We wait for them to—" He sucked in a breath. "Look!" The unmarred part of the panel lit up with symbols. Gus frowned. "Wait. It says they don't have the key. It says we do." Shit! He reached for the leather strap around his neck and tugged to reveal the key we'd retrieved from Fertilis. "There's a hole in the panel. I saw it. We can—" His body jerked, and his eyes flew wide with shock.

I stared at the crimson stain blooming across his shoulder in confusion for a second before it hit me that there was an arrow sticking out of his back.

"No!" I made a grab for Gus, but an arrow whizzed between us and connected with the panel behind.

"Don't move!" Trystin bellowed. "Step away from the hub. Now." He had a crossbow pointed at us, and several maras holding spears flanked him.

The guards he'd recruited, no doubt. The fact that he was here without warning told me that he must have rumbled Lynal. Was the maras still alive, or had he been dispatched?

Gus slumped to the floor by the machine, unconscious and bleeding.

Anger raced like fire through my blood, and I slowly raised my head and fixed my gaze on the daimon. "I'm going to kill you, Trystin."

His eyes narrowed in a smug smirk. "You won't get the chance."

"Where's my father?" Jysten demanded.

"Your traitorous father is indisposed," Trystin said. "Temporarily, for now, but I'll happily make it permanent if he refuses to cooperate."

"Cooperate with your plan to keep everyone trapped in the abyss?" Mallini asked.

He sneered at her. "This is our home. The wards were the best thing the fallen ever did for us. They gave us autonomy from their false rule. This is our world, and we will *not* invite them back into it."

The maras around him nodded in agreement.

He'd spun them a pretty lie, and they'd bought it. "You're all fools. He doesn't care about keeping the abyss pure. He wants control and status, something he won't have if the hub is working. You'll have the choice to leave. To come to the demon realm and start a new life away from the infected, free from fear of being infected. The princes will more than likely set up a rotation of demon guards to come and help man the city and patrol, to keep the infected in control." I had no idea if that's what the princes would do, but it seemed like a reasonable assumption, and the flicker of doubt on the maras' faces told me it resonated with them.

"Pretty lies," Trystin said quickly. "The fallen serve only themselves."

He wasn't wrong there, but agreeing with him wasn't going to get us out of this pickle.

"Now move!" He used his crossbow to wave us away from the machine.

Keelan stepped forward. "No."

"What?" Trystin looked thrown.

Keelan raised his chin and addressed the maras. "If you want to stop us from contacting our home, then we will not fight you. We will not hurt you, because every life here matters to us. If you want to stop us, you'll have to kill us. Here. Now. In cold blood. Like cowards."

A murmur broke out among the maras. Disconcertion and doubt. I saw the flash of unease then the light of pride in their eyes as they lowered their weapons one by one because Keelan had just spoken to the warrior inside them all and challenged their sense of honor.

"What are you doing?" Trystin said. "Raise your weapons. I am your liege!"

"You're nothing but an imposter," Jysten said. "You killed Ione."

Trystin paled. "How...Liar!"

The maras he'd brought with him turned on him now, spears pointed at his torso. Trystin's eyes went wild. "Stand down. Stand down, damn you."

There was movement behind me. Gus was awake and reaching for the panel.

"Stop!" Trystin raised his bow and fired.

I stepped into the path of the arrow, biting back a cry as it punctured my thigh. Silence permeated the air for a long beat in which I took in the maras' faces, tight with shock. Keelan let out a roar and thundered toward Trystin, who let out a shriek and fired at him, but a maras shoved him, and the shot went wild.

"Gus..." I staggered back, my leg a dead weight of agony. "Gus, are you okay?"

He was slumped against the open panel. "The key..." His voice was a whisper of pain.

I grabbed it from around his neck, shoved it into the hole in the panel, and twisted. There was a soft snick, then the four crystals lit up. The room erupted in a low-grade hum.

"It's working." Gus smiled, then his eyes rolled back in his head, and he passed out again.

"Stop it. Damn you, get off me!" Trystin cried.

But the maras had him pinned, their eyes on the machine.

I swayed on my feet, fighting a wave of dizziness as the larger crystals on the hub began to glow. Light shot out of each one, lancing across the room to converge in a brilliant spot of white light.

There was something inside it.

A figure.

A male with horns...

Sin...

He appeared a moment later, larger than life, glorious, powerful, and fuck, my heart was doing all kinds of crazy shit.

His gaze swept over the occupants of the room, searching until it landed on me, and then his mouth tightened, rage filling his beautiful silver-kissed eyes.

"Who did this to you?" he demanded.

Fuck it. I pointed at Trystin. "That bastard." My vision darkened. "He broke the hub too."

Sin's lips curled in a sadistic smile. "Then he shall pay with his life."

I wanted to see this. I needed to...

Darkness swept across my vision, and my face met the floor.

NINETEEN

There were ashes in my mouth and a bitter taste in my throat. I opened my eyes on a groan and stared at an unfamiliar ceiling. How much had I had to drink last night and whose bed was I in?

No.

That wasn't right.

That wasn't me anymore.

My leg throbbed. Oh crap, I'd been shot in the leg by a power hungry daimon and then the doorway to the demon realm opened and...Sin...I sat up, wincing as the motion made my leg hurt even more. Someone had taken off my trousers and bandaged up my thigh, leaving me in a strappy top and panties. The bed beneath me was firm and covered in fancy silken sheets that smelled like...Sin? Wait, was this his room? No, I'd been in his quarters. This room was different. Decorated in muted gray and silver accents and minimally furnished with just the bed, a large dresser, and an armchair by the window.

Stars twinkled against the blanket of night outside. How long had I been out? Couldn't have been that long if it was still nighttime. There were two doors leading out of the room. I swung my legs to the side, biting back a cry as pain shot up my thigh. I needed clothes, boots, and answers.

Where the fuck was everybody? Oh crap, Gus had been shot. Was he okay?

I had to check on him.

The door opened, and Sin filled the frame. He was so tall he had to duck to enter the room. His ferally beautiful face was set in stern lines, and his dark eyes, swimming with flecks of silver, were hard and unforgiving as they roved over me.

That look made me feel like I'd been caught with my hand in the cookie jar, and that pissed me off. "What? Why are *you* mad? I'm the one who got shot."

"You stepped into the path of the arrow," he said tightly. "It was not meant for you."

Was he serious? "And that matters how?"

"You intentionally put yourself in harm's way."

What the fuck? "I protected my brother. He's okay, right?" Please tell me he's okay.

His jaw ticked. "He lives. But I won't stand for this behavior. No more."

"Excuse me?"

"If you put yourself in unnecessary danger again, I *will* punish you."

"You'll *punish* me?" Indignant rage numbed my pain. I scooted off the bed to face off with him. "I'm not a pet you can discipline."

He looked down his nose at me, making me feel small and insignificant.

I returned the glare, refusing to be cowed. "You can't punish me for protecting my family."

"Yes, I can."

Rage momentarily stole my words, and when I finally spoke, they exploded from my lips like bullets. "Well, you can just fuck right off, Sin." His eyes flinched. "You might be all big, bad Lucifer and stuff now that you're here, but *I* know you from your blacksmith days. From when you were hammering out metal in a workshop and trading with me for sexual favors. Do *they* know? Do they know about the workshop?" I glared up at him through narrow eyes. "What were you doing there, anyway?"

His hand was around my neck in a blink, his face close to mine. "You have beautiful lips, Nyx, especially when they're wrapped around my cock, but you talk too much. You need to learn to keep that pretty mouth shut."

His grip was tight enough to feel intimidating but not tight enough to hurt. "Are you threatening me?"

"No, I'm warning you. Keep your nose out of matters that don't concern you."

"And you keep your nose out of my relationship with my siblings."

"Not when it puts your life at risk," he said. "Because your life belongs to me."

The hand around my throat was now a caress, thumb sweeping back and forth across my skin. "You are my electus." Heat bloomed across my breastbone where his damned mark lived. He brought his mouth close to mine. "If you hurt, they will hurt. If you die, they will die, do you understand me?"

I couldn't breathe with him this close. Couldn't think straight with his scent filling my head with carnal images. My traitorous body softened and leaned toward him.

Focus, dammit. "No."

He flinched. "No?"

"You won't hurt them."

His smile was cruel. "Oh, Nyx, you have no idea what I'm capable of. Test me and see what happens." His lips brushed mine. "I dare you."

My eyelids fluttered closed at the contact, heart lurching, breasts swelling. "Let me go." My voice was a thick rasp that contradicted my words.

"No," he said. "I don't think I will."

And then he kissed me, knocking all sense from my brain and turning my knees to jelly. I grabbed at his powerful biceps, clinging to him as he snagged me around the waist and hauled me against his powerful form. I molded to him, softening against the hard planes of his body, fingers flexing against the rounded muscles in his arms as he devoured my mouth as if it was a feast. He tasted like cinnamon and coffee. I sucked on his tongue, and his chest rumbled in approval, the vibration spreading through me, down to my pussy, where it flooded me with slick heat.

He broke the kiss, nostrils flaring in triumph. "I can smell your arousal."

"Yeah? So what?" I was still pissed at him. Pissed off and horny as fuck. I wanted his mouth on my cunt and hated myself for it. "What are you going to—"

He lifted me off my feet and carried me to the bed. My heart pounded as he sat me on the edge of the mattress and knelt before me. There was something undeniably erotic about this powerful male kneeling between my thighs, and the smirk on the fucker's face told me he knew it.

He gently gripped my thighs, his huge hands easily wrapping around them.

"This will help with the pain." His voice was a low hungry rasp that deepened the pulse between my legs.

He spread me wide, exposing my arousal in the way my panties clung to my pussy.

I needed him to touch me.

A talon sprouted from his thumb as he slid his hand up my uninjured thigh. My breath quickened. Yes. Do it. Tear them off.

He sliced at the fabric, but it clung to me still. I made a sound of frustration in the back of my throat.

His chuckle was deep and wicked. "Patience, Nyx." He slowly peeled away the fabric, and cool air kissed my slick heat. "Patience," he growled, pushing my knees up to open me wider. "So fucking good." His hot breath beat against me. "Get ready to scream, Nyx."

He covered me with his mouth and pushed his tongue deep into me. My cry lodged in my throat, hips rising to take him deep as he fucked me with his tongue. I fell back onto the bed, hands on my breasts, squeezing and kneading as he ate me out. He withdrew and claimed my clit, sucking and flicking before sinking his tongue back into me, over and over, until my mind fractured and my body was a writhing mess of whimpering, gasping need beneath him.

Please, please. Oh...

Stars exploded in my vision, and I ground my hips against his face, desperate to ride the orgasm to infinity. He continued to feast, lapping at me as I came again and again.

Once it was over, he stood, looking down at me, his mouth glistening with my juices. "There are fresh clothes on the dresser. Put them on and meet me in the next room. We have business to discuss."

My legs were still shaking from the orgasm. "That's it? You eat me out and leave?"

He licked his lips and headed for the door.

"Sin?" I sat up. "Are you fucking serious?"

He closed the door firmly behind him.

I slumped back on the bed. The bastard. I hated him, but he was right about one thing. The pain in my thigh was no longer my main concern.

TWENTY

The view from the window told me we were still in the abyss, which was good, because we had issues to sort through here.

I donned the male's shirt and britches someone had left for me. They were a little large, but I made some adjustments. They'd do for now. I wasn't going to complain. Better these than a dress. Although I was starting to like dresses, especially if I was in the Court of Flame with Ignatius. I didn't mind them then.

The thought of the efreet brought a pang to my chest. I'd get to see him again soon. I'd get to see all the guys...my guys. Yes. That felt right. Sev already had my heart, and Ignatius knew that I wanted to consummate our bond, but it was more than that. I was falling in love with him too. When it came to Artimus, I'd been skirting romance ever since we met. Fighting our attraction with words and banter, but it was time to take the next step. He belonged to me, and I was ready to claim him. And Zepar? There was no denying our chemistry. It had been simmering between us from the moment he dunked me in Lake Morbidus to cleanse my body of poison. But the last few days before the final trial had changed the dynamic between us. He'd come to my rescue in Libidine, standing up to his father, Ramiel, on my behalf. He'd saved my life in the Court of Ivory when some fucker had shoved me off a bridge. He'd earned my trust, and I was done fighting our attraction. Things would be different going forward, because if I'd learned anything since coming to Morningstar, it was that life was too short.

But first I needed to speak to Sin about Tristeene and the entity she was connected to. He was from Inferis. He'd been trapped there after the rest of the daimon found their way into the abyss. Lucifer reopening the door had let him out, so maybe he'd have some insight.

It was a long shot, but it was all we had.

I found him in a room across the hall from mine, but he wasn't alone. Ramiel and Lynal were with him. The room looked like a lounge and dining room mushed together, and the males were sitting at an oval table nursing cups of...tea? I mean, there *was* a large teapot on the table, so...

Sin indicated the seat beside him and then drew the tea tray toward him.

"Sugar? Milk?" he asked me.

Wait, was he going to make me tea?

He arched a brow, waiting.

"Two sugars and milk, yeah."

He made the tea and passed it to me. "Lynal has filled us in on Tristeene's situation."

"This is a first," Ramiel said. "The succubus is now very important."

Good. "So you agree. They can't kill her."

"Yes," Sin said. "Tristeene will be kept here. Kept comfortable. But she will need to be locked up."

Ramiel prompted Lynal to speak with a nod.

"We've transferred her to cell quarters," Lynal said. "She won't be in the dungeons any longer. Jysten will be overseeing her care."

At least she'd have some creature comforts. "Where are my other siblings?"

"Back in Morningstar," Ramiel said.

They'd left me here? No. They wouldn't have gone, not if they'd been given a choice. "You made them leave."

"We would have sent you with them," Ramiel said, "but the arrow you were hit with was dosed with a toxin, and the antidote was only available here. The first shot that pierced your sibling was a warning shot, the second was a kill shot aimed for his head."

Lynal nodded. "You saved your brother's life."

"But we were beginning to think you'd never wake up," Ramiel said. "That we'd have to transport you unconscious through the portal."

I looked to Sin. "How long was I out?"

"Two nights," Sin said. The corners of his mouth tightened. "You were delirious most of it."

"But Sin tended to you," Ramiel said with a slight tilt of his lips. "The perfect nursemaid."

Sin slow blinked but didn't bite.

He'd taken care of me. Had he slept in the bed with me? It would explain the scent of him all over the sheets. My chest fluttered, but I shut it down. "So what now? How do we free Tristeene from this sentient infection?"

A look passed between Sin and Ramiel, and alarm bells went off in my head. "Sin, did you know that the infection was alive?"

He gave me a flat look. "How could I have known that?"

That one was easy. "Part of you is a high daimon. You were trapped in Inferis long after the daimon left."

His jaw ticked. "Yes. I was. I was one of many."

"You're saying there are more daimon trapped in Inferis?"

"Of course there are." His tone held a hint of impatience. "It's a whole world. Only a fraction of us made it out. The rest of us survived as best we could, but the infection is stronger there."

"Why?"

He sighed. "Who knows? And it matters little now. The succubus has a direct line to the entity driving the infection, and we'll find a way to use that connection to gather more information and do what we can to help her in the process."

"We?" I looked from Ramiel to Sin. "You mean the princes."

"Yes," Ramiel said. "Your only concern is returning to Morningstar and preparing for the coronation, which will take place three days from now."

"The succubus can no longer be considered a potential Satan," Sin said. "Not that it matters now."

"What? Why?"

"Because we've made our decision," Ramiel said.

I'd been about to pick up my teacup but stalled. "You've picked a Satan?"

"Yes," Ramiel said.

My pulse pounded in my throat. "Who?"

Sin's smile was slow and deliberate, his eyes lighting up with stars. "You, Nyx. The new Satan will be you."

Twenty-One

I'd taken on the challenge of Satan to prove a point to Artimus. To show him that even a human could be worth something. Back then, I'd been mad at the father who'd left me to a mother who'd abandoned me to the streets, but between then and now I'd discovered a family. I'd fallen in love with my competition, and now the idea of my being chosen over any of them felt wrong.

"Why me?"

Sin blinked sharply. "Excuse me?"

Sin wasn't the focus of my question. "Why me, Ramiel? What did I do that was better than the others?"

Ramiel sipped his tea. "Everything."

I wasn't buying that. "Tristeene charmed the serpent in the first task, and Keelan saved my life. In the second task, Gus worked out how to get us in and out of Fertilis, and Mallini risked her life to make sure we made it out. All I did was teleport us into the abyss, into danger, where my sister got infected."

Sin sighed. "Ramiel, if you could..."

Ramiel leaned forward, bracing his forearms on the

table. "In the first task, you identified your siblings' strengths and encouraged them to use them. You say that Mallini risked her life to save yours in the second task, which tells me that she deemed you worthy of living in her place. You are a natural-born leader, Nyx, and your siblings admire and love you, which was evident during your trial and the evidence that the imp gave. And then there's the question of your heritage and power." His gaze fell to my wrists. "You broke out of the shackles to save your siblings from lava. Which tells us you could have broken out of them at any time to save yourself from Levistus and his sword, yet you did not, because your power is driven by the need to protect others."

"But—"

"It's decided," Sin said. "And your siblings have been informed. They're happy with the decision."

"We're confident now that you won't use your abilities against us," Ramiel said.

Bullshit. I'd just shattered their cuffs, and I bet they didn't have anything stronger to slap on me. That coupled with the fact I was Sin's electus meant they couldn't touch me. They had no choice but to play nice.

Still, being chosen as Satan didn't sit right with me. Gus was the one I'd have picked. He was logical, methodical, knowledgeable, and a natural-born peacemaker. Morningstar was about maintaining that peace, of being a neutral party. Leadership, although useful on the battlefield, wasn't a priority for the role of Satan.

I lifted my chin. "You've made a mistake."

Sin's eyes flashed. "I do *not* make mistakes."

The fleeting expression on Ramiel's face said differently, but it was gone too soon for me to be sure of what I'd seen.

"Go see your sister," Ramiel said. "We leave in an hour."

"I'll have a troop of maras ready to go with you," Lynal said.

Wait, he was sending maras to the demon realm? "No!" I pushed my chair back. "No maras."

Sin looked at me in surprise. "Why not?"

But my attention was on Ramiel. "Why don't you tell him why not, Ramiel? Tell him where the maras you took from here centuries ago are now. Tell him how they're treated."

Lynal stiffened. "What is this about?"

"Nyx…" Ramiel warned.

But fuck him. I wasn't about to let him take more maras into the demon realm to be mistreated. "The maras are kept like animals in the Court of Shadows and are owned by Duke Umbrane."

"Maras in the demon realm…Owned?" Lynal's eyes narrowed.

I crossed my arms and looked down my nose at Ramiel. "Go on. Explain why more maras should be sent into the demon realm."

Ramiel made a sound of exasperation. "It was a mistake gifting the maras to Umbrane. Merihem realized this once he discovered how Umbrane was treating them, but the gift is bound by contract, and there is nothing we can do." He looked to Lynal. "The maras that you send with us will not be treated as objects to be gifted. You have my word."

Lynal pushed back his chair and stood. "There should be no maras in the demon realm. None were sent with you."

I looked over at Ramiel, but he didn't meet my eyes. "You may not have sent them, but they came nonetheless."

Lynal's eyes flashed, and his jaw ticked, but he exhaled through his nose, calming himself before speaking. "My people are not cattle. They cannot be owned, and the fact that a fallen felt it within his right to gift them to anyone..." He shook his head. "You will not get any aid from us until the mistreated maras already in your care are freed."

"We are your only way out of the abyss," Ramiel reminded him.

"And we have survived the abyss for centuries without your help. Your kind may rule over the demon realm now, but the abyss will only ever be ruled by the daimon." He looked over at me as he said it. Ramiel opened his mouth to speak, but Lynal held up his hand. "Now if you'll excuse me, I need to speak with our new regent before she leaves."

Why was he looking at me again?

"Oh, yes," Sin drawled. "Nyx, now that Trystin has been...dispatched, you're the only surviving Knightwood."

"Wait...What?"

Sin sat back in his seat, head canted to one side. "Why so surprised, Nyx? You have Knightwood blood. And the abyss throne belongs to the Knightwoods."

And now it all made sense. The reason they wanted me as Satan. They hoped I wouldn't put the interests of the abyss above the interests of Morningstar, and they could continue to hold the reins to this realm through me.

Or so they thought.

Because they were going to find out that I was done being pushed around the chessboard.

TWENTY-TWO

Lynal escorted me through the corridors of the royal tower. The sun was rising, lighting up the marble floors and glinting off the silver walls.

"What is this material?" It was abrasive to the touch but not brick or any stone that I'd ever seen.

"Shilana stone," he said. "Native to the abyss and highly durable. It keeps the buildings cool in summer and warm in the colder months. There are quarries to the east filled with vast amounts of it. The bridges are also constructed of it."

We walked in silence for several seconds. "Lynal, what did Sin do to Trystin?"

"Broke his neck," Lynal said. "He deserved to die for what he did. Ione was...She was a good woman. Kind and generous." His throat bobbed.

There'd definitely been more to his relationship with Ione. "Did you two have a thing?"

He snorted softly. "I would have been honored to, but she was faithful to Trystin, and unlike most other daimon, she chose not to take any more mates."

"But *you* loved her?"

"Yes. I never stopped."

"But you met someone, right? Jysten's mother?"

"Ah, yes, Yana was sweet. We spent a year together. Long enough for Jysten to be born, but her heart was elsewhere, just as mine was. She's mated to a good maras now." He fell into silence for a long beat. "The maras in the demon realm...How bad is it?"

"Bad. I managed to free one of them. His name is Sev."

"You smile when you say his name. He's important to you."

"I love him."

Lynal's eyebrows shot up, and then his face broke into a wide smile. "Then you have impeccable taste."

I matched his grin. "Not always. Sev is...He's special. I've vowed to find a way to free his kin, your kin, from Umbrane's clutches."

"How many maras does this Umbrane have?"

"I don't know. I've always assumed he had no females, but now...I'm not so sure. It was a mistake for them to go with the princes."

Lynal's jaw tensed. "I do not believe they did so willingly. During the Chaos War, we loaned a troop of maras to the fallen to fight beside them against the infected. The troop was made of males and females. They never returned. We assumed they died. I believe now that your princes took them into the demon realm during the exodus. Took them by force somehow."

"Or tricked them. Who knows?"

"How can you trust them?" he asked.

"I don't trust them, but I trust that they'll act in their own interests, and that makes it easier to predict their actions."

"You never saw any females in the Shadow Court?"

"No. None. And Sev never really spoke about it. He's never spoken about his mother. All I know is that he was preadolescent when Umbrane took an interest in molding him." My lip curled. "The stables are filled with maras of the same generation."

"He must have been born in the demon realm," Lynal said. "Only the adult marasguard were taken."

Sev had told me about the stables and his maras brothers, all the same age as him. He'd never mentioned older maras, only ones younger than him. But from what he'd told me about the abyss and the maras who'd lived here, I'd assumed he'd lived here too. But if Lynal was saying no younglings had been taken, then how could he know?

"Sev told me about the abyss and how the maras operated here."

Lynal blinked sharply. "He did? Maybe he had contact with one of the original maras who were taken."

"No. He told me he'd been raised in the stables with that generation. The only influence he had was Umbrane himself."

Lynal's gaze sharpened. "What did Sev tell you about the maras?"

"He told me you were morpheses, and how you could dream walk, about the baku who swallow nightmares, and how the maras worked with General Dhuma..." The look on Lynal's face had me trailing off. "What?"

He swallowed the lump in his throat. "Only a select few recall the baku. They went extinct such a long time ago. If your lover knows all this and hasn't been taught it by an abyss resident, then he must be experiencing hereditary memories."

He looked excited. Awed, even. "What does that mean?"

"Only the maras bloodline directly bonded to the royal Knightwood bloodline hold these memories. The first maras bloodline is able to command all others. They are, in all effect, a royal bloodline...My bloodline."

"Sev is royal? He's related to you?"

"He must be," Lynal said. "He has to be."

We'd come to a halt beside a large window, and the sun streamed in to kiss his skin, so it shimmered a blue shade so similar to Sev's that I was surprised I hadn't seen the similarity before.

"There was only one royal maras in the troop that was allocated to the fallen. She was their general. And my older sister. They found her bloody helm on the battlefield but not her body. All this time, I've been searching..."

"You thought she was infected?"

"Yes..."

If Sev was royal, then Lynal's sister must be his mother, which would make Lynal... "You're Sev's uncle."

Sev had family. He had an uncle and a cousin and many more relatives, according to Lynal. But what happened to his mother and the other females in the troop that the princes took?

Umbrane must have them locked up somewhere. It was the only explanation. I needed to get back and speak to Sev about this. Sev had spent his life in the stables or dancing to Umbrane's tune, but the Court of Shadows was a large place, and Umbrane could have hidden the females elsewhere. He might even have more than one stable. My heart pounded with the implications.

A long time ago, Sev told me that Umbrane had wanted him executed because he was afraid of him. Had Umbrane realized that Sev was a royal maras with the ability to lead his people in an uprising if need be? Killing him would have been the safest option in this respect. Did Sev realize he was different? He must.

"You must bring him home," Lynal said. "I would love to meet him."

"I'm going to do more than that, Lynal. I'm going to find out what happened to your sister, and I'm going to bring all the maras home, no matter what it takes."

TWENTY-THREE

So many revelations in such a short space of time had my head spinning, but once I stepped into Tristeene's new prison, all those thoughts fled, leaving me focused on her.

She was a beautiful butterfly trapped in an opulent, windowless room. Caged behind thick iron bars. This chamber had obviously been custom designed to hold prisoners of high standing, dignitaries and nobles maybe, but it was still a prison.

Tristeene sat at a small table drinking tea. They'd removed her shackles, and the muzzle was nowhere in sight, which was a good thing.

She rushed to the bars when she saw me. "You're okay. I was so worried."

She was worried about me when she was the one in the predicament here. "Forget about me, how are you? Are they treating you well?"

She smiled wryly and shrugged a slender shoulder. "It's not too bad in here." Her shadow-drenched eyes said differently. "The princes will find a way to keep the infection at bay until they find a cure." There wasn't much conviction in her tone.

There had to be something we could do sooner to help her. Wait a second... "My blood stopped the infection taking you completely. Maybe if you have more, then—"

"No blood!" She held up her hands. "It brings *it* out. I can't feed while infected. It's too risky."

Not feed? "Tristeene, if you don't feed, then you'll die..."

"Eventually, yes. But you'll find a cure before then." This she said with confidence. Confidence in me.

My chest tightened. I wouldn't fail her. I couldn't. "I'll do everything in my power to make sure you're freed."

"I have complete faith in you. In the meantime, I'm going to see if I can tap into it. Go back to that place...that strange collective consciousness..."

"Tristeene, please be careful. If it senses you—"

"I know." She smiled to reassure me. "I'll be careful. Just...find a way to cut it out of me. Use your clout as Satan if you have to."

"I promise."

Leaving her behind felt wrong, but taking her with us was too dangerous. We'd kept the infection out of the demon realm all these years, and knowingly walking it through the wards would be a foolish move.

I'd tell Sin my theory about my blood helping Tristeene. Maybe there was a way to use it to create a pill or an herbal concoction to keep the infection at bay until we figured out a permanent solution. Fuck it, once I was Satan, I'd order the conji to work on the problem personally.

I didn't trust the princes, and there was no way I was leaving Tristeene's welfare in their hands.

Lynal met me outside Tristeene's fancy prison. "I'll

escort you back to Sin now, but I've been thinking, and I have a favor to ask."

"Anything."

"I'm a leader to the maras, and I'm happy to stand in for you while you rule Morningstar, but I'm not a daimon, and I fear my ruling in your stead may wear thin quickly."

"What do you suggest we do?"

"You mentioned Dhuma was with you?"

Oh... "You want him to rule in my stead?"

"He is high daimon and was also Queen Soreena's consort. The people will accept him. They'll listen to him."

It was an excellent plan. "I'll speak to him when I get back."

"Thank you."

It was time to go home and get the many wheels in motion.

ARTIMUS

My eyes are gritty from lack of sleep, but the message in my hand makes the anxiety of the last few days melt away.

Nyx is awake. She's awake and coming home.

I need to inform the spawn. They've been on tenterhooks ever since they returned from the abyss without her.

"What is it?" Ignatius pads out of the guest room. He looks like I feel, rumpled and exhausted.

We've been roommates for the last few days with Ignatius popping back and forth from the Court of Flame while they prepare for Hrath to make a spy trip into the breach there. There's a second breach forming, and Hrath wants to go through the first to gather intelligence. But Ignatius is making him wait until his conji have created a spell that can pull him out forcefully if need be.

We've spent the nights talking about Nyx, about the future, about...us, because I'm done shying away from what I want. I want Nyx, and I know she wants me. Ignatius is a huge part of her life. Her twin flame. I like the male. He's no-nonsense, straight-talking, and trustworthy so I wanted to be sure my advances wouldn't be a problem for him. He's given me his blessing, and even though I may have gone ahead without it, it feels good to have.

"Artimus?" He frowns. "What's wrong?"

"Nothing's wrong, for once. Nyx is awake. Sin's bringing her home today."

Ignatius's shoulders sag in relief. "Thank the stars. The spawn—"

"We'll go now. I'll send a message to the Ivory Court to let Zepar know."

Ignatius nods, then grins. "She's coming home."

I match his grin, probably looking like a fool but not caring. "Yes. She's coming home. Coming to claim the throne."

Our Nyx is going to be queen.

ZEPAR

Nyx is coming back. She might already *be* back. I exit the portal from Ivory to Morningstar and head toward the spawn quarters. The door directly into her chambers is still shut down. I don't trust that I've rooted out all the spies. I can't risk them using this door to get to her. It grates that the Court of Flame doesn't have the same issue, but they have a breach, and in a twisted way, that fact makes me feel better.

I take a flight of stairs and pause at the sound of voices. My skin pricks.

"We do it tonight." The voice is insidious and raspy.

"I do it." The second voice is gruff and thick.

"We both do it. The daimon bitch must not become queen."

Fire races through my veins. I take the steps two at a time and burst out into the hallway beyond. But the corridor is empty. I know what I heard, though.

There are assassins in the keep, and Nyx's life is still in danger.

ARTIMUS

We're headed out of the door when Erinea materializes on the threshold. She looks...nervous. Strange. I don't believe I've ever seen her look nervous before.

"Artimus." Her gaze flicks to Ignatius, and I catch an element of surprise in her eyes before she masks it, dismissing the duke. "Can I please have a moment of your time?"

Please? Who is this female? If she'd *demanded* my time, I'd have told her to go fuck herself. I no longer need to eat her pussy to keep Nyx safe. But she *asks.* She said the golden word—*please.*

I have to hear what she's got to say. "Ignatius, I'll meet you there."

I don't say where, because Erinea doesn't need to know our business. As far as we know, she's working with Umbrane. She hates Nyx and wants her dead.

"Very well." Ignatius doesn't even grace Erinea with a glance before walking past her. She jumps aside to avoid being knocked over.

The efreet has no love for this Erinyes either.

I step back to let her in and close the door. "Make it quick."

She gives me a doe-eyed look. "I believe you had genuine affection for me when we first started sleeping together. I know much has changed since then, but if you ever loved me, then help me now. "

I throw up a little in my mouth.

The idea that I could ever feel anything for this conniving bitch makes my stomach turn. But I guess I deserve an award for my acting skills.

Still, it's time for some home truths. "I *never* loved you, Erinea. I don't even like you. I fucked you to stay in your confidence. To protect Nyx."

Her throat bobs, and she lifts her chin. "You're lying. We were together before she came to—"

"Yes. I did what I had to."

Comprehension dawns on her face. "You *knew* about her?"

"Yes. I did. Satan asked me to watch out for her, and the best way to do that was to have the Erinyes council on my side."

"You're a bastard, Artimus."

"And you're a conniving bitch. But then, you know that."

She pales. "Yes. I did what I felt was right. Protecting the throne from someone unworthy, dangerous even. And I stand by that. Nyx is a ticking time bomb, all that power... And now the princes have decided to give her more. To give her access to the Morningstar power." She takes a shuddering breath. "I don't agree with their decision, but I'm no traitor. They've made up their minds, and Nyx will be our queen. The monarch to the Erinyes. But not everyone is willing to back down. Which is why I'm here."

Unease pricks at my senses. "Go on..."

"I believe Umbrane is planning to attack Nyx before the coronation."

Of course he fucking is. "Do you have evidence?"

She shakes her head. "Only my word based on the fact that we were once working together." She pauses, waiting for my reaction. I roll my eyes and wave my hand in a 'move it along' motion. "You knew?"

"Yes, I knew."

She licks her lips. "Well, then you'll understand why I can't give evidence."

"Because it would paint you in a bad light to the princes?"

She doesn't try to deny it. "I lost a son to this farce, and then I lost my daughter too. She despises me, and in truth... I'm starting to wonder if any of this was worth it."

If I didn't know her better, I'd have believed her bleeding-heart maternal story.

But I *do* know her better. "Cut the theatrics, Erinea. You're here because you're afraid that if Umbrane is caught, he'll drag you down with him. You're afraid what Sin will do to you if he discovers you had a hand in hurting his electus."

The conflict plays out across her face so quickly that if I wasn't attuned to reading her, I'd have missed it.

"Fine," she says finally. "I admit it. I'm afraid. But the

fool, Umbrane, is like a hound with a bone. Not even the threat of Sin or the princes seems to deter him. He's determined that his zuni betrothed be placed on the throne. He said we'd rule together, using the zuni as a figurehead, but I'm beginning to think he has other plans. I just don't...I don't know what those plans are."

Plans that involved getting me killed. He'd orchestrated the redirection of our carriage when we'd gone to Libidine, stranding us in Old Forest and putting all our lives in danger. He'd been after me and Nyx. Wanting us dead. But unaware that all the spawn, including his custodia, were with me.

But Erinea has no idea I know about that.

I need a moment to think. For all I know, this is a ploy and she's working with Umbrane to throw us off the real trail. But if it *is* a ploy, then it's a bold one. No, there's genuine disconcertion in her eyes. The worry that the throne will be compromised and that Umbrane is planning something that will damage the power even more than Nyx can.

The fact that Umbrane is still gunning for Nyx, despite the potential consequences, are the actions of a man who either has nothing to lose or way too much to gain. A man secure in his position and whatever rewards success will bring.

My suspicions that he's working with the fawda grow tenfold. He must be banking on some sort of protection from them. What kind of deal did he have with them? One that involved the throne's power no doubt. But as slimy as Umbrane was, I couldn't see him handing over our power to outsiders...but they wouldn't know that. *He* could be using *them.*

There is no way of knowing for sure right now. "What do you know about Umbrane's plans?"

"Nothing. Just that they'll be taking place before the coronation." She locks gazes with me. "I need you to vouch for me if he's caught."

If he's caught, not if Nyx dies. I bite back the instinct to snap her neck. "Let me make one thing clear. If he succeeds in hurting Nyx in any way, then the princes' wrath will be the least of your worries."

Twenty-Four

NYX

Sin towered over me as we walked to the hub. "How is your succubus sibling holding up?" he asked.

"Do you really care?"

"Care is too strong a word. I'm concerned. She poses a vital lead on this infection."

The suspicion that had been niggling at the back of my mind pushed to the surface. "You don't have any intention of freeing her from the infection, do you?"

"Efforts to do so will be wasted. There is no cure."

I came to a stop. "You don't know that."

"Yes, I do." He glared at me, his silver-flecked gaze cold. "I know because I tried for decades to create one."

"I knew you had more information on it."

He looked away, jaw ticking. "There is no cure, Nyx. But maybe we manage her symptoms and keep her from succumbing long enough to find a clue, or some weakness within the infection that we can exploit."

"You knew the infection was sentient too, didn't you?"

"I suspected."

There was so much I didn't know about this male. So much he was hiding, but I knew enough to understand that any attempts at dragging information out of him would be a waste of energy. Sin only gave what he wanted, when he wanted.

"You can use my blood to synthesize a blocker."

"I intend to."

Of course, he'd already thought about that.

"I'll have Odette take a sample once we return," he said. "She'll oversee the synthesis of the blocker. I'll be gone until the coronation."

Where was he going? I desperately wanted to know. "Oh?" I waited for him to elaborate, but he didn't.

Instead, his mouth curved in a small, knowing smile. "Ask."

Fine. "Where are you going?"

"That's none of your business."

Bastard.

"Did you know Soreena left a message for her guards to stay and reclaim the abyss?"

He frowned. "Her final act. I remember. She knew she wouldn't return, but she believed the abyss could be saved. In time. She trusted her marasguard."

This was the Lucifer part of him speaking. These were the Morningstar's memories. At least the princes hadn't tricked the maras into staying.

"And here we are," Sin said.

Two maras stood on either side of the hub room entrance. They inclined their heads as I passed.

"Already getting the respect that befits a queen," Sin said dryly.

Wait...they were bowing to me?

"It will take some getting used to," Sin said. "But Lynal will keep the abyss in order in your absence."

"I will be coming back here, though."

Some emotion flickered across his face, fleeting and hard to define. "Undoubtedly." He tapped symbols on the panel. "But for now, you belong to the demon realm, and Morningstar awaits its Satan."

The portal lit up, a bright circular vortex.

The heat of his hand kissed the small of my back. "Shall we?"

I looked up at his beautifully harsh features. "Yeah, let's do this."

We stepped through the door together.

I wasn't a crier. I didn't get overly emotional, but I'd have to be made of stone not to shed a tear at the welcome I got from my siblings. They'd set up a long table laden with food and drink in the entranceway outside our rooms, and the smell of delicious food saturated the air.

But the best part was all the hugs. Hugs were now my new favorite thing, especially group sibling hugs.

But it wasn't just the siblings waiting for me. Sev, Zepar, Ignatius, and Arty were there too. Nugen, the weapons master, stood by the windows with Dhuma, both in identical poses, arms crossed over their chests, watching the reunion. But that's where the similarity ended because the fawn-legged Nugen barely came up to mid-thigh on Dhuma.

Ignatius waited for my group hug with my siblings to break before drawing me into his arms. He rested his chin on my head, heart pounding hard and steady against my chest.

"You have no idea..." he said.

I closed my eyes and breathed him in. "I think I do. I thought I'd never see you again."

He kissed the top of my head and lifted my chin with the crook of his finger, his ember eyes swimming with emotion. "We'll talk later."

I nodded, not trusting myself to speak past the lump in my throat because his presence made my heart swell with a cocktail of emotions.

Sev swept me away from Ignatius and into a hug that squeezed the breath from me. He buried his face in the crook of my neck and inhaled. "Missed you." His voice was a ragged whisper.

I stroked his silver locks. "Missed you more."

He pulled back, his pupils large and dark against silver irises. "Later..." His tone was gruff with need and hunger. How long since he'd fed? He pressed his lips to mine softly, uncaring of the audience we had, and hot tears stung my eyes.

This was home.

Here with him. With all of them.

He released me when Chase nudged us. Just in time, because the damn tears were about to fall.

"Fucking hell." I crouched to hug Chase, while secretly using his fur to wipe my eyes. "You guys sure know how to make a girl feel welcome."

"Of course, Your Majesty," Veena said with a giggle.

"Not yet." I smiled at her. "If there's one thing I've learned, it's that it's not over until it's over."

Dhuma, who'd been silent up until now, made a gruff sound of agreement.

"Yes, you're right about that," Artimus said. He looked

across at Ignatius then Zepar, who both gave him a slight nod. "It's not over."

I stood slowly, stomach tightening with nerves, because what was that look that passed between them? "What's happened?"

"Umbrane has a hit out on you," Dhuma said bluntly.

Artimus's brows shot up. "I thought we agreed that I'd deliver the news."

"You were taking too long," Dhuma said. "We need to strategize. Now."

"I'm sorry," Mallini said. "It's shitty news to come back to."

"I can't say I'm surprised." I crossed the room to the table and took a seat. "So what do we know?"

"It'll happen tonight," Zepar said. "I overheard someone talking."

"And Erinea paid me a visit earlier that confirmed it. She's not willing to give evidence, though."

Afraid that Sin would have her head for colluding with Umbrane, no doubt.

"We should get you somewhere safe," Zepar said.

"You can come to the Court of Flame with me," Ignatius said. "Sin appointed me your secundum."

They wanted me to hide. Again. But I was done hiding. "No."

"No?" Artimus frowned.

Ignatius locked gazes with me, and my solar plexus heated. "You're going to play bait, aren't you?"

I smiled sweetly. "Yep. The time for hiding and evading is over. I say we catch these fuckers in the act, torture Umbrane's name out of them, then nail that fucker's balls to the wall once and for all."

Twenty-Five

The plan was simple. Act normal and make it seem as if everyone was going about their own business. Ignatius and Arty would head back to Artimus's quarters, and because Ignatius had been staying with Arty for the last couple of days, any spies who saw them together wouldn't think anything of it. Ignatius had also been appointed as my secundum by Sin, so they'd expect him to stick around Morningstar. Zepar, on the other hand, would need to be seen headed back to the Court of Ivory. Dhuma would remain in his room, and Sev and Chase would stay in my room while I went for my late night 'walk' all alone, needing to clear my head and give the killer the opportunity to strike. But I wouldn't be alone, because Sev would be tracking me from the shadows.

Sev wouldn't be the only one trailing me. Nugen had picked out a route for my walk that ran alongside the secret passages, and he'd guide Arty and Ignatius through those to make sure they stayed abreast of me.

The assassin would strike, and we'd nab the fucker.

Simple.

If all went to plan.

"It will work," Zepar said, his tawny eyes bright in his tanned face. "We won't let any harm come to you."

"She can handle herself," Sev said. "But we'll be there to help."

I loved Sev's confidence in me, but it was his tone when addressing Zepar that had alarm bells going off. It was obvious that Sev wasn't a fan of the fallen, even though I'd warmed to him. We'd speak later, but for now, I wanted to push aside the looming attack on my life and relax with my family.

We ate and drank, and the conversation flowed easily.

Mallini leaned across the table and caught my attention. "How's Tristeene?"

Keelan made a grumbling sound. "They said they were moving her to proper rooms."

"Yes. They have." I filled them in on the plan to find a way to keep the infection at bay and what Sin had told me about his time in Inferis and his suspicions about the infection being sentient. "But that's all he'll tell me. I don't even know where he's gone."

"I had a message to watch over you in his absence," Ignatius said. "I do wonder what business would call him away just before the coronation. It must be important for him to risk leaving you, knowing that there are forces eager to keep you off the throne."

It didn't matter that Sin was gone because my siblings and the males who'd become so important to me were all here, around the table with me. A warm, fuzzy feeling filled my chest.

I'd never needed anyone to watch over me. It had always been me and Chase against the world, even when Babs took us in. I'd taken care of business, kicked ass, and knocked heads. I didn't need a protector, but damn, it was nice to have the backup.

"He knows I'm in good hands." I smiled.

"He knows you," Dhuma said. "From before. He must know you're capable enough."

That was also true.

"You're going to be queen," Veena said excitedly. "Three short days."

My stomach trembled with nerves, but I'd been thinking about this for a while now, and I had plans. "I can't say I'm not nervous. But I'll have my new council to help me rule."

Mallini blinked at me in surprise. "A new council? What about the Erinyes?"

I gave her a look that said, *Are you serious?*

She rolled her eyes. "I suppose there is a conflict of interest there."

"A huge one," Keelan said.

I nodded. "Exactly. That's why I'll be asking the people I trust the most to take their place." I smiled sweetly at my siblings. It took a moment, but then comprehension dawned on their faces.

"You want *us* to be your council?" Mallini asked.

"Yes. The seat's council."

Mallini let out a low whistle. "Mother is gonna be enraged by this. I'm totally in."

"I'd be honored," Keelan said.

"Me too," Gus added. "Wait, do I get access to Satan's private library?"

"There's a private library?"

His eyes were round with excitement. "Yes, there's a private library. Some of the rarest texts are held there. The books all belong to Satan. Gifted to Morningstar."

"Then it's yours."

He blinked sharply in surprise. "Mine?"

"Yes. Once I take that throne, the library is yours."

Gus beamed at me. "Have I told you I love you?"

Veena was the only one of my siblings who hadn't said anything yet. "Veena?"

She looked unsure. "I don't think it's a good idea for me...With Umbrane as my betrothed..."

She was worried he'd exert influence through her. "Umbrane will be locked away or dead. Depending on what Sin does to him when we prove his murderous, traitorous plans."

Veena looked up with hope. "If he's convicted, Mother will certainly break the betrothal even if he doesn't."

"Yep."

Veena exhaled and smiled. "Then yes, please. I would be honored."

Finally, I locked gazes with Dhuma. "I have a favor to ask of you too."

"Anything," he said. "Name it."

"After Sin killed Trystin, it left the abyss without a ruler, and apparently the people will only accept a Knightwood or someone who carries the name." I gave him a pointed look. "They want me to rule, but I can't be in two places at once. Now, the leader of the marasguard is holding the fort, but he asked me if I could send you."

"Me?" Dhuma sat up straighter in his seat. "You want me to go to the abyss? To go...home?"

I nodded. "You're a high daimon, and you were Soreena's consort, which makes you a Knightwood by marriage. Will you rule in my stead?"

When he spoke, his voice was thick with emotion. "If that is what you wish."

"Lynal believes that—"

"Lynal?" Dhuma's eyes flared. "He's alive?"

"Yes. He suggested you as a stand-in, and I agreed. You'd be perfect."

"Yes," Dhuma said. "I will do it. I'll be your regent."

I could do this. I could be Satan *and* rule the abyss with the help of my family and my friends. Now all I needed to do was to stay alive long enough to take the throne.

Twenty-Six

Artimus, Ignatius, and Zepar left just before eleven, and Zinichi arrived with several zuni to tidy up. She gave me a hug, her eyes wet with unshed tears.

"I'm so very proud of you, child," she said. "But there's so much to do in preparation for the coronation. I'll need you for a few hours tomorrow so we can get you fitted for your coronation ensemble. And we'll need a separate outfit for the ball afterwards too." She swept her gaze over my siblings. "You'll all need new outfits. I'd best inform Chesra."

Chesra, the head seamstress, was a wizard with fabrics.

The zuni had already finished packing up the table and food, and Zinichi ushered them out of the room. "Two tomorrow afternoon. I'll come for you all."

It sounded like a threat. "A ball?"

"It's going to be opulent and decadent," Veena said.

Keelan snorted dust from his nostrils. "Dancing." He shuddered.

I bit back a smile.

"We should retire," Dhuma said. "It's getting late." He gave me a pointed look.

Oh yes, my little assassin would be waiting for me to take a stroll.

Mallini hugged me and whispered in my ear, "Be safe."

It wouldn't be easy for them, hanging back when we'd been a team for so long, and in truth, it made me a little squirrelly too. But this was the way it had to be.

We said our goodnights and retreated into our separate rooms. Chase stopped at the door and dipped his head. He was giving Sev and me some privacy. That hound was way too smart.

Sev closed the door before gathering me in his arms and crushing me to him. He claimed my mouth in a heated kiss that shot straight to my core.

It was zero to sixty with Sev, cold to hot in a flash as our bodies collided. He backed me toward the bed. My thighs hit the mattress, and I went down with him on top of me, tearing at my clothes, talons scraping my skin leaving delicious trails of heat. I was naked in seconds, the rough abrasion of his skin against the softness of mine leaving me gasping as every inch of me awoke, sensitized and ready for him.

He fisted my hair and pulled my head to the side to slide his mouth along the column of my neck, leaving a trail of wet heat.

"Need." His fangs pressed to my jugular, and his cock teased my entrance.

"Take it."

He thrust into me and bit down at the same time, piercing my jugular.

My cry lodged in my throat, becoming a guttural vibration. The endorphins in his bite hit a moment later, and my eyes rolled back. He fed and fucked, pinning me to the bed, taking complete control. I let him have me. Let him feast until my head was swimming and my cunt was throbbing with release.

We lay tangled in a heap for long minutes afterwards. He was still hard inside me, seated like he belonged there while my body continued to pulse around him. I ran my fingers through his silken locks as he nuzzled the spot below my ear.

"Missed you." His voice was a sensual purr.

I turned my head to kiss his temple. "I missed you too."

He raised his head, looking down at me with moonlight eyes and lips stained red with my blood. "Not done yet..."

He pinned my wrists above my head and took my nipple in his mouth, rolling his tongue around it before suckling hard. My hips jerked up, and I tightened around his thick length.

He growled and moved to the other breast, nipping and sucking until I was weeping all over his cock.

"Dammit, Sev. Fuck me."

He kept me pinned in his control as he gripped my hip and slowly pulled out, leaving me aching with emptiness and anticipation. I didn't have to wait long before he was sinking deep again, building a tempo that rocked my body against his, rubbing me in the perfect places to help me lose my mind. I brought my knees up higher, taking him deeper, and sucked in a breath as something hard and smooth ran over my clit.

His tail was between my legs, circling and rubbing while he kept his tempo. He was beautiful, eyes at half-mast, jaw clenched in focus as the pleasure built between us.

"Nyx...Oh fuck..."

I let out a moan as he hit that elusive spot inside me,

sucking in air between my teeth as cold fire raced through my body, tightening and twisting me into knots.

"Yes, there, don't stop. Oh...Sev, please..."

I came with a guttural cry, and he joined me, slamming his mouth over mine in a desperate kiss as we climaxed.

I loved this male. Loved him with every fiber of my being.

I SHOWERED and pulled on fresh clothes. Chase was back in the room, lying at the foot of the bed while Sev sharpened his blade at my dresser.

"Are you ready to go?" Sev asked.

I was. "There's something I need to tell you first."

He set his blade down, concern flitting across his features. "What is it?"

"I met your uncle in the abyss."

He stared at me dumbly.

"Sev? Did you hear what I said?"

"I...How can you know that? How can you know he's my uncle?"

"You were born here in the demon realm, right? You had to have been because according to Lynal, no younglings were taken out of the abyss."

"So?"

"But you have memories of the abyss, of the order of things there."

He lifted his chin. "Yes."

"Did someone tell you? Did they teach you? An older maras maybe?"

He shook his head. "I told you. I've only ever been with my brothers in the stable. Or Umbrane." His lip curled in disgust as he said the duke's name. "I just...I remember things. The knowledge surfaced a year ago. It was when I knew Umbrane was treating us wrong. That we were better than he claimed us to be."

"And it's why Umbrane wanted you killed. Why he was afraid of you. He was scared you'd cause an uprising and lead the maras against him."

Sev's smile was wry. "That *was* my plan, until he had me sentenced to die. But how does this relate to my having an uncle?"

"Because those memories you have are hereditary memories, and only one maras bloodline has them: the bloodline bound to the Knightwood royals. Lynal called them royal maras. And only one royal maras was in the unit of maras taken into the demon realm by Merihem. Lynal's sister."

Sev absorbed this for several long seconds. "You're saying my mother was a royal maras..."

"Yes." Which brought me to my next question. "Sev, where are the female maras? You never spoke about them, and there were only males in the stables at the Shadow Court."

He frowned. "I don't know. We were raised by demons. By the time we thought to question who our mothers were, we were forbidden to do so on pain of death."

"So you just...left it? Stopped thinking about it?"

A flash of anger crossed his features, a reminder of the person he'd been when we'd met. "Yes, I stopped thinking about it. My energies were best channeled elsewhere."

I crossed the room and cupped his face. "Hey. I'm not making a dig. I'm just trying to understand."

He closed his eyes, allowing his body to relax. "I know." He covered my hands with his. "I'm not proud of backing down. Not proud that back then the pain was too much."

My throat tightened. That bastard Umbrane had a lot to answer for. "I will find a way to make him pay, Sev."

His eyes snapped open, blazing bright silver. "When the time comes, when his duplicity is revealed, I want his head. I want to take it."

"I promise you." I kissed his forehead.

He sighed. "I had a mother," he said softly. "We all did."

"He must have them holed up somewhere, the male maras too. The original troops gifted to him."

"He's breeding them," Sev said with a twist of his lips. "He conditioned us not to question. To fall in line. To forget." He looked up sharply. "She could still be alive. My mother could be trapped in the Court of Shadows."

"And I promise you I'll do everything in my power to find her and free her. To free all the maras from Umbrane's clutches."

His jaw ticked. "When you bound me to you with the blood debt, I told myself you were a means to an end. I planned to use you to free my people. But then I fell in love with you, and for a while I forgot about them...How could I forget?" The torment on his face made my heart ache.

"You're allowed some happiness, Sev. You were treated like shit, so it's only natural to want to forget for a while."

His fingers curled around my hands, and he gently drew them away from his face. "But no more. We'll find a way to get them out."

I allowed my lips to curl in a cold smile. "Once he's convicted of attempted murder, I'm sure the princes will convince him to burn the contract that allows him to keep the maras."

"A contract?"

"Yes. Ramiel told me. It's the only reason they haven't been able to take the maras away from him. Ramiel admitted they realize it was a mistake to gift the maras to him."

"But does Umbrane have to be the one to burn the contract?" Sev asked.

"I...I don't know."

"We need to find out. If it's just a case of destroying it..." His silver eyes lit up. "Maybe we can find a way to get to it?"

"Yes."

"We'll figure it out," Sev said. "But right now, we have an assassin to trap."

Twenty-Seven

Sev was good at the stealth stuff. I couldn't sense him trailing me, and at one point, I was tempted to call out and check that he was there, but that would blow his cover, so I kept my mouth shut, trusting that he had my back.

The corridors were empty and silent at this time of night, which left plenty of opportunity for an attack to occur. We'd agreed I'd go for my walk at one in the morning, and we'd agreed on the route too. One that had a secret passage in the walls so that Arty and Ignatius, guided by Nugen, could be close by.

Knowing I wasn't alone didn't take away from the nerves while I waited for the attackers to pounce. Not knowing what they looked like or what weapons they'd employ made it hard to plan a counterattack. Still, I had my blade strapped to a holster at my waist and hidden beneath my bathrobe. Yep, I'd gone for the whole impromptu walk in my pj's thing.

I looked like easy prey.

Come on, fuckers. I'm all alone here. Come get me.

I took a left at the next intersection.

Nothing happened. No shadows. No prickle of awareness.

What if we were wrong? What if tonight wasn't the night? The assassins could have changed their minds and—

The hairs on my nape quivered.

Danger.

Bingo.

There was a turning up ahead.

Time to slow my pace. Come on...

A figure jumped into my path and ran at me with a needle-blade knife. It was a demon, four foot in height and crimson all over. I let out a shocked yelp and sidestepped, but that one demon turned into two and blocked my path.

I jumped back, pulling my blade free of its holster just as Sev materialized in front of me like a shield. He swiped at the demons with his talons.

They leapt back to avoid getting sliced but couldn't avoid being swept off their feet by his tail. They hit the ground and multiplied, becoming four, then six.

"Fuck!" I spun and slashed the air to ward them off.

Arty and Ignatius burst out of a tapestry up ahead and charged toward us, but there were so many tiny demons filling the corridor now that they'd have to fight their way through.

Ignatius's hands lit up. He was going to fireball them.

"Don't," Nugen yelled. "You kill the wrong one and we lose our lead. Find the one with the blue mark on its neck."

Blue mark. Okay. But it was hard to check for a mark when they were coming at me in a wave of blades, eager to get a stab in. These fuckers were relentless.

Sev kept his body between us, but he couldn't stop them

all. They slipped past, weaving between his legs. What were these things?

Ignatius and Arty were close but slowed down by their search for the demon with the blue mark.

"Nyx, watch out!" Zepar cried from behind me.

I spun in time to see a demon leaping at my face, needle blade aimed at my eye. My heart pulsed in my throat.

Sev shoved me out of the way, and the blade sank into his shoulder. He didn't make a sound, simply grabbed the demon's wrist and twisted it with a snap. The demon threw back its head and screamed, revealing a blue mark under his chin. Sev gripped the creature's throat and squeezed until his eyes bugged. Half the demons in the corridor evaporated, leaving just a small bunch of them between Arty, Ignatius, Nugen, and us.

"Stop!" Nugen yelled at the mass of creatures. "Or your brother dies."

Sev held the creature aloft and shook him.

The mass turned to look at us, then one by one they evaporated, leaving a single demon standing in the corridor.

"Let him be," the demon said. "Ye put me kin down, ya bastard."

An authoritative booming voice echoed down the corridor. "What is the meaning of this!" Ramiel bore down on us, two Minorax in tow. "What is this disturbance?"

"The wards," Artimus said with a groan. "They must have picked up on the chaos."

Ramiel joined us, taking in the scene, confusion etched across his features. "Seneschal, what is the meaning of this?"

"These chima just tried to kill Nyx," Arty said coolly.

Ramiel frowned. "And you all happened to be close by?"

"We knew of the plot," Zepar said. "We laid a trap to catch them."

Ramiel's whiskey eyes darkened in rage. "You knew of a plot against our chosen Satan, and yet you failed to inform me?"

"*That's* what you're focusing on?" Zepar said in disgust.

"Enough," Ignatius snapped. "As secundum to Nyx, I authorized this coup. We had to keep the information within our circle of trust." He looked Ramiel right in the eye as he said this, making it clear that the prince wasn't in the circle.

Ramiel's jaw ticked. "Very well. What's done is done. But had this gone badly, it would have been your head on the block, Ignatius."

"If you think you can have my head, Ramiel, then you're more delusional than I thought. Need I remind you that I'm done taking orders from the fallen?"

"And yet you act as secundum for Sin."

"For Nyx," Ignatius said. "Only for Nyx."

For fucksake. This was a waste of time. "We have the culprits, and Sev is bleeding. Can we just get on with this?"

Ramiel turned his attention to the chima, who stared up at him with wide, frightened eyes.

"Don't hurt us," he said. "We claim proxy."

I looked to Nugen. "What does that mean?"

But it was Ramiel who answered. "It means they're acting under contract for someone else and cannot be held liable for their actions."

Devils then. "Where's the contract?"

The chima looked at his brother trapped in Sev's grip, then held out his hand. A scroll appeared across his palm, which he passed to Ramiel.

Finally, the truth would come out. Finally, Umbrane would get his comeuppance.

Ramiel opened out the scroll and read it quickly. His

mouth tightened, and his nostrils flared. "This is unfortunate. I would not have expected this."

"Umbrane is good at hiding his tracks," Artimus said coolly.

Ramiel looked up sharply. "Umbrane? What has he to do with..." He looked down at the contract in his hand, then back up at us. "You thought *Umbrane* was the orchestrator?"

My pulse quickened. "He is. He wants me dead."

Ramiel pressed his lips together. "Maybe so, but it isn't his name on this contract."

"What?" Artimus frowned. "Then who?"

"The contract is signed by Erinea."

Twenty-Eight

HRATH

The female writhes beneath me, clutching on to my shoulders as our bodies meet. Her skin is slick with perspiration, her cunt a tight sheath around my cock, but I'm focused on her mouth and her breath as it filters into my body.

There is no emotion in this sexual act. No connection aside from a physical one. I prefer it that way. But sex produces a potent rich quality of willing breath that will sustain me longer. If I could survive without it, then I would. I can go months between feeds, but the trips across the hottest sands of the Court of Flame have drained me. I need fuel, and the female beneath me is more than willing.

Our lips are fused as I feed, and she pants and moans into my mouth, hips rising to meet mine over and over as she takes her pleasure and I take my fill of her willing breath.

There may not be emotion in this act, but there is pleasure. The tightening at the base of my spine, the tingling in my shaft as she rides it, but it isn't pleasure I want from her. I've taken my fill of her breath, and I want this over. I grasp her hips and thrust, once, twice, hitting that place inside her that makes her cry out in release.

I give her a moment to ride the wave, then I withdraw.

"Hrath..." She reaches for me, dark, silken hair spilling across the white pillows like an inky river. But her face is oval, not heart-shaped, and her lips aren't as plump and rosy as...

What am I doing?

Disgust claws at my chest because I can no longer deny why I chose her or who she reminds me of. The dark-haired succubus has haunted my subconscious ever since she offered me willing breath when we were trapped in the Old Forest. I declined her then because I hadn't trusted myself to be close to her. She's the only reason I'm able to harden for this female now.

Her expression closes off. She thinks I'm disgusted by her. I don't have the energy or will to explain something I don't yet understand myself.

"I'll get dressed and leave," she says stiffly.

I turn away and button my pants before striding out from beneath the canopy of my tent.

There's a carriage waiting to take the djinn female back to the keep. No doubt she'll tell the others how callous I am, and they'll be lining up to prove her wrong. To be the one that can thaw my icy heart.

Little do they know I no longer have one.

The breach is a quarter of a mile away. A short flight, which I've been making daily in order to keep an eye on it. I don't need to be here. There are efreet guards and conji on standby, but my gut tells me I must stay close.

It warns me that something is about to change. I always

knew creating the Court of Flame to act as a haven was a bad idea. Our court is the only one that connects to all the demon realms; it's supposed to be a Plan B if our world is attacked. Our court is to act like a sanctuary, housing all the inhabitants of the demon realms if need be because there are layers to our court, catacombs beneath the earth that extend for miles. A place we can live if the need arises, and the harsh climate above will help us ward off threat.

But being a haven comes with a cost. It makes the fabric of our court weaker than the others and now...Now the fawda have breached it.

I'm about to take to the air when a shadow appears on the horizon.

Ugar, my sylph brother, hurtles toward me.

My heart sinks. Something's wrong.

He lands, and the vortex of air around him dissipates. "We have a problem."

"Tell me."

"The breach is shrinking."

If it leads to the fawda as suspected, and if it vanishes, then we'll never know where they're camped. We won't know who they're working with or what they're planning.

There's only one thing to do. "I'm going in."

"Hrath, you can't. The spell isn't ready, and Ignatius—"

"Will understand. This is our last and only chance."

"If it closes with you on the other side, you'll be trapped."

I allow my lips to curve in a wicked smile. "I'll find a way home."

I'll have to.

NYX

Ramiel took Zepar and Artimus to find Erinea and investigate the allegations, and we were ordered to remain in some empty guest quarters.

On the surface, the case looked cut and dried. Erinea's name was on the chimas' contract along with her blood. But unless she pled guilty, she'd be tried for attempted murder. No ordinary charge because the target had been me—the princes' chosen Satan. If she *was* convicted, then she'd be executed.

I should be happy about it. The bitch had conspired to have me executed barely a week ago, but it was impossible to feel any satisfaction when I knew the real mastermind behind all this might give us the slip.

Umbrane would go free if the blame fell solely on Erinea's shoulders.

There was no doubt in my mind that Erinea was merely a pawn in his game, but my reticence to have Erinea convicted was deeper than that. I'd seen the look on Mallini's face earlier when Arty had revealed Erinea's partnership with Umbrane. There'd been conflict in her eyes. She might say she hated her mother, but I couldn't help but feel there was a part of her that wished things could be different.

If Erinea died, she'd never have the chance to make amends to her daughter, and Mallini would be left wondering *what if?*

Erinea was no friend of mine, but I loved Mallini, and she didn't deserve to lose another member of her family.

So we waited in the opulent guest room decorated in cream and gold and furnished with comfortable sofas and cushioned chairs. A room occupied by several large imposing paintings of people that looked like they should be important.

There was one portrait that drew my attention. It was of a dark-haired man with storm-gray eyes. He was looking right out of the canvas at me. There was a smile playing on his lips as if he knew a secret. He was dressed in Morningstar colors, and a large pendant with a red gem in it hung around his neck.

"He was a regal male," Ignatius said.

"Who was he?"

Ignatius looked at me in surprise. "Beelzebub." He glanced back at the painting. "Your father."

This was my father? This man who looked the same age as me? Bloody immortals.

Still, it was nice to put a face to the name. Did I look like him? I didn't spend enough time staring at myself in the mirror to be able to tell for sure.

Almost an hour passed before Artimus finally returned with Dhuma in tow, which meant my siblings had been informed of what had happened.

"What's happening out there?" Ignatius asked them.

"We found Erinea in a carriage outside the gates," Arty said. "It looked like she was running even though she says she was headed to the market. They're questioning her now. To give her credit, she looked stunned by the allegations." He shook his head. "This is bullshit. She wouldn't be so stupid as to tip me off about her plan to kill Nyx."

"She has nothing to gain from doing that," Ignatius agreed.

"Ramiel will figure that out," Dhuma said.

I could tell that he was still annoyed about having to sit this one out. But his large size would have made navigating some of the passages in the wall difficult.

"I haven't told Ramiel that Erinea came to see me," Arty said. "It's up to her to reveal her involvement with Umbrane. It's in her best interests to do so, especially if she wants to assert that she was framed."

"We should torture the chima," Dhuma said. "They're lying, and we can get the truth if we hurt them."

"The conji fed them truth serum, and they still assert that Erinea came to them with the contract and signed it in blood."

"So it must be her," Ignatius said.

It made no sense. "She must have known that if we caught them, the contract would come to light."

"It has to be a trick by Umbrane," Sev said from his spot leaning up against a dining table. "But how did he pull it off?"

There was no way to know. The chima had been released. Proxy status meant they couldn't be punished for attempted murder. Morningstar law was fucked up. I'd be changing that as soon as I took the throne.

Sev reached up to rub his shoulder. It was healing but slowly. The needle blade had been coated in a toxin which might have been lethal to me but was a minor irritant to a maras, simply slowing down the healing process. The wound wasn't deep, thanks to his thick skin.

I parked my butt beside him and took his hand. If he hadn't jumped in to take that blow, I'd have lost an eye.

He squeezed my fingers and looked across at me, opening his mouth to say something when the door to the room was flung open.

Zepar entered, his expression tight. "The princes want to see us all in the Convectus Locus. Now."

Twenty-Nine

Oh, how I hated the assembly room. I'd been here a handful of times, and each experience had been awful. My first visit had been for the custodia choosing ceremony, and I'd ended up in the arena helping Sev fight off demibeasts. The second time had been after our first trial when we'd lost Charod. The third, and most recent time, was *my* trial, where I'd been found guilty of being an abomination, judged as too dangerous to let live, and almost executed by Levistus.

Yep, this room sucked.

But at least this time it wouldn't be sucking for me.

Erinea stood in the judgment box, the same spot I'd been standing in a week ago. Her dark plumes were ruffled, her eyes red-rimmed, but she held her chin high and proud. I had to give her props for composure.

Ramiel and Levistus sat opposite her in their special throne-like seats, looking all powerful and groomed in tailored dark suits. Levistus's golden hair gleamed in the chandelier light as if he'd given it a thousand strokes of a brush, and his eyes sparkled like gems against his alabaster skin. Ramiel's chestnut locks were brushed back off his forehead, and they looked darker because they were wet. He'd obviously showered recently, and his skin had a dewy look to it. His whiskey eyes flicked my way briefly as Zepar led us across the room to the witness section.

It was strange standing on this side of the room. Strange not to be in the spotlight, but heck, I'd take it. There were wooden benches to sit on, but I chose to stand by the railing instead. Sev took the spot to my left, and Artimus stood to my right. Ignatius and Dhuma were close behind us, and Zepar stationed himself beside Sev.

We were all in place now.

The door on the far side of the room opened, and Zepar's mother entered, trailed by an Erinyes carrying paper and quill—the record keeper, no doubt.

She parked herself at a small desk and set up her supplies, not once looking across at her leader about to stand trial.

There was no jury. Only us, the princes and—

"Motherfucker."

Umbrane ducked into the room via another entrance. What was he doing here?

But the princes didn't bat an eye, which meant they knew he was coming. They'd probably invited him.

Why?

"They'll want to see how he reacts to Erinea's accusations," Artimus whispered. "To gauge his guilt."

"Why can't they just give him the truth stuff they fed the chima?"

"It probably won't work on him," Arty said. "The fallen are immune to most remedies and mystical concoctions."

"Great, so they have to rely on his word?"

"And their deductions of his body language."

Well, this would be interesting.

Umbrane took a seat on the opposite side of the room. His dark gaze locked on to me, and a small smirk curved his cruel mouth.

Bastard.

"Erinea," Odette said. "You've been accused of conspiring to murder our new Satan. How do you plead?"

"Not guilty," Erinea said.

Odette stepped back to stand beside Ramiel's seat.

"The evidence against you is strong," Ramiel said. "A contract with the chima signed with your name *and* in your blood, along with their word, under truth serum, that you were the one to liaise with them. How do you explain that?"

"I cannot," Erinea said. "All I can do is assert the truth and my innocence. I did *not* conspire with the chima. I did not sign that contract. But I cannot deny that the blood in the ink is mine. I simply cannot explain how it got there."

"The chima claim that you signed the contract three days ago at four in the afternoon. Do you have an alibi for that time?" Levistus asked.

"Yes," Erinea said. "I was with Duke Umbrane."

Oh fuck.

"Umbrane?" Ramiel asked. "Can you confirm Erinea's alibi?"

Umbrane looked confused. "I'm afraid I cannot."

Erinea's jaw tightened. "Of course you won't," she said. "Because this was your plan all along."

"Excuse me?" Umbrane said indignantly.

"I am not guilty of this crime," Erinea said to the princes. "But I am guilty of conspiring to rid Morningstar of Nyx. I believed her to be unworthy of the throne, and I colluded with Duke Umbrane to have her removed."

Umbrane's brows shot up, and he sat forward in his seat looking the picture of shock.

"Umbrane?" Ramiel turned his attention to the duke. "What have you to say about these allegations?"

Umbrane's dark eyes flashed with anger. "The allegations are false. I will not be used as a scapegoat for your crimes, Erinea. I admit, at first, I was not keen on the idea of a Nephilim being in the running for Satan, but once I noted Duke Zepar's interest in her, I knew she must be a worthy candidate. Since then, Nyx has proven herself worthy time and time again, and now that we know her true nature, I believe she will be an asset to Morningstar."

The door behind us opened, and Nugen stepped in. I caught sight of Mallini and Veena behind him.

"What now?" Levistus said, throwing up his hands in irritation.

Nugen stepped forward and cleared his throat. "Nyx's siblings would like to bear witness also," Nugen said.

"Why not?" Levistus said sarcastically. "In fact, why don't we invite everyone to come bear witness?"

"Levistus." Ramiel gave him a stern glance. "These are Satan spawn, and Nyx's fate is tied to theirs."

Levistus sighed and shook his head. "Very well. Let them in."

My siblings entered the room and squeezed in behind us. Veena pushed through to stand between Sev and me, and Erinea's attention fell on her, a lightbulb moment crossing her features.

"If you felt that Nyx was worthy, then why did you choose the zuni as your custodia instead of her?" Erinea asked Umbrane.

Silence filled the chamber.

Ramiel looked across at Umbrane. "Well? Answer her."

Umbrane smiled and spoke smoothly. "She'd accepted Duke Zepar before the ceremony, at least that is what my sources told me." He shrugged. "I was simply being polite in not intruding on the arrangement."

"So you picked the weakest candidate?" Erinea said.

Umbrane looked across the room at Veena. "I picked the sweetest." His smile made my skin crawl. Veena moved closer to me, and I put my arm around her shoulders. Umbrane's smile widened. "I'm a proud male to call her my betrothed."

Both princes looked surprised. I guess that piece of information hadn't filtered up to them yet.

He broke eye contact with Veena to look up at the princes. "I have no issue with Nyx as choice for Satan. Not now that she has proven herself. I have no reason to want my betrothed's sister dead."

Veena whimpered softly, and my gut clenched.

I couldn't let him have her. "That's bullshit, Umbrane, and you know it. Veena doesn't want you, but you convinced her mother to give you her blessing, and now Veena is trapped."

Umbrane's mouth turned down. "Is that how you feel, little one?" he said to Veena. "Do you feel trapped? Why didn't you tell me you were unhappy?"

The bastard sounded genuinely concerned and appropriately shaken that the female he loved had less than complimentary feelings for him.

Veena's body trembled, but she met his gaze. "You never asked me what I wanted. You locked me in a dark room and left me there."

Umbrane sighed. "For your own protection, sweet one. The Court of Shadows is a dangerous place, and now, on reflection, I see that I've been selfish, thinking of only my needs and wants." He nodded as if to himself, as if he'd just come to a decision. "I free you from our betrothal. You have my word on that." Veena stiffened and looked up at me, her eyes shining with hope.

What on earth?

"Th-thank you," Veena said.

Umbrane inclined his head, his dark eyes sad. "You're welcome, little one."

Someone hand the fucker an Oscar. He almost had me convinced he was in love with Veena. But he was a liar and a conniving, murderous bastard. Sev had heard him colluding with Erinea. But if we brought that up, it would be Sev's word against Umbrane's, and the princes knew there was little love lost between those two. I couldn't even voice my suspicions that Umbrane was working with the fawda because, once again, we had no proof.

We were stuck.

Umbrane was going to get away with this, and the only positive thing that would come out of it was Veena's freedom. Erinea needed to 'fess up and tell them she'd tipped Artimus off about the attack. Why wasn't she saying anything?

"What I want to know," Levistus said, "is how this attack was thwarted." He looked over at us. "How did you discover this plot?"

Good question.

Artimus had his attention on Erinea, a question in his eyes. She sighed and nodded.

"Erinea came to see me earlier," Artimus said. "She warned me that Umbrane was planning to murder Nyx. If she *is* the orchestrator, then warning me would be counterproductive."

"Did she tell you when the attack would take place?" Ramiel asked.

Artimus frowned. "No."

"Then how did you know?"

"I didn't. Not until Duke Zepar told me what he'd overheard."

"Zepar?" Ramiel prompted.

Zepar stepped forward. "I heard two voices in the stairwell plotting the attack, but I wasn't able to catch the culprits."

My mind was whirring because I saw exactly where this was going. Ramiel confirmed my suspicions a moment later.

"This proves nothing," he said. "The accused told you of a plan to assassinate Nyx but gave no details. If Zepar hadn't overheard the chima plotting, the attack would have gone as planned, and Erinea would have been in the clear, having already pointed the finger at Umbrane."

He was right. That was exactly how it looked.

"There is no evidence to prove Duke Umbrane's involvement," Levistus said. "But there is solid proof to implicate Erinea."

"We've come to a decision," Ramiel said.

Wait, they hadn't even conferred yet.

Ramiel was the one to deliver the verdict. "Erinea, for the crime of attempted murder, you are sentenced to death."

"No!" Mallini slapped a hand over her mouth, eyes wide with shock, whether at her outburst or at the verdict, I wasn't sure.

Erinea looked across at her daughter. Her dark eyes filled with sorrow.

This was bullshit. "You can't execute her."

"Excuse me?" Ramiel said.

"It's hardly fair with just the two of you judging. Merihem and Sin should have a say too."

"Sin isn't here, and Merihem is indisposed. The evidence speaks for itself."

"What about me?"

Ramiel's lips curved. "You aren't Satan yet, Nyx."

"I know. But the crime was against me. What if I don't want to press charges?"

Ramiel blinked in surprise. "That isn't how it works."

"May I speak?" Gus asked.

Ramiel inclined his head. "You may."

"Crimes committed in Morningstar are usually tried by Satan and Satan's council."

"The princes can step in at any time if they wish," Levistus said sharply.

"*If* Satan agrees," Gus said firmly.

"But there is no Satan yet," Ramiel pointed out again. "The coronation takes place in three days."

Think, think. Ah. "Then I ask that we wait to sentence the accused until then." I smiled tightly. "It would be my first official act as Satan. A lesson in procedure for me."

Ramiel arched a brow. He knew this wasn't about lessons but about control. Question was, would he give it to me? He leaned to the side to whisper to Levistus, who pursed his lips but nodded.

"Very well," Ramiel said. "Satan will pass sentence after the coronation and festivities."

I exhaled in relief. "Thank you."

"Take the accused to the cells," Levistus said.

Two Minorax appeared to guide Erinea from the room. She looked back at us once before she was ushered out the door.

Ramiel pressed his palms to the arms of his chair, ready

to rise. "Court is dismissed."

"If I may..." Umbrane said. "While we're all here, I have a request."

Ramiel sat back down. "What is it?" His tone was long-suffering. It was obvious he'd had enough of this whole experience.

I couldn't help the pang of annoyance at his attitude. As if deciding if someone lived or died was a chore.

"As you're aware," Umbrane said, "I have a contract giving me rights to the nightmares."

My scalp pricked. Why was he bringing this up now?

"Yes," Ramiel said. "And?"

"One was taken from me not long ago." He smiled my way. "A blood debt bound him to Nyx."

The pricking across my scalp settled into a cap of ice as realization dawned. "No..." The word was a whisper.

"Nyx..." Sev took my hand. "It's all right."

But it wasn't. It fucking wasn't. How could I not have realized? How didn't I feel the absence of our bond and make the connection? His wound...the blood. He'd stepped in front of that blade to save me, which meant—

"That blood debt is now paid," Umbrane said.

His words punched me in the gut. "No."

"He belongs to me," Umbrane said. "But I may need assistance in getting him to comply."

"NO!" I stepped in front of Sev. "You can't have him. He's mine." My voice deepened to a growl, and the air around me fizzed with power.

"Nyx!" Ramiel's tone was sharp with warning, but his expression was wary. "Stand down. Please."

Please...He was scared, and he should be. His power...all their power was an illusion. I could burn them. Would burn them all to protect what was mine.

Sev pressed his chest to my back. "It's all right," he whispered in my ear. "Let me go. Let me go, and I can find it."

It? The contract holding the maras in Umbrane's control? He wanted to go back so he could infiltrate the Court of Shadows, but how could he find anything if they locked him in the stables?

"Nyx..." Ramiel stood slowly. "You *must* stand down."

Umbrane's smug smile slipped, and unease entered his eyes. Yes, he should be worried. They all should, because there was power in my veins that even I didn't understand, and it wanted to be unleashed. It wanted out.

I wouldn't let it out, of course. The risk of hurting my family was too high because the power was unknown and unpredictable, but the princes and Umbrane didn't know that.

I tore my gaze from Umbrane's smug face and fixed it on Ramiel. "I have one condition."

"The nightmare belongs to Umbrane by law," Levistus said tightly, but I could tell from his tone that he also found the whole thing distasteful.

I swallowed the lump in my throat. "I understand, and he can have him on one condition."

"Name it," Ramiel said.

"A vow that Sev won't be harmed, locked away, or confined."

Umbrane's eyes narrowed. "I have a contract and—"

"And you will have your nightmare," Ramiel snapped. "On the proviso that you keep him unharmed and unconfined."

Umbrane dropped his gaze, probably working through the situation, figuring out whether it was worth pushing back on this. Would I follow through on my threat? Did he want to risk finding out? In the end, he simply shrugged.

"Very well. I vow that no harm will come to him, and he will not be confined."

I let my rage go, and the power fizzled out. Sev made to move past me, but I grabbed his hand and turned to him, wrapping my arms around him tightly.

My heart thundered in my chest, and a chasm opened inside me. There was so much I wanted to say in that moment. So many words that tumbled over themselves to be uttered, but in the end, only two surfaced and coasted on a whisper. "Be safe."

He kissed my temple. "Always."

It took everything I had to let him go and watch him walk across the room to Umbrane. The horned fallen didn't even bother to hide his smirk of triumph, and the way he looked at Sev, the hunger in his black eyes, made my stomach hurt.

The door opened behind the princes, and a small zuni entered and scurried across the room, head down, to pass a note to Odette. She leaned down so he could speak to her then passed the note to Ramiel, speaking to him in hushed tones.

Ramiel looked across at us. "Duke Ignatius, it seems you have an important message." He held it out, and Ignatius crossed the room to take it.

He read it quickly then tucked it into his pocket. "There is an issue at the Court of Flame."

Beside me, Artimus tensed. Did he know what Ignatius was talking about? Wait, did this have something to do with the breach there? If it did, he wouldn't say so, not with Umbrane here and our suspicion that he might be in league with them. It seemed far-fetched, but we had to be wary.

"Of course," Ramiel said. "Then you must leave to attend to it."

Ignatius looked across at me, his gaze filled with conflict.

"Ah." Ramiel smiled tightly. "Your secundum duties. I'm sure now that our culprit has been caught, Nyx is no longer in any danger. An attack on her now would simply prove Erinea's innocence. Or that she wasn't working alone, and then..." His gaze slid toward Umbrane. "Then we'd be forced to reopen our investigation." He knew Erinea's conviction was a trap, and this was his warning to Umbrane.

Ignatius nodded. "In that case, I leave her in good hands." He looked over at me again, his expression torn. "I'll be back as soon as I can."

It seemed as if fate was determined to keep us apart for now. I smiled and nodded to let him know it was okay. That I'd be okay, even though this felt like a double whammy.

Sev and now Ignatius.

Ignatius swept from the room, and the knowledge that he was free to return was a comfort, but it took every ounce of willpower not to chase after Sev as he was led out of the room by the Duke of Shadows.

My nightmare didn't look back. Not once. But his white-knuckled fists left me in no doubt that leaving was hurting him as much as it was hurting me.

If I'd known this would happen, if I'd realized...What would I have done? Held him tighter. Hidden him away in my chambers. Loved him harder. Urgh.

The door closed behind them, and silence deep and unsettling filled the room.

"I'm going to kill Umbrane one day." The words slipped from my lips loud enough for everyone to hear, and I didn't give a shit. "I'm going to kill him and enjoy doing it."

THIRTY

HRATH

The sand is so hot the air above it is like fire. But thanks to the willing breath I've consumed, I'm able to create a cocoon of cool air around my body as I fly toward the breach.

It's certainly smaller than before. But large enough to let me pass. I close my eyes as I hurtle toward it.

Any moment no—

The world fractures and tips, and I land on something soft.

Blades of grass peek from between my fingers, and the world forms around me, spilling out and taking shape like a sketch suddenly flooded with color.

There's a golden pillar up head, and beyond that, I see the peaked tips of colorful tents. Tinkling music drifts toward me.

What is this place?

It reminds me of a bazaar or a fete, yet the air smells of nothing, and the grass...it has no scent either. I move quickly and stealthily toward the pillar and stand against it for cover, scanning the area beyond it. There's an empty stall hung with colorful scarves and bangles. Tables and chairs are set out to invite visitors to sit, but shining brightly beyond it all is a carousel lined with majestic war horses, set in fierce poses where they paw the air, hair flying out behind them. Black, gold, silver, white, and gray horses turn slowly to the tinkle of eerie music.

Why am I walking toward it? Why have I broken cover?

There's someone here. Someone behind me, but I'm unable to turn around.

Pressure explodes at the back of my skull.

Darkness.

THIRTY-ONE

NYX

Artimus was gone. Summoned by Ramiel to discuss the coronation arrangements. As Seneschal, it was part of his duties to organize the event of the century. There were dignitaries to invite, not just from the demon realm but from the human realm too. Three days to organize it all, because the event had to take place on a full moon, and if we missed this one, then we'd have to wait weeks for the next.

Back in the spawn quarters, panic swelled in my chest. I needed a moment. Just a moment alone to process, gather my wits, and work through the storm inside my chest.

This was supposed to be a time of celebration. The worst was over, and yes, Umbrane had given us the slip, but he'd also boxed himself into a corner that had led to Veena's freedom. Yes, he had Sev, but being in the Court of Shadows would allow Sev to find the contract that was keeping his people prisoner. It would give him a chance to find out where the female maras were kept and maybe...Maybe he'd find his mother and father.

This was good.

All good stuff.

He'd be safe. Umbrane couldn't hurt him.

I sat on the edge of my bed, and Chase rested his head on my lap with a soft whine. I stroked his coarse fur, breathing through the tightness in my chest. This is what love did to a person.

"I'm sorry," Zepar said from the doorway. "I know how much he means to you."

There was something undeniably solid and comforting about the way he filled the doorway. How his broad shoulders stretched the dark material of his T-shirt and how the denim clung to his muscular thighs. The normality of his attire reminded me of the human world, of the Fringe and all the places beyond, and nostalgia ballooned in my chest, chasing away the panic.

"Nyx?" He stepped into the room, bringing the scent of ozone with him. Fresh and wild at the same time.

I closed my eyes and swallowed the lump of emotion in my throat. "He'll be fine. We have a plan. This is just a temporary separation." I sounded like I believed it, and that helped.

"A plan?" Zepar canted his head. "What plan?"

A couple of weeks ago, I'd have smiled sweetly and buttoned it. Trust had come slow with Zepar, but it *had* come, and now he was part of the team. "Sev is going to find the contract binding the maras to Umbrane and destroy it."

Zepar's brows flicked up. "That's why you set the condition of not having him confined?"

"Yes. If anyone can find it, Sev can. I know it."

"I believe it too," Zepar said. "It's about time the maras

were freed. Umbrane gives all fallen a bad name." He moved closer and crouched in front of me. "You probably don't know that once you're Satan you can visit with any court with impunity. Without an invite."

The urge to touch his face, to trail my fingers down the planes of his high cheekbones, had me curling my hands into fists. "I can?"

His tawny eyes warmed as if he could read my thoughts. "Yes. You're not an original fallen, but you hold the seat of one, which gives you as much power as they have."

Which meant I could visit Sev and make sure he was okay. "Thank you." This time I did touch him lightly with my fingertips.

His eyes fluttered closed in a long blink, and the corner of his mouth lifted. "I've dreamed about you touching me like this so often this almost doesn't feel real."

"You have?"

He reached up to gently grip my fingers and brought them to his lips. "Yes, Nyx. I don't believe I've kept it a secret how much I want you."

"No. You've been quite open about that."

"It hasn't changed." He kissed the tips of my fingers, and a delicious shiver ripped through me. "I'm here for you. I won't let any harm come to you. I promise."

I believed him. I leaned down and rested my forehead against his. "Letting my guard down hasn't been easy."

"I know." His breath was warm against my lips. "But I promise you, it will be worth it. You and I...we have more in common than you realize, and once you're Satan, I'd like to show you just how alike we are."

Color me intrigued.

He pulled back and kissed my forehead. "It's late. You

should get some sleep." He stood smoothly and headed for the door. "I'll see you at breakfast."

It was on the tip of my tongue to tell him that I was fine. That I didn't need to sleep, but exhaustion chose that moment to dig in its claws, reminding me that even high daimon abominations needed sleep.

"Thank you."

"Anytime, Nyx." He retreated and closed the door behind him.

I kicked off my boots, stripped down to my underwear, and crawled under the covers. Chase lay on the floor at the foot of my bed, but after a few moments he nudged my hand.

"Up you come, boy." I patted the bed beside me, Sev's side, and Chase jumped up and lay down. He made a soft, sad sound. "Yeah, I miss him too. But he'll be back soon. He'll be okay. Everything will be okay."

I'd make sure of it. I settled down and closed my eyes, and Chase's deep, even breath soon had me drifting off to sleep into a memory.

The Ministry loomed large and forbidding before me, supernaturals kitted out in the academy colors spilling up the steps and through the grand doors.

The sky was gray and gloomy like my mood. "You're seriously going to make me go through with this?"

Babs sniffed. "You need an education, and you need to make friends, and this is the best place to get both."

"I have friends." I placed my hand on Chase's neck. "Chase and you."

"And you're lucky they'll let you bring him here."

Because I'd refused to come without him. "Let's just get this over with. The sooner I start the term, the sooner it'll be over."

"That confident you'll hate it?"

I smiled sweetly up at her. "Oh yes."

The deal was simple. I do one term, and if I hated it, she'd let me leave. One term was eight weeks. Eight weeks was nothing in the grand scheme of things.

I'd do my time. It was the least I could do for Babs. The very least after all she'd done for me.

Someone bumped into me in their haste to get up the steps.

"Watch it." My voice was a growl.

The girl turned to look at me and walked slowly backwards. "Hey, sorry. You're new, right? I'm Orina."

Babs nudged me. I guess this was the 'making friends' part. I resisted the urge to roll my eyes. "Nyx. My name is Nyx."

"Cool name." She glanced at Chase and smiled. "Cool hound. He staying?"

"Yeah."

"You know what dorm you're in?"

"Blackwood."

Her eyes lit up. "Me too and—"

"Orina!" Another girl slammed into the first. This one had golden hair with pink stained ends. The two hugged, and a strange, empty feeling spawned inside me.

"Quinn, this is Nyx. She's in our dorm."

Quinn turned to me, raking me over with a curious gaze. "Hey..." She looked down at Chase. "Wow."

"Yeah, she gets to keep him here."

Quinn's brows shot up, but she didn't say anything.

"Oh, don't mind her. Quinn's a shifter. She's probably smelling all sorts of things right now."

Well, that explained why Chase had gone so tense and

still. Quinn stepped forward and held out her hand, slow and easy.

Chase dipped his head and sniffed her. His body relaxed.

I exhaled, not realizing until that moment that I'd been holding my breath.

Chase chuffed his approval.

"Come on," Quinn said. "We'll show you around."

"Blackwood is just us," Orina said. "We've got the whole dorm, so it'll be fun."

Fun...

Babs smoothed a hand over my head then stepped back. Her cue for me to go. I picked up my suitcase, gave Babs a nod, and trailed after the girl, the knots in my belly easing a little.

Maybe the next term wouldn't be so bad after all.

I WASN'T sure how long I slept, but my dreams were filled with memories of my childhood at the Ministry, and when I woke, it was with a deep ache in my heart. I missed them. My friends. The first sisters I'd ever known. I missed Babs too, the only mother figure I recalled.

Chase slept soundly and didn't wake when I slipped off the bed into the early dawn light. I needed to see Artimus and ask him to send out three extra invites, because if I was going to be crowned Satan, I wanted my best friends and Babs to be there.

I pulled on my clothes but faltered by the large, ornate mirror.

I hadn't seen Loke since before the trial. The fact that he hadn't come to see me probably meant he was busy with

Tarrifel business, but I could pop to his room and leave him a note.

I pressed my palm to the glass and said his name. The smooth surface shimmered and melted, allowing me to step through.

The empty room was filled with the gray light of dawn. Not just empty of life but stripped bare of sheets and any personal items.

It looked unlived in.

It no longer smelled like him either.

Loke was gone.

THIRTY-TWO

ARTIMUS

The Erinyes calls out names from a never-ending list. Demons, devils, fallen, abyssbloods, Mageri, shifters, and so many more. The list is endless, and the names are all beginning to sound the same, but it's my job to focus and make sure we don't miss an invite. Next will come the seat placements for the grand meal and then the music.

Erinea usually organizes the music.

Can I make her do it from her cell?

Fuck it. Why not?

"Seneschal?"

I look up at the Erinyes holding the list. "What?" There's a snap to my voice.

"Are you...um...listening?" She's young, probably in training. No point snapping at her. "I need a moment. Why don't you—"

The door to my study bursts open and Nyx storms in

like a whirlwind. How can such a tiny frame command such power?

"A word. Now," she says.

A tight smile is all the cue the Erinyes needs. She nods and hurries from the room. I push back my seat and stand. "What's happened?"

"Where's Loke?"

Ah, this... "Yes. About that. I meant to tell you—"

"He's gone? When? He wouldn't leave without saying..." Her eyes go round. "It's the source, isn't it? She's punishing him for helping me." She walks over to one of the armchairs framing my impressive hearth and drops into it. "This is my fault."

"No. Loke made a choice. He knew the risks."

She runs a hand through her hair then winces when it snags. "Fuck. I need to get it together. Look at me." She indicates her rumpled clothes. "I look like a hobo, not the Satan-to-be."

"We can fix that."

"No." She stands abruptly, clearly still agitated. "We need to do something about Loke. We have to help him."

If only that was possible. "There is no way to help him. Tarrifel is out of bounds to the living or anyone not affiliated to it. There is literally nothing we can do to find out what's happened to him."

"I don't believe that. There's got to be a way to speak to the source. To explain...I don't know. There's got to be some way to find out that he's okay."

There is one way. "Satan has a relationship with Tarrifel and the source. I'm not sure what it is, but once your coronation takes place, you'll be invited to visit."

She sits up straighter. "I will?"

"Yes. You can choose to take an emissary with you."

Her eyes light up and lock with mine, and my heart squeezes in my chest because it's obvious she wants to pick me, and that fills me with a strange heat. But as much as I might want to, I can't go.

"It can't be me or Ignatius."

"Why not?"

"There are terms set out for the meeting, they've been in place ever since the seat of Satan was created. Only a fallen may cross over and return unscathed."

"And I'm part fallen…"

I could see her mind ticking, thinking over which sibling to take with her. But I'd be doing her a disservice if I didn't point out a better candidate to advocate on her behalf.

"Duke Zepar would be an excellent choice. He's familiar with the etiquette, and I do believe he accompanied Satan once or twice."

She looks up at me in surprise. "They were close?"

Close would be pushing it. "They were on friendly terms. I believe now that Zepar was attempting to annoy Ramiel by cultivating a relationship with Beelzebub."

She snorts. "Yeah, I can believe that. Fine. I'll ask him." She chews on her cheeks. "I hate that we've got to wait. Loke could be in trouble. Do you think she'd hurt him?"

I've known Loke for some time, and from what I've gleaned, the source may have power over him, but he also has power over her. It's what makes him bold and confident enough to go up against her. I'm not sure what their true relationship is, but my gut tells me she wouldn't hurt him.

"I don't think his punishment will be physical torture. I think, if the source does punish him, it'll be something of a more subtle nature."

"Like keeping him away from me…" She gives me a wry smile. "I can't wait to speak with her."

"You won't have long to wait. The true coronation will take place at dawn. It's a closed affair with the princes and select dignitaries as witnesses. This is where you'll connect with the power in the seat. After that, you'll receive your summons from Tarrifel. There'll be plenty of time for a visit before the official ball that evening."

"Okay. Fine." She relaxes against the cushions. "Two days to kill till then...How will I pass the time..."

Our gazes collide, and all the naked ways we could pass the time tumble through my mind. My pulse speeds up, and hunger rises within me. My gums throb as my fangs ache to slide out. I'm leaking pheromones into the air without meaning to, and I don't fucking care.

Her eyes darken as she slowly gets to her feet and approaches me. "You and Erinea are completely over, aren't you?" Her tone is low and suggestive.

Her vanilla scent fills my head, and I'm immediately thick and heavy with desire.

"Yes." My heart pounds inside my ribcage.

She stops right in front of me and places her palm on my pectoral, the heat seeping through the expensive cotton of my shirt and starfishing out across my chest. I should stop this, claw it back and release her from my influence, but I don't. I want her.

I want to be inside her. Now.

"Arty..." She offers me her mouth, and I sip at her sweet breath.

"Nyx..."

She makes a soft, needy sound in the back of her throat, and I lose it.

I grab her and crush my mouth to hers, sucking on her bottom lip before sliding my tongue into her mouth. She's soft, sweet, and luscious, and I want her. I want her so badly it's painful.

She groans and sinks her fingers into my hair before raking her nails across my scalp. The perfume of her arousal fills my head. I want to taste it. I want to suck on her clit, push my tongue into her heat, and eat her out until she screams my name and comes all over my to—

There's a sharp rap on the door. "Seneschal?"

No. Go away.

"Seneschal?"

I tear my mouth from Nyx's. "Fuck off!" The words come out a feral growl.

There's a squeak and the clip of heels as the Erinyes runs away.

Nyx lets out a bark of surprised laughter. Her eyes are bright as gems, her mouth rosy red and plump from my kisses. I don't want to let go. But I do. I force my power to ebb and wait for her indignant rage at being manipulated by my 'mojo.'

It doesn't come. Her eyelids remain heavy, her expression dreamy and soft. "Later?" she says breathlessly.

This is her. All her. Nothing to do with my power. She wants me just as much as I want her. My cock jerks to life in my pants as I dip my head and press my mouth to her jugular and hold it there so I can feel the pulse of blood beneath her skin. I inhale her heady scent. Her blood, so fucking sweet and intoxicating. It will drive me wild. It will tip me over the edge. But as much as I want her, I can't risk hurting her.

I've known it ever since the first moment I smelled it. Tasting it the last time that we kissed confirmed it, but I pushed the knowledge aside and hid from it. Lying to myself. Telling myself I can have her, when in truth...

I pull away from her, regret a knot in my throat. "We can't."

She frowns in confusion. "I thought you and Erinea—"

"This isn't about Erinea. Your blood…" I lick my lips. "It's too intoxicating. I can't trust I won't lose control."

She studies me for a long beat. "I understand, but can you trust *me* not to let you lose control?" The corner of her mouth lifts. "I'm stronger than I look…especially now."

She is right. Maybe…No, stop it. Putting the onus of control on her is wrong. "It wouldn't be fair."

Annoyance flashes in her eyes. "And it's fair for us to deny what's between us?"

I run my thumb across her bottom lip. "No. It isn't fair, but Nyx, if I hurt you…If I lose control, then I'd never forgive myself."

"Then we take it slow." She caresses my cheek. "One step at a time." She leans in so I can't help but be engulfed in her scent. "Let's acclimatize your incubus to the scent of my blood."

I close my eyes and press my nose to her jugular and breathe. My cock is so hard I'm afraid it'll explode, and then she grips it through my slacks and my body spasms.

"Fuck."

She turns her head so her lips graze my earlobe. "Soon, Arty. Once I have the seat's power, you and I, we're going to fuck all night long."

She releases me and steps back, her eyes dark with need, her mouth parted on short, sharp breaths. We're fully clothed, and we've done nothing but kiss and talk, but this… this is the most intimate experience of my fucking life.

She backs away then turns and heads for the door. "Oh, and Arty, can you add three more invites to that list for me?"

I clear my throat. "Of course."

She smiles sweetly over her shoulder. "I'll find your assistant and give her the names."

She slips out of the room. I cross the room into the ensuite bathroom, close the door, and flip the shower on to cold.

Ice fucking cold.

THIRTY-THREE

MALLINI

I don't know what I'm doing here. I should turn around and leave. The Minorax guard simply watches and waits for me to decide. One nod, and he opens the dungeon doors to admit me.

The last time I was here was to see Nyx. The last time I'd been eager, but not this time. This time the conflict is real.

Am I a traitor for coming here? A traitor to Charod? To myself? The small child inside me doesn't believe so. She needs this.

My mother sits silently in her cell, the same cell that Nyx occupied not so long ago. She's been provided with blankets, but it's cold down here, and my plumes puff up to counter the chill.

She looks up in surprise as I approach.

"Hello, Mother."

"I didn't do it," she says. "I didn't plan the assassination, I swear it."

The tightness in my chest recedes a little. "I believe you."

She exhales heavily. "That's all that matters to me."

"Is it?"

She gives me a small, dry smile. "I'm no saint, child. I don't want to die, especially not for a crime I didn't commit, but if I were to be executed, then it would be a comfort to know that you believed in me."

"I never said I believed *in* you, Mother, just that I believe you didn't plan the attack. Not this time, anyway."

She drops her gaze. "I've made some mistakes."

A bitter laugh escapes me, and she cringes.

"Power corrupts, child. It makes you hungry. It makes you want things that don't belong to you."

"So much for wanting what was best for the realm."

"I told myself that. Lied to myself. I made the wrong choices and trusted the wrong people."

"Umbrane."

She grips the bars with one pale hand. "Yes. Umbrane. I was a fool to think I was the one in control."

"You've always been arrogant, Mother."

I expect her to bite, but she merely nods wearily at that. She's given up.

The last thing I expected to feel for her was pity. "Nyx won't let them execute you, you know."

"It doesn't matter. I'm as good as dead. I'm a loose thread now. Someone that knows Umbrane's true face. He won't allow me to live, even if Nyx does."

"He wouldn't dare try to kill you."

She makes a small, incredulous sound. "You have no idea what that male is capable of. He revels in inflicting pain. He feeds off it. His court is a cesspool of sadism." She leans closer. "He has secret prisons. Places where he keeps his playthings. He goes there sometimes and returns reeking of sex, blood, and white jasmine." She sighs. "I might escape these bars, but I'll never be free, not as long as he lives."

I've had enough of her defeatist attitude. "You messed up, Mother. No doubt about that, but you're being given a second chance, and you're an Erinyes. We don't give up. We fight. Remember? So if Umbrane wants to take you down, you best make sure he has to fight for it."

Her chin lifts, and her dark eyes glitter with pride and determination. "You're stronger than I thought, child. Maybe it's too late to say it, but I'm proud of you. I wish I'd shown it more often. I wish that instead of being a general, I'd been more of a mother to you."

I used to wish that too, but I've realized now that mothering isn't who we are. We aren't soft. We do not coddle. We're blunt and brash at times, but when it comes to protecting family, we don't back down. And that...that *is* how we love.

"Not loving us was never the problem, Mother. Your problem was that you put the seat above your family. But that must change, not for me, not for Charod, but for you."

She swallows hard and then smiles. "When did you get so smart?"

I return her smile with a wry one of my own. "It's my secret weapon."

The door above us clangs, and the Minorax's voice drifts down the steps. "Time's up."

Already? "I have to go."

I head for the steps.

"Will you come visit again?"

Do I want to come back? Do I want to spend more time with her? "Yes." I look over my shoulder and nod. "I'll come back."

THIRTY-FOUR

VEENA

Today I'll put my hair up. No hiding today. It's so early. The sun is barely awake, but the kitchens will be teeming with life.

I've avoided returning for weeks, but it's time. I've been afraid of what they'll say for too long. Of how they might treat me...different, now that they know.

But it's time to be brave.

I take the hidden passages and come out by the kitchens. A strong wave of nostalgia washes over me. I've stood in this same spot countless times and walked through those doors too many times to count.

This was my haven before I was plucked from obscurity and elevated to Satan spawn.

Before the trials, before it all, these kitchens were my home.

I enter to the hum of conversation, the clang of pots and pans, and the smell of fresh bread, and I'm given maybe thirty seconds to revel in it before all ambient sound ceases and every eye is on me.

Why did I pull my hair back? Stupid, stupid. I shouldn't have come.

Symone, my old baking buddy, shoots me a grin. "I was wondering when you'd come pay us a visit," she says.

"Glad to see you haven't forgotten us," Bari adds.

In the next moment, I'm surrounded by my zuni and demon friends. Someone hands me an apron, and the doubts fade away, replaced by a warm, full feeling in my chest. For the next few hours, I forget about ascensions, coronations, and thrones. For the next few hours, all that matters is pastry.

NYX

We ate breakfast in the hallway where a fresh table had been set with delicious food and drink for us all to consume. Zepar hadn't joined us yet. Maybe court business had called him away. It was a little disappointing. I'd been looking forward to seeing him.

"Nyx, try the porridge," Veena said. "I helped make it."

"You did?"

She blushed and nodded. "I helped out in the kitchens this morning."

Zinichi placed a fresh basket of bread on the table. "You shouldn't have been down there, love. You're Satan spawn now."

"I'm still a zuni," Veena said. "I'm still me, and I missed them. Missed the work."

Just when I thought I knew all there was to know about her... "You like to cook?"

"Oh yes. I love it." Her eyes shone bright with enthusiasm. "Baking, particularly. I enjoy making pastries."

"Veena was on the way to being head chef before Satan's demise," Zinichi said with a proud smile. "Her sweet apple and bitter cherry pie was the best I'd ever tasted."

I held out my bowl. "Well, load me up."

Veena leaned across the table to ladle some porridge into my bowl when one of our Minorax guards approached.

"There is a visitor for Mistress Veena," he said.

Fear tightened Veena's face. "Umbrane?"

"No, he wouldn't," Keelan said. "He released you."

"It is not the duke," the Minorax said. "It's a zuni claiming to be your mother."

"Oh..." Veena sat back and looked up at the Minorax. "Oh, right..."

The Minorax gave her a sympathetic smile. "She's insistent that she must see you."

"You don't have to see her," Mallini said. "We can make her leave."

Veena shook her head. "No. Best get it over with. Let her in." She climbed off her seat and stood to one side as the Minorax headed back to the doors.

A moment later, a whirlwind of indignant rage barged into the room and stormed toward Veena.

Veena flinched, and I sat forward, ready to spring into action. I wasn't the only one. The others were on guard too.

"What did you do?" Veena's mother demanded. "What did you do to make him break off the betrothal?"

Veena lifted her chin and met her mother's gaze levelly. "I told him I didn't want to marry him."

Her mother's chest expanded on a gasp, then she

slapped Veena in the face so hard that the sound echoed around us.

I leapt up. "What the fuck?"

Keelan and Mallini were already on their feet, and Gus had jumped onto the table to get closer to Veena.

Veena held up her hand to halt us. "Don't." She turned her face back to her mother, her pale cheek emblazoned with a red hand mark. "Are you done?"

Her mother stared at her, seething with rage. "No. I am not." She made to strike her again, but this time, Veena caught her wrist.

"No," Veena said. "I let you have that first blow in deference to your status as my mother. But the second blow is *not* free. Strike me again, and you *will* be punished for striking a daughter of Beelzebub and a sister of Satan."

Her mother jerked her wrist from Veena's grasp. "You dare to use your status as a weapon against me? *I* made you who you are today."

"Yes, Mother, which is why I'll allow you to walk out of here with your hand still attached to your body."

Whoa. Go, Veena.

"Now get out," Veena said. "And don't come back. I *never* want to see you again."

"You forget that I own you," her mother sneered. "As your matriarch, I make your matches. I choose who you marry. You may have convinced Duke Umbrane to release you from the betrothal, but the next male I choose will not be so easily swayed."

Oh fuck. She still had the power to tie Veena to any guy she wanted.

"Thank you for the reminder, Mother," Veena said. "I am, of course, in your control as long as I am part of your bloodline." Veena took a step closer to her mother, looking her dead in the eye. "So you will sever my tie to you, or I will sever your head from your body. Are we clear?"

Her mother stared at her in dumb shock. This was one of the most beautiful moments I'd ever experienced in my fucking life.

"Well?" Keelan demanded gruffly. "Do it. Now."

Her mother looked about the room, noticing us as if for the first time. Her daughter's new family. The one that loved her and would protect her no matter what.

"Now!" Mallini boxed the zuni in.

Finally. Veena's mother raised her hand and placed it on Veena's forehead. She muttered a few words, and the area beneath her hand glowed.

Veena let out a soft cry and clutched at her chest, tears filling her eyes.

Her mother's lip curled. "You're free now. Untethered, with no family."

I walked around the table to stand beside Veena. "Well, that's a load of bullshit."

The others gathered close to illustrate my point.

"Goodbye, Hunara," Veena said.

The Minorax placed a hand on Hunara's shoulder. "Time to go," he said.

We stood in solidarity until the door closed behind her, and then Gus let out a soft whoop.

"Veena, you were amazing."

Veena's smile was small and sad. "I wish it hadn't come to that."

I lightly touched her red cheek. "We should get some ice on that."

"No," she said. "It'll heal on its own."

Yeah, Veena was going to be just fine.

THIRTY-FIVE

Zepar arrived just as we were finishing up breakfast, and for a moment, I didn't recognize him. He was dressed in dark jeans, ankle boots, and a long-sleeved polo top and was carrying a jacket. His wings were hidden, and he looked like a male model who'd just stepped off the cover of an otherworldly magazine.

"I'm sorry I missed breakfast," he said.

"No worries." I drained my mug. "There's plenty left if you want some."

"No time." He smiled. "We have to go."

"We..." I arched a brow. "As in you and me?"

"That's right." He pulled three crisp cream envelopes from his jacket pocket. "We have a delivery to make."

"What are those?"

"Your three special invites."

Wait... "How did you—"

"Artimus told me, and we both thought it would do you good to get out of Morningstar and visit your friends."

"I can leave?"

"Yes, Nyx. You can leave. The trials are over. You're about to be crowned Satan; you can leave if you have protection. Which in this case will be me."

"Now, wait a moment," Zinichi said. "Dress fitting is this afternoon."

Zepar aimed his smile at her, and I swear she simpered. "We'll be back in plenty of time, I promise."

She threw up her hands. "So be it."

"Now, dress warm," Zepar said. "It's freezing out there."

I was already out of my seat and headed to my room. I was going back to the Fringe, and I couldn't wait to see Orina and Babs.

ORINA

Quinn's empty mug sits on my kitchen table. She left last night after being with me for three days. Pack business. I miss her. Her presence filled this room with warmth and made my tiny apartment feel like a home. But then, Quinn was always the warm, gooey center of our friendship triangle, with Nyx and me being the hardened crusts.

She grounded me before Nyx came along, and once Nyx joined us, she grounded her too. The funny thing is, she always thought she was the weakest of us. It took her time to realize just how strong she is.

I'm glad she's found herself. So glad she's found her home.

I pull my phone from my pocket. Should I call Micah again? The Mageri haven't bothered to get back to us yet, but fresh posters popped up overnight informing us that the trials are over, and a Satan is about to be crowned.

It's killing me not knowing if Nyx is all right.

Fuck it. I'm going to call. But before I can dial Micah, my phone rings, and Quinn's name flashes on caller ID. "Hello?"

"Have you heard anything?" she asks.

"Not yet. I'm gonna chase Micah. Again. How are things in Hawthorne?"

"There's shit going down here. Stuff with the Raventhorn pack."

"The high pack?"

"Yeah, I might be out of contact for a few days. If you hear anything, drop me a message, and I'll pick up when I can."

"I'm sure Nyx is fine. I'll let you know if I hear from her."

"Okay, love you."

"Love you too."

I hang up and stand in my spotless kitchen staring at Quinn's mug. Washing it up erases her, as if she was never here.

I'll leave it. Just for a little while.

I'm about to hit speed dial for Micah when the doorbell rings.

Fucking hell. What now?

I yank open the door and stare at the woman standing on my doorstep.

Nyx grins up at me. "Miss me, bitch?"

NYX

The look of shock on Orina's face melted to relief, and in the next moment, she was squeezing the life out of me. She must have been worried because Orina wasn't usually a hugger. I closed my eyes and reveled in the contact.

She tensed and released me, her gaze on Zepar standing a little way down the path. "He with you?"

"Yeah. That's Zepar."

Her eyes narrowed to slits. "What is he?"

She was still tense, as if ready to fight or flee. "He's with me, Orina. He's not a threat. He's a fallen."

She blinked sharply and tore her attention from Zepar to fix it on me. "What? Fallen? As in...fallen angel?"

"That's right."

Some of the tension drained out of her. "Angels are real?"

Seriously? "You're angel-blessed. Surely you should know."

"Angel-blessed is a term they use to..." She shook her head. "I didn't realize they were real. I thought it was just some Order anointing ritual."

"To be fair, their existence doesn't seem to be common knowledge."

She mulled this over. "What's a fallen angel doing in the demon side?"

Wow. How to summarize that one? "Long story, but I promise I'll fill you in over lunch."

"Is he coming with us?" Her tone said clearly that she'd rather he didn't, and I couldn't help the stab of annoyance that pinched my chest.

"What is your problem, Orina?"

She sighed. "I'm sorry. He makes me feel...odd."

To be fair, many people had given us a wide berth as we walked here. Maybe fallen angels had that effect on the general populace. Maybe his presence didn't bother me so much because I was part fallen. Maybe being part fallen didn't have such a disconcerting effect on people.

Zepar was looking back down the street, hands tucked into his pockets. "I've noticed he's drawn quite some attention here. I think you're probably picking up on his otherworldliness. But he's here for my protection."

"Protection? When have you ever needed protection?"

She had a point. "I guess being the new Satan comes with security whether you need it or not."

It took her a moment, and then... "I knew it! I knew you'd win that damn tournament."

There'd been no winner. No clean lines. I'd been chosen, and I wasn't entirely convinced of the reasons why. "It's complicated."

"And Chase? Is he okay?"

"Yeah, back at Morningstar." I'd left him with Veena for the day. I figured she could do with the company and the distraction after her altercation with her bitch of a mother.

Her gaze flicked to Zepar again. This time he raised a hand in greeting.

She gave him a terse smile. "Let me get my coat."

WHERE ELSE COULD we go for a hearty lunch than the Hole in the Wall? My favorite haunt with the best crisp ale in all the Fringe. I'd come here countless times with Orina.

We'd camped out at a table in the corner and enjoyed a

meal in relative anonymity, but today was different. There would be no melting into the background with Zepar in tow.

Even without his wings on display, the fallen was a compelling visual treat. Males and females stared as we walked to a corner booth, and it was only when we got to the table that I realized how ill-equipped it was to house his larger-than-normal frame.

"You may need to sit on my lap," he said.

I expected to see mischief in his topaz eyes, but he was deathly serious.

"We can get you an extra seat." Orina hurried off to find one while I slid into the booth. "Here you go." She plonked a large armchair beside the booth. She'd obviously stolen it from the hearth at the back of the bar.

Zepar smiled warmly. "Perfect."

We took our seats, and I'd barely glanced at the menu when a waitress appeared by our table. "Hi. What can I get you?" She spoke directly to Zepar, *at* Zepar, as if Orina and I weren't even there.

Zepar's gaze flicked my way, and a ghost of a smile played on his lips. "I'll wait until the lovely ladies have ordered." He sat back and fixed his gaze on me.

Even though he wasn't giving her any attention, the waitress continued to stare at him. The woman was mesmerized, and heck, I couldn't blame her. Zepar was a visual feast. The beauty of his chiseled face was enhanced by the fact that he kept his dark hair super short, and his eyes were fire surrounded by a forest of dark lashes. He had a lazy confidence about him, a charisma that demanded a double take, and here, in the Fringe, a place filled with the average supernatural Joe, Zepar was a rare gem.

"Hey," Orina snapped at the waitress. "You know it's rude to stare, right?"

The waitress blushed and looked genuinely mortified. "I'm sorry. I don't...I—"

"It's all right." I smiled up at her. "How about a jug of ale and some of your house special stew?"

She nodded quickly. "Coming right up." She hurried away but not before shooting another look Zepar's way.

Orina shook her head. "I suppose you get that reaction often?"

Zepar ducked his head with a smile. "Not from the people that matter." He shot me a sidelong glance.

He had no idea.

"Well," Orina said with a knowing smile, "how about you fill me in on your adventures?"

The spotlight was on me, and my mind went blank.

Where to start? "Okay, so that night after we cleared out that vamp nest, I was attacked by demibeasts..."

The story tumbled out of me. My meeting with my siblings, the trials, the murders. I left out the part about Veena being possessed by a shiqq and skipped over the in-depth stuff, giving her the Cliff's Notes of horror and awesomeness.

The food arrived, and I filled her in between bites of delicious stew and gulps of fresh ale. By the time I got to the part about my trial for being an anomaly, Orina had stopped eating and was sitting forward in her seat, hanging on my every word.

"And then Sin burst in and stopped Levistus from turning me into a kebab."

"Sin? *Your* Sin?" Orina asked.

My Sin...That sounded right. "The one and only."

'That's something I meant to ask you about," Zepar said. "How *do* you know Sin?"

"I came across him when looking for information on a particular artifact a while ago."

"Here, or in the demon realm?"

"Demon realm. He ran a smithy close to the station."

Zepar's eyebrows shot up. "Right under our noses." He frowned. "I can't help wonder why he didn't make himself known sooner."

Yeah, that was bugging me too, but although Sin had squared things with the princes, he hadn't been inclined to explain himself to me. "You'd have to ask him that."

"Can we get back to the story please?" Orina said. "So Sin showed up, then what?"

"He saved me by telling them I'm his chosen mate."

Orina's eyes went round. "What the fuck?"

I filled her in on the electus mark, the final trial, the lava, the abyss, everything. "And now, I'm here with you."

"Bloody hell, woman." She took a swig of her ale. "And I thought Quinn getting tangled up in all the Hawthorne business last year was an adventure."

She looked almost wistful. Almost...but it passed because Orina was a creature of habit and plans. She didn't do spontaneous unless it was related to the sisterhood pact —a document we signed a long time ago promising to be there for each other no matter what. We'd stuck to it too.

"Do you know why Morningstar won't liaise with the Order?" Orina asked Zepar suddenly.

He looked momentarily thrown by the shift in topic. "I didn't know that was the case."

"Never mind," she said.

I passed her the invite. "This is your VIP invite to the

coronation and ball, and this one is for Quinn. If she can make it."

She took the invites. "She was here, you know, but had to leave for pack business. She called before you turned up, said she'd be incommunicado, but I'll leave her a message just in case."

Pack business when it came to Quinn was rarely an easy ride. "Is everything okay?"

"You mean, do we need to rush to her aid?" Orina smiled wryly. "I think her pack has it covered."

True. Only a fool messed with the Foaladh, the unique breed of shifter our buddy was bound to.

"We should go," Zepar said. "Zinichi will be waiting."

Orina gave me a questioning look.

I rolled my eyes. "I have a dress fitting for the ball."

She pressed her lips together and smiled, showcasing her dimples. "There is no way I'm missing seeing you in a dress. I'll be there with my camera to snap plenty of pictures."

"Fuck off." I pulled the third envelope from my pocket. "I have to see Babs before I head back."

Orina's smile dropped. "Babs is gone."

"She'll be back. I'll drop this through her door and—"

"No, Nyx...She's gone for good."

What was she saying? "What do you mean, *gone for good*?"

Orina had that look on her face, the one she got when she delivered shitty news. "I went to see her a week ago after I got your note, and she'd vanished into thin air. I went back to the house a few days later, and it'd been cleaned out. No furniture, nothing. It's as if no one's ever lived there."

Babs wouldn't just vanish like this. "Something must have happened to her."

Orina shook her head. "I don't think so. It was almost as if...as if her business here was complete. She told me to watch out for you, that you'd need me and Quinn. She's gone, and I don't think she plans on returning."

I pushed back my chair. I needed to see for myself.

THIRTY-SIX

The front door to Bab's house wasn't locked, but that wasn't the first sign that something was off. There were no drapes on the windows, and the flowerpots that usually lined the path were gone.

Babs loved those plants.

The welcome mat with kittens on it was missing. The umbrella stand was gone too. By the time I got to the homeless people camped out in the empty living room, there was no denying that Babs had vacated this building.

The three men huddled in threadbare sleeping bags didn't react with any urgency as we entered the room. Instead, they glared at us as if we were invading their space.

"Fuck off," one of them said. "Squatters' rights."

"You want a boot in your face?" Orina asked.

He ducked under cover of his sleeping bag with a whimper.

Orina groaned. "Look. I'm sorry. There's a food kitchen on North Street run by the Order. Get yourself a meal."

The whimpering man peered over the lip of his blanket. "Been there, got sent away. They said we smelled too bad."

The room did smell bad. Like urine and unwashed bodies. But that was par for the course when you were homeless.

Orina's mouth tightened. "Did you catch the name of the person who sent you packing?"

"Nah. But he had strange pale eyes."

Orina nodded sharply. "Yeah, I know him. I'll speak to him. Go back at four and tell anyone that asks that Orina sent you."

The man blinked up at her. "S'pose. Thanks."

We left the trio to huddle in their sleeping bags for warmth and made a quick sweep of the rest of the house. There wasn't a shred of evidence of the home I'd grown up in. No evidence of Babs.

"This makes no sense." We headed outside, away from the smell of sweat and piss. "Why would she do this?"

"I don't know," Orina said. "But I've asked around, and no one's seen her. In fact, I spoke to several people on the street about Babs, and they had no idea who I was talking about. It was...strange."

Zepar joined us on the garden path. "Those people are starving and cold." He said it as if it was a strange concept.

I snorted. "Yeah, Zepar, this is the Fringe. Walk down any alley, and you'll find more just like them."

His mouth turned down. "And your governing body lets this continue?"

I guess Morningstar had it cushy compared to here. "Haven't you visited this side of the river before?"

He shook his head. "I've meant to but...Now I don't think I'll return. It's all too...depressing."

He had that right.

There was hunger and homelessness here. The Mageri may have created order by splitting the city into territories and giving humans a semblance of protection from the predators that roamed the streets, but putting food in everyone's belly and a roof over everyone's head was, unfortunately, still a stretch. Bounty hunting, to help those that needed it, and working for the Order to keep the monsters in check was our way of doing our part, but it was never enough.

"You don't have homeless in Morningstar?" Orina asked.

"No," he said. "There is a roof for everyone, food for everyone, and a role to be played by everyone in the demon realm."

"Nice," Orina said. "Maybe your leaders should speak to the Mageri and give them some tips."

Zepar looked down at me with a small smile and warmth in his topaz eyes. "I'm sure our new Satan would be happy to liaise on our behalf."

Me. He was talking about me doing political stuff. Crap. Is that what my life would become?

Orina nudged me. "It'll be okay. You're going to do great."

She read me so well.

"We should get back," Zepar said.

I looked back at the house I'd spent the best years of my life in. "Once the coronation is over, I'm going to find her."

"I'll help," Orina said.

"And you'll have Morningstar's full resources at your disposal," Zepar added.

"I've got some things to tie up," Orina said. "But I'll be there for the coronation. I promise."

"I'll have a carriage wait for you at the other side of the bridge on coronation day."

We parted with a hug, and Zepar and I headed back to the station.

NOW THAT ZEPAR had pointed it out, I saw sorrow at every corner. I guess I'd become desensitized to it while living here, among it all. But after spending time in Morningstar and seeing how the creatures there lived, the Fringe felt like a horror show.

"Are you nervous about the coronation?" Zepar asked.

"Not really. More about what happens afterwards. The responsibilities."

"You won't be alone in any of that."

"I know. It'll still be an adjustment." I sidestepped to avoid a woman with a cart piled high with knickknacks.

Zepar's hand went to the small of my back. "I imagine you've had to make plenty of adjustments in your short life."

He had no idea. "I've learned to be flexible, yes."

His hand fell away after a moment, and it niggled that I missed the reassuring heat and pressure. I wasn't one to need reassurance. Being around the males of Morningstar was spoiling me. Making me crave things. Things I could totally have if I wanted which made them more dangerous.

We walked in silence, taking the main street toward the station. The markets were setting up for the afternoon, and the street buzzed with activity as it filled with shoppers. Someone whizzed by me on a hoverboard, and Zepar pulled me against his side.

"Fool!" he bellowed at the man.

The guy on the board didn't look back but gave him the finger.

"I assume that's a nonverbal curse," Zepar said tightly.

I bit back a smile. "You assume correctly."

We continued, but Zepar kept his arm around me, and I let him. It felt nice.

"Have you ever wondered about your mother?" he asked.

He meant my bio mother, of course, not the human who'd abandoned me. "Sure, I have. From what I learned in the abyss, there are no more Knightwoods left. Just me. I can only assume Beelzebub smuggled her over here, and she died, maybe giving birth to me?"

"But he would have had to keep her hidden. He kept *you* hidden..."

Yeah, he had. Protecting me from the princes. "I don't know, Zep. And dwelling on it doesn't help me in any way."

"Zep?" He drew me to a halt and looked down at me, his gaze a questing caress. "You've given me a nickname."

I couldn't hide my smile. "I guess I have."

"You know what that means, don't you?"

"Why don't you tell me?"

He leaned in and brushed his lips across my cheekbone, leaving a trail of heat that seeped into my skin with a tingle. "It means you like me, Nyx. It means you want to keep me."

He had us walking again before I could respond, and it took a few moments for my pulse to slow.

Yes, the fallen was most definitely having an effect on me.

The archway to the station came into view a few moments later, but the gates were closed.

"That's not right." I picked up the pace.

"What?"

"Those gates are never closed."

Zepar lengthened his stride to keep pace with me.

There was a sign on the gates saying *Closed for Maintenance.*

"Well, that's a first." The woman at the ticket booth was

busy cashing up her till. "Excuse me? When will the Shooting Star be running again?"

She didn't bother to look up. "Six-thirty tomorrow morning."

"No," Zepar said. "That is not acceptable."

This time, she did look up, probably startled by the change in voice. Then she got a starstruck look on her face. "Oh...oh...my..."

Urgh. "Look, we have to get back to Morningstar."

She stared dumbly at Zepar.

Really? "Hello? Over here."

She blinked, snapping out of whatever fantasy was playing in her head. "Wh-what?"

"The Shooting Star shouldn't be out of commission for this long," Zepar said. "It's part of the terms of the Accords."

"I...I don't know anything about that. I just sell tickets."

"Who's in charge here?" he demanded.

She picked up the phone and punched in a number, barely taking her gaze off Zepar, but she was more wary than anything else now. "Gary, can you come out here please?" She smiled tersely. "He'll be with you in a moment."

We stepped back, and I turned to Zepar. "This is weird."

"It's a breach of our contract. The Shooting Star is designed to need minimal maintenance. An hour at most every few weeks."

A portly man appeared on the other side of the gates. He had the pointed ears of a faeblood and the look of a male who was running short on patience. "What's the problem?" he demanded. Then he got a better look at Zepar, and the anger shifted to surprise.

"Hello, Garminali," Zepar said. "How have you been keeping?"

Garminali grinned up at him. "Glad ta see you got my message." Confusion puckered his brow. "Wait a second... When *did* you get here? Train's been outta commission for two hours." His eyes went round. "Tell me you didn't fly."

"I didn't fly," Zepar said. "We got here this morning."

I looked between them. "What's wrong with flying over?"

"It's forbidden," Garminali said. "Morningstar peeps aren't allowed to use their power here. It's a breach of the Accords."

"You sent me a message?" Zepar asked, getting us back to the point. "What about?"

"The train, that's what, you numbnut."

"I didn't get the message," Zepar replied. "What's happened?"

Whoa, had he just cursed out Zepar? And was Zepar seriously being this zen about it?

"One of the, er..."—he slid a glance my way— "thingamabobs is gone."

Zepar made a sound of exasperation. "This is the new Satan. You can speak freely."

Garminali looked at me with new interest now. "Oh, well in that case. One of the crystals was taken."

Zepar ran a hand down his face. "How could they know where to look?"

"It's my fault. I left the safe unlocked, and the thieving fucker found the schematics. I should never have hired a lone shifter. Should have trusted my gut, but we were short-staffed and...Never mind. It's gone, and we need a new one."

Was he seriously just going to let this go? "Someone stole one of these crystal things, that I assume is vital for making the train work, and you're just going to replace it so he can sneak back and steal another?"

Garminali blinked sharply at me. "Do I look like a bounty hunter to you?"

"Garm." There was warning in Zepar's tone.

Garm sighed. "Sorry, sorry. Look, I can't afford to hire a hunter to go after the bastard. That's something Morningstar needs to pay for."

I could feel my feet slipping into familiar boots. "How about we get you one for free."

He arched a brow my way. "You know someone?"

"Yeah. Me."

Zepar looked down at me in surprise. "You want to go after this scum?"

"Hell yes, I do."

Garminali smiled. "In that case, let me get you his last known address."

Zinichi was gonna be pissed, but this was out of our control. The dress fitting would have to wait.

I had a rogue shifter to hunt.

THIRTY-SEVEN

The shifter obviously wasn't at the address he'd provided, but we did get a lead on his favorite hangout from the landlady he'd stiffed on the rent. The Mole—a rat-infested excuse for a bar on the south side of the Fringe—was where she was sure we'd find the weasel. Her words, not mine.

"Drinking away his rent money, no doubt," she said, taking a drag of her cigarette and flicking the ash directly onto the carpet. "Beat his ass for me. The weasel owes me."

I couldn't quite place what breed of supe she was—not a vamp, shifter, or faeblood, but not human either.

There was plenty of interbreeding now, and new supes were being born every day. I was evidence of that.

Zepar looked slightly nauseous by the time we exited the block of flats. "The air here is sick," he said.

"Oh, you're gonna hate The Mole. It's unsavory, unsanitary, and perfect for the likes of our thief."

"Great," he said dryly. "I'll be needing a hot bath when we get back." He dropped me a sidelong glance. "You could join me. The baths are huge in the Court of Ivory."

I arched a brow his way. "Bathe with you?"

"Uh-huh."

I smirked. "Naked?"

"It's preferable."

We'd slowed to a halt by now, standing still in an ever-moving sea of bodies. The wise move would be to say no. I had enough on my plate, but I wanted him.

I shrugged. "Maybe."

His brows lifted. "Maybe? I'll take that."

We took a tram as close as it would get us to our destination, because only the criminal types and those looking to hook up with them went this far south into the Fringe.

It was getting colder, but my daimon blood kept me warm. Still, I tucked my hands into my coat pockets because it felt like the right thing to do in deference to the chill. "How do you know Garminali?"

"He worked on the construction of the Shooting Star using my designs," Zepar said. "We became...friends."

"And the crystals? Fuel?"

"Yes. Native to the demon realms. It's how we power our world. The crystals recharge themselves through movement, which made them perfect to power a locomotive. They're clean energy. What I don't understand is why someone would want to steal them."

"The fact it can't be found in this world makes it a collector's item. There is no way this rogue shifter's a collector. But he's probably working for one."

The streets were dingy and quiet here, and it felt much later than mid-afternoon. As we turned down the skanky alley that housed the entrance to The Mole, my nape tightened in warning.

Something was off.

"Well, what do we have here?" a gruff voice said from behind us.

Three shifters blocked our path out of the alley. "Seriously?"

"Oh, we're serious, little Satan-to-be," the stocky one in the middle of the trio said.

How did they know that?

"Come closer and I'll rip your spine from your body," Zepar said calmly.

"You can try," the stocky shifter said. "Or you can just"—he drew a spray bottle from his pocket—"breathe."

He sprayed.

I caught a whiff of aniseed, and my mind dredged up the related intel—a rumor about a drug that could incapacitate any creature.

Surely it wouldn't work on a fallen. They were immune to most everything, but still...

"Cover your nose and mouth!" I slapped my hand over mine, but the potent fumes had already entered my system.

The lights went out.

"NYX. WAKE UP," Zepar said. "Now."

My head. What the...I'd been drugged. Where were we?

Zepar lay on his side on dusty floorboards, hands pinned behind his back. A dark angry bruise stained his cheekbone. It had to be fresh, or it would have healed by now, surely.

There was only one window in this gloomy room, and it was too high up and too small for escape. A staircase ran up out of view to my right.

"Basement."

"I think so." Zep sounded pissed. "They have me shackled, and I can't break free. This is no ordinary metal. It must be enchanted."

"I thought fallen were immune to enchantments."

"I'm not pure fallen, Nyx."

"The knockout spray worked on you?"

"Yes," he said tightly. "This is not good."

"Someone tipped them off that we were coming."

"Garminali wouldn't do that."

"He would if he was in on it. Sell the crystal, get paid, then have it replaced. No fault of his own. Get Morningstar to pay for the bounty hunter but never actually hire one."

Zepar shifted on the ground, trying to work on his shackles. "I refuse to believe that. I know him."

"People change." I needed something to pick the lock on the handcuffs they'd put on me. Idiots had shackled me with my hands in front of me. If I'd been wearing a bobby pin, I'd be all set, but I'd come here unarmed and unadorned.

I was getting soft. Not good.

It wasn't hard to break free of the rope around my ankles and shuffle across the dusty floor to Zepar.

"I'm going to try to get these chains off you." But they were knotted tight, and I'd need a moment to untie them. "I can just—"

A door slammed, and bootfalls echoed down the steps.

"Move away," Zepar said urgently.

I shuffled back to my spot and quickly wrapped the rope around my ankles to make it look like I was still bound.

The stocky shifter who'd sprayed us appeared at the bottom of the steps, trailed by two figures: a slender female with eyes like silver pennies and long crimson hair and a shorter male who had the look of a toad about him.

He had the kind of eyes I liked to call dead eyes or fisheyes.

My nose told me they were faebloods.

"Oh, my," the female said. "This is a haul indeed. A native of Morningstar and the new Satan." She walked over to stand opposite me, scrutinizing me.

I glared back. "What do you want from us?"

She smiled, showcasing a row of small, triangular teeth. "I want to cut you up and sell the pieces."

THIRTY-EIGHT

The Fringe could be a fucked-up place. I'd lived in it long enough to know. But this...selling supe parts. This was new.

"Bracelets made from your hair and skin will fetch a pretty price in the right circles," the faeblood said.

The right circles? There were circles for this shit now?

"The rest you can keep," she said to the toady guy.

He licked his lips with a wide, flat tongue. "Good. Kiba hungry."

"What about this one? The bodyguard?" the shifter asked.

"Meat market will pay well for demon flesh."

They thought Zepar was a demon. So the shackles they had on him were either generic or designed to hold a demon, which meant he might still be able to bust out of them.

Our eyes met, and it was obvious he was thinking the same.

The toady man moved toward me and drew a blade

from his pocket. "I'll make it quick. Slice clean. You won't feel that part. But when I feed, you'll scream."

I waited for him to get closer, then kicked out, hitting him in the shin.

He yelled and hit the ground, blade slipping from his grasp. I scrambled toward it, but my fingers had barely grazed the hilt when a boot came down on my hand.

"*Tut, tut.* I leave you alone for one moment, and this is what I come back to?"

Who the fuck was this guy? Another faeblood by the smell of him. Slender, wiry, with a shock of white hair and eyes like cold emeralds. He ground his boot onto my hand.

I bit down on a gasp of pain. "You're fucking with the wrong woman, faeblood."

"I don't fuck your kind, filthy demon whore."

They thought I was a demon too. Of course they did. The existence of the fallen wasn't common knowledge. Probably only the Mageri knew about it, and a select few like Garminali, which meant...Garminali wasn't the one who sold us out. It had to be...the ticket woman. She must have overheard part of our conversation. She must be working with these freaks.

The toady creep hurried over and grabbed the knife. "I do it. I can do it good. Let old Kiba slice."

"Shut up," the emerald-eyed faeblood said. "I'll do it. You'll just make a mess."

Zepar tried to free himself, his moves subtle and controlled but evident to my expert senses. The others remained oblivious, their focus on me, the main prize for making Satan bracelets to sell on whatever fucked-up black market these bastards operated.

"Do you really want to get your hands all dirty, love?" the woman crooned.

The man rolled his eyes, but with his back to her, she was oblivious of the derisive curl of his lips, and when he spoke, his tone was smooth and seductive. "A little blood never hurt anyone, Sorcha."

She smiled thinly. "I do love watching you work."

Kiba handed the male faeblood his blade. "Here. Here, take and cut."

The faeblood grabbed me by the hair and forced my head back. "We'll start with the face."

Adrenaline flooded my veins, hot and potent as the reality of this situation hit hard. I couldn't break free of this. He was going to cut me, and there was nothing I could do. The impotence, the vulnerability spawned ice in my chest. But like fuck would I give him the satisfaction of hearing me beg or scream.

I gritted my teeth and glared at him. "Well? What are you waiting for?"

He studied me in a cool, detached way. "I'm just calculating how to best remove your skin in one large peel. I think I have it." The blade kissed my temple, and terror clamped a fist around my heart.

"No!" Zepar bellowed. "Let her go. Take from me instead."

The fae pulled the blade away from my cheek. "You? You have nothing to offer me."

"Are you sure about that, faeblood?" Zepar sneered. "Take a closer look. A deeper whiff. Do I honestly smell like demon, or does the scent of demon simply linger on my clothes?"

The faeblood's eyes narrowed to slits. He jerked his head at Sorcha, who approached Zepar.

She grabbed his chin, forcing his head up to run her

nose up the column of his powerful throat. Anger tightened my belly.

"Oh..." She made a soft sound of delight. "Oh..." She licked his neck.

"Stop that!" My voice was a warning growl.

The male's grip on my hair tightened. "Shut up, bitch."

Anger raged through my blood, but my daimon power was barely a sizzle beneath my skin. It felt distant and out of reach. I'd been strong without it, but even that strength felt muted somehow.

It had to be these cuffs.

"He smells like the earth and the sky," Sorcha said. "Like stars and the moon."

"A fucking celestial?" The faeblood male scoffed.

Sorcha licked him again, then straddled him, forcing him onto his back. "I want him, Puck. I want him now."

She tried to kiss him, but Zepar turned his head to the side. Our gazes collided, his helpless rage matching mine, but there was also something else in that look.

Defeat.

No.

He couldn't be giving up. Not Zepar.

"Let her go, and you can have me," he said. "Every part of me."

What? "No. Stop it. Let him go. If they find out what you've done, they'll kill you. All of you."

"Your kind can't hurt us," Puck said. "Not on this side of the pond."

"Why? Because we aren't *allowed* to use our power? You think that'll stop the princes of Morningstar when they discover what you've done?"

"You really have no idea, do you?" Puck said. "It's not just that you aren't permitted to use your power. Your power is weakened here. This air. This earth, it saps your strength."

Oh earth, that's why I couldn't access my daimon power. The rest must be these damn cuffs.

"No one will come for you." He smirked. "No one."

Sorcha fumbled with Zepar's pants.

"Stop it!" Puck and I said in unison.

She ignored me but pouted at him. "Fine. But I want his wings."

"Do it," Puck said.

My heart stopped for a moment. Did she say...Ice filled my veins. No...

The shifter grabbed Zepar and hauled him up. "He don't have wings."

"He does," Puck said. "And he'll reveal them if he wants his precious woman to live." Puck pressed the blade to my throat. "Won't you, *celestial*?" He said the word as if it was a dirty one.

Zepar responded, but his gaze was locked on me. "Give me your word that you'll let her go if I give you my wings."

"Oh, you have our word," Puck said. "A celestial's wings are worth a thousand demons, even if she is the new Satan."

This couldn't be happening. This was insane. "Zepar, don't. You—" My head rocked on my shoulders from the blow Puck delivered.

The world stopped spinning to the whoosh of unfurling wings. "No..." I hated how weak I sounded. "Stop..."

Zepar stood with his hands behind his back, wings flared, the span so large it took up most of the room.

"It's okay," he said to me. "It'll be okay."

"No, it won't," Sorcha sing-songed, drawing a blade from her waist. "This is gonna hurt like a bitch." She disappeared behind him.

My heart thumped in my throat, making it hard to breathe. "Stop. Please. Don't do this. Please don't do this." They didn't know what I was. That I was unique, different. If they did, then they'd leave him be. "You want me. I'm—"

"I love you!" Zepar said.

My heart stalled in my chest.

His throat bobbed. "I love you, Nyx. You have to go back and take the seat. Please…"

Please don't tell them. Please don't give them the power.

My gums ached from how hard I ground my teeth. "Puck, don't do this." I blinked back tears. "I'm begging you."

This was my fault. I'd taken this job, come here on this job, rusty and out of practice. I should have picked up on the shifters trailing us. I should have—

Zepar's scream shattered my heart and fractured my thoughts. The wet sound of tearing flesh and the crunch of cartilage filled the room.

Someone screamed shrill and horrific. The sound filled my head and my ears.

My sound.

My scream.

Zepar thrashed, his body in the grip of survival mode, wanting only to get away from the object of his agony.

"Hold him!" Puck ordered.

The shifter grabbed Zepar around the waist as Sorcha laughed and continued to hack at his wing, releasing the coppery scent of blood into the air.

They were killing him. He'd bleed out.

My screams turned to sobs that clawed at my throat. "Stop. Please. Stop."

Zepar went limp in the shifter's grip.

"Zepar! Zep, please…"

"One down," Sorcha said. "One to go."

I grabbed at Puck's wrist. "He'll bleed out. Make her stop. Make her fucking stop!"

The slap dislodged my tears and left my head ringing. "Enough!" Puck hauled me up. "I'm a fae of my word. We have what we need. You can go." He shoved me hard toward the stairs. I stumbled, but someone caught me before I could hit the ground.

"Nyx..." Orina gripped my shoulders tightly.

I stared up into her beautiful face through a haze of tears, then held out my cuffed wrists. Her jaw flexed, eyes flashing in anger as she stepped back, then brought her blade down to cut me free.

Bootfalls echoed around the room as angel-blessed filled the basement.

"We've been looking for you, Puck," Orina said.

Puck made a dash across the room, probably toward a hidden door. I was there in a blink, my hand around the back of his neck. I slammed his face into a pillar once, twice, then a third time, until his blood decorated the brick.

"Nyx. Hey, Nyx. Let go." Orina grabbed at my shoulders. "He's out cold. Let go."

I dropped him, chest shaking, hands trembling. "Zepar."

"He's bleeding badly. We've got to—"

I crossed the room to Sorcha, who was held between two Order members. "Her arm. I want it."

"What?" the male said.

"She took my guard's wing. I demand recompense."

"That's not—"

"Shut up, Ian." Orina handed me a blade. "Do it."

"Orina?" Ian glared at her. "What the heck?"

"If you don't like it, get out of the room," Orina said. "Anyone have a problem, you can leave now."

No one moved.

I gripped the hilt of the dagger. The blade was sharp enough to do the job, but the serrated edge meant she'd feel every bite of it.

"No. Stop," Sorcha said. "You can't do this." She wriggled, trying to get free of the Order members.

Orina grabbed Sorcha's arm and yanked it out.

I looked the faeblood bitch in the eyes and then brought the blade down on her shoulder.

It took a few minutes.

It was bloody, and her screams hurt my head.

But I took it.

I took off her fucking arm.

Thirty-Nine

Zepar lay sprawled on his front, unconscious from the pain of cauterization. It had been the only way to stop the bleeding. One of the Order medics had bandaged him up to keep the area clean, and now we were at an inn close to the station, with guards posted at the door.

Orina was concerned that Puck's associates might come for Zepar or the wing they'd cut off him. It lay across the large dresser, wrapped and bound carefully in cloth. It was a piece of Zepar. A part of him, and they'd severed it.

If they came for it now, they'd be sorry, because I was ready for them. I might not have my daimon power on this side of the river, but I was still stronger than the average supe, fast too. They wouldn't get the drop on me this time, and they wouldn't get out alive.

I'd make sure of it.

I fingered the vial of resistor in my pocket. A new tincture that the Order took once a day to prevent them from being affected by the new take-down spray on the black market.

Turned out, Puck was the one responsible for its

circulation, and the Order was after him. They had toady, Sorcha, and the shifter in custody, but Puck had slipped away even after I bashed his head against a post. They'd interrogate his cronies to get intel. They'd find him.

It wasn't my problem.

My focus was on getting Zepar home. They may have closed his wound, but he had internal injuries that we needed to address. Back home, we'd heal him. There'd be a way to put his wing back on. His mother, Odette, was a powerful conji. She'd regrown his hand when he was younger. She could regrow his wing too. She had to.

It was the only thought keeping me going right now, because if I stopped focusing on the solution, then my mind took me back to the moment when it happened. When Sorcha cut off his—

No. Don't think about it.

The crystal that powered the Shooting Star was back with Garminali. The train would be up and running soon. We'd be out of here.

There was a knock on the door, and Orina entered. "Hey..." She closed the door behind her. "How're you holding up?"

"I'm fine. He's the one that..." My throat pinched. Fuck. I would not cry.

"It's okay to be upset, Nyx. What happened today was...barbaric."

"If you hadn't found us..."

"I heard the station was shut. Seemed odd, so I went down to investigate, spoke to Gary."

"You know him?"

"Yeah, Order keeps tabs on the station and the Rim border too. I asked if he'd seen you and got half the story out of him. He didn't tell me about the crystal, but I recognized his description of the shifter."

"And you tracked him?"

"Yeah. We got lucky. So lucky." She pressed her lips together. "I was so scared. I know these bastards. They're dangerous. Lethal. And Puck is the worst."

"He wanted to peel me like a grape, but Zepar saved me by offering them his wings." My vision blurred. "I can't even..." I exhaled sharply and blinked back the tears. "He did that for me."

"He's in love with you," Orina said simply. "But I think you know that already."

"He said it. He told me just before they...I wasn't sure how I felt about him before, but now..." The weight on my chest, the pain in my heart, the wrenching in my gut all screamed that I was falling for the arrogant son of a—

"Nyx..." Zepar groaned. "Nyx!" He tried to push himself up and made a strangled sound of pain.

I rushed to his side. "Easy. You've got to take it slow."

He flopped back onto his front and cracked open an eye. "Where?"

"An inn close to the station. I'm taking you home as soon as the train is running."

"The faebloods?"

"The male escaped," Orina said. "We got the other two and the shifter, and Nyx took the woman's arm off in recompense for the loss of your wing."

Zepar's eyes widened. "You cut it off?"

I clenched my jaw, unrepentant. "Yeah, I did."

The corner of his mouth lifted. "Good."

Yes, I was falling for him, hard.

Orina cleared her throat to get our attention. "We've

contacted the Mageri. An attack like this could constitute a breach of the Accords."

Really? "I don't buy that considering it's the Accords that gave them the balls to come after us in the first place. They knew we were powerless on this side of the river. The Accords made it so. The terms need to be changed. Once I'm Satan, I'll be making sure of it."

Zepar's eyes lit up with pride. "You're going to be a formidable Satan." He covered my hand with his. "I always knew you would."

"The underdog?" I smiled slightly, recalling the conversation when I'd asked him why he'd picked me as custodia. He'd said he wanted to champion the underdog.

He gently squeezed my hand. "You'll never be the underdog again. You were born for great things." His pupils dilated. "I'm so glad I found you."

We locked gazes in a connection that was deeper than any look we'd shared so far. A connection that made my heart flutter and my throat constrict with emotion.

"I'll let you know once the train is ready." Orina ducked out of the room.

I dropped my gaze to Zepar's hand covering mine. "How bad is the pain?"

"Excruciating, but it helps when you hold my hand."

He was making light of it, but I could tell how bad it was by the tightness around his eyes and mouth and the pallor of his skin.

"I'm so sorry, Zep."

"You have nothing to be sorry for."

"I should have picked up on the tail and—"

"What ifs serve no purpose. Everything will be all right."

The way he said that, with such confidence. I believed him, even with the evidence of butchery in front of me. Even with the pain etched onto his face. I believed that everything would be all right.

The hair on the back of my neck quivered, and my skin pricked.

Zepar tensed. "Something—"

A loud crack was followed by a blast of bright light. Zepar hauled me onto the bed with him, wrapping me in his arms and curling his body around mine to shield me from whatever was about to attack us. The rapid pound of his heart and the soft hiss that fell from his lips were the only indication of his discomfort in moving so fast and suddenly.

Oh earth. I was in love with this male.

The light died, and Odette stood across the room from us with a portal blazing behind her.

"Mother?" Zepar's grip on me tightened. "How are you here? The portal?"

She raised her chin, looking stiffly down her nose at us. "A concession made by the Mageri on this occasion considering the circumstances."

The door opened, and Orina entered. "Well, that was fast. I only just got the call."

A Minorax stepped through the portal. "Help my son," Odette said.

I gently extricated myself from Zepar. "His wing..."

Her eyes flashed. "Where is it?"

I crossed to the dresser, but a second Minorax got there first.

Zepar got to his feet, braced by the first Minorax. His intact wing was hidden, but he looked off balance.

"Nyx..." He glanced back at me.

"No." Odette said. "She takes the train."

"*She* is *your* Satan," Zepar snapped. "And just in case that means nothing to you, she's also the woman I love."

He'd said it earlier, but we'd been in danger, in the heat of the moment, so hearing it now said so easily, so simply, as if it was nothing more than an everyday fact had my pulse skipping into a gallop. "I'm not leaving here without her."

Odette's delicate nostrils flared. Boy, she was pissed. "Fine." She turned and strode into the portal. The Minorax carrying the wing followed her.

Zepar shooed off the Minorax trying to help him and held his hand out to me.

"Go," Orina said to me. "I'll see you soon."

I fit neatly under his arm, as if the spot had been made just for me. He kissed the top of my head, a soft press of his lips, brief and natural, as if it was a habit. My eyes misted.

"You ready?" he asked.

"Yes. I'm ready." We walked into the portal together.

FORTY

SIN

I'm eager to return to Morningstar, and it would be a lie to say that isn't related to Nyx.

But seeing her will wait.

I have business to attend to.

Levistus and Ramiel are cloistered in Merihem's lounge. The Prince of Libidine looks much better. His skin is healing, and his hair has grown back. He's sitting up and sipping from a goblet.

All three look over at me with interest as I enter the room.

"Well?" Ramiel asks bluntly. "Is it done?"

"Yes. We'll be ready when the need arises."

Ramiel nods slowly. "Good. That's good."

"Let's hope it doesn't come to that," Merihem says.

I couldn't agree more. My plans are a failsafe, a backup, and I want them to remain that way. "Are all the preparations for the coronation taken care of?"

"Artimus has it under control," Ramiel says. "But while

you were away, there were a couple of incidents involving our Satan-to-be. Two attacks. One here, in Morningstar, and one in the Fringe."

What was she doing in the Fringe? "Tell me."

"Two chima attacked Nyx last night. They were caught, questioned, and the contractor was tried and convicted."

"Who?"

"Erinea."

"Bullshit."

"We know," Levistus says. "But we have no evidence to prove the orchestrator was someone else."

I've been around Erinea enough to know that the female has an authoritarian personality. She follows rules, and now that Nyx has been chosen to be Satan, she'll respect our wishes, like them or not.

She wasn't the killer. "Who do you suspect?"

"Umbrane," Merihem says sourly. "I rue the day I put him in a position of power. How could I have been so blind?"

"We always are when it comes to our offspring," Ramiel mutters.

Umbrane is his bloodline? That explains why he'd gift him the maras. A show of faith and confidence. The fool. "Keep an eye on the Duke of Shadows. One false move is all we need to bring him in for a proper questioning."

"I agree," Merihem says. "If he is responsible for this, which my gut tells me he is, then I refuse to protect him."

If his twisted offspring is found to be guilty, I'll gut him myself. "What was the second attack?"

Ramiel answers. "Nyx went to the mainland with Zepar to deliver some invites to the coronation. They were both knocked out and captured."

"Knocked out? A fallen and a high daimon?"

Levistus's jaw clenches. "We are not at full power beyond the golden bridge. It's part of the Accords."

The fucking Accords. Of course. "We need to change those terms, and this attack gives us the ammunition to do so."

Ramiel smiles wryly. "That's what Nyx said. She's adamant on a meeting with the Mageri after she's officially crowned Satan."

He sounds proud of her. In awe of her. I don't like it.

"Don't get attached, Ramiel. She's mine. She can play with the maras and the efreet, but she belongs to me."

"So no playing with the big boys, is that it?" Levistus sneers. "You were always awful at sharing, Lucifer."

His feelings don't matter to me. "Ramiel? What happened after they were captured and who captured them?"

"Faebloods. They wanted to sell Nyx's"—his nose wrinkles in disdain—"parts on some black market. Apparently, demon parts are now a collectible."

"She's no demon."

"They didn't know that. Zepar revealed his fallen nature and offered them his wings in exchange for her freedom."

Wings are a part of who we are and what we are. They're connected to us in a spiritual way that can't be described, and a celestial without wings is...He gave them up for her? For Nyx... "They took them?"

"They took one before the Order arrived," Ramiel says. "Nyx is friends with an Order member."

"Ironic, considering the Order wants nothing to do with us," Levistus says.

"I heard that Nyx took the arm of the faeblood who took Zepar's wing," Merihem says.

"Oh yes," Levistus confirms with a gleam in his eyes. "She demanded it in recompense."

Pride swells my chest. "And Zepar? How is the duke faring?"

"He'll heal," Ramiel says. "But he'll never fly again. Not even Odette can help him this time."

"This time?"

"He lost a hand once, and she helped him regrow it. She thinks I don't know, but I kept tabs on them. She healed him by giving him back his hand all those years ago, but a wing is a celestial limb. It doesn't conform to the same rules as a flesh and bone body. Once severed, it cannot be reattached or regrown."

To never fly again? To never take to the skies? It's an awful thought. The duke's actions tell me that Nyx has another champion for her heart. "Where was Duke Ignatius in all of this? I appointed him secundum. He should have been with her."

"He was called away to the Court of Flame to deal with the breach," Ramiel says. "The fawda are a thorn we must pluck out before they take root."

"And we will. Once Nyx has the seat's power, we'll be ready."

"And what if that doesn't happen?" Levistus asks. "Maybe we should warn her about—"

"No!" I stare him down. "We do this my way. The less she knows, the better."

"I agree," Ramiel says. "We don't want to cloud her mind before the coronation."

"You think it might muddy the result," Levistus says. "But what if keeping it from her doesn't help, what if—"

"Enough." I'm done here. "We stick to the plan."

"That's it? You're leaving already?" Levistus says.

The door closes behind me. I have no need to explain why I need to leave right now. Especially because I can't explain it myself. Nyx is a magnet for danger. Being tested over and over and coming out stronger.

She'll survive what's to come until...

I shut down my thoughts.

I need to see her and reset the balance between us, and the best way to do that is with sex. Me in control. Her submitting.

That's how it needs to be for my plan to work. There can be nothing else.

FORTY-ONE

NYX

Chase sprawled at the foot of my mattress. Veena sat beside me, her back against the headboard, and Mallini took up the dresser chair, busy smoothing her plumes.

Dhuma was with Artimus, and Gus and Keelan were at a fitting for boots or something. I'd missed the dress fitting, and Zinichi had rescheduled for first thing in the morning, but that was the last thing on my mind.

All I could think about was Zepar.

Conji had surrounded him and swept him away as soon as we got back. I'd wanted to stay, but it was obvious he was in pain, and with me there, his focus wouldn't be on himself. It would be on me, because that's the kind of male he was.

I'd let Odette take over, allowed her to shut me out because right now, she was the only person who could help him.

He'd been given quarters here in Morningstar while he recuperated so he was close. I'd check on him first thing in the morning. What he needed tonight was sleep, and I was sure Odette would be able to dose him up for that.

"He'll live without his wing," Mallini said. "But you would have died if they'd taken you apart. There'd have been no body for you to come back to, even if you'd done the high daimon thing and resurrected yourself."

I knew this. It didn't help, and my expression must have said so because Mallini sighed and shook out her plumes.

"Look, I'm just glad you're alive. That might make me selfish, but I don't care. I won't lose another sibling."

I'd been there too many times in the past few weeks, so I understood. "I thought she'd be able to fix him. He'll never fly again..." A part of him was gone for good, and despite what he said, I still blamed myself.

"We need to focus on the coronation." Veena said. "It's the day after tomorrow."

She was right. I needed to get my head in the game, and I would, once I knew that Zepar was healing properly, that Umbrane had kept his word about not harming or locking Sev up, and that all was well in the Court of Flame with the breach. Then there was the issue of Loke. What if the source refused to tell me where he was or if he was all right?

Focusing on a ball seemed irrelevant right now.

I just wanted it over.

The door to my room flew open, and Sin stood on the threshold, staring at me. My stupid heart fluttered with joy, and my mouth wanted to smile, but I schooled my features into one of polite inquiry.

"Can I help you?"

He closed his eyes and inhaled, and when his dark lashes swept back up to reveal his night sky eyes, they were filled with a familiar demanding heat.

He fixed that attention on me but spoke to the others in the room. "Everyone but my electus. Leave. Now."

Veena and Mallini looked to me for confirmation, and Chase slowly raised his head to look at Sin as if to say, *Who does he think he's speaking to?*

Sin growled low in his throat. "Fine, stay and watch if you like." He advanced a step, and it didn't take a genius to read the intention in his eyes.

The pulse between my legs throbbed in anticipation. "Guys, you need to leave."

"Yes, I think that's a great idea," Mallini said.

"Come on, Chase." Veena led him out, and he let her.

They exited quickly, closing the door behind them.

Sin tugged his shirt over his head, expertly managing to not snag it on his horns. "Take your clothes off," he said. "I need inside you." He pushed down his trousers. No boxers, everything on display. My heart hammered, and my pussy flooded with heat.

Words like *get lost, go fuck yourself,* and *I'm not your bitch* scrolled through my mind, but when he was like this, sensuous heat beating off his delicious body, the only words that would do were, "What are the terms?"

He made a sound of exasperation. "I fuck you and make you come."

"What?"

He climbed into the bed. "Take off your clothes, or I'll tear them off."

There was a wild, untamed sense to him tonight that teased the beast inside me.

I shrugged and smiled. "If you want me, you'll have to unwrap me yourself."

His chest vibrated, and in the next instant, he was on me,

his weight pinning me to the bed, his hands tearing at my clothes.

They snagged and ripped, leaving friction burns across my skin, but the pain was fleeting, forgotten as his skin kissed mine, and his mouth me. He was all over me, every inch of his body pressed against me, his tongue deep in my mouth, his cock sliding between my folds and opening me wide. He pinned my hands above my head and palmed my breast before tearing his mouth from mine to claim my nipple.

My head spun with sensation, small whimpers escaping between gasps of pleasure.

"Sin…Oh, fuck…"

He entered me, thrusting hard and deeply so my body jerked up the bed. My cry was cut short by a bruising kiss. He broke it and cupped my jaw, his eyes flashing in anger.

"Look at me," he ordered.

There was nowhere else to look but at him. He took up all the space in my field of vision leaving me trapped and vulnerable.

He rolled his hips, ending in a thrust that seated him as far as he could go. A moan parted my lips, hanging between us like validation of his skill. He rocked against me, and my eyes fluttered closed.

"Look at me while I fuck you, Nyx."

SIN

Our gazes connect, and heat blooms in my chest. A forgotten emotion. Unreliable. Unwanted. But it's here. It's here, and it flares for her.

I should run. This isn't part of the plan.

But I don't. Because I want this. I can control it.

Just this once. Just a taste.

I fuck her while devouring the play of emotion on her beautiful face. The desire, the need, the vulnerability, because in this moment she is giving herself to me. Putting her trust in me. Submitting, just like I want her to.

Need her to.

This is the moment to hurt her. Hold her down and go so deep she bruises, but I don't, because...I don't want to hurt her.

Oh fuck.

She cries out, cunt squeezing my cock in undulating spasms as she comes.

Fuuck. My thoughts fracture as I find my release inside her.

Mine.

She's mine, and I'm so fucked.

FORTY-TWO

IGNATIUS

The heat is so intense this close to the breach that even I, as an efreet, can feel its effects. It's been hours and no sign of Hrath. In that time, the breach has shrunk by a significant amount. If this continues, it'll be gone by sunset.

"He should have waited," Pelar says. "Another two hours and we'd have been done." The spell is ready, and so is the potion that accompanies it. The conji would have kept up a chant on this side, and Hrath would have carried the potion in his blood. That was the plan.

But now he's alone on the other side. Trapped unless he finds his way out. Maybe even captured. We have no way of knowing. Unless... "Will the spell work for two djinn?"

"What do you mean?"

"If someone else were to take that potion and go into the rift and find him, could they carry him back?"

"No," he says. "You need another potion and more conji to power the spell. We have neither."

Dammit.

"You would do it, though, wouldn't you? If you could?" His metallic silver eyes gleam in the dying sunlight.

"Yes. Yes, I would. Hrath is my bond brother."

There is nothing more to say. No way to explain how the bond brotherhood works. It's more than a vow, it's a symbiosis of souls. It's why he feels responsible for Nyx. Why he feels connected to her, because in a way, he is. If he dies, it will break me.

"There must be a way to stop the breach from closing."

"I've already considered the problem," Pelar says. "A breach either opens because of a natural tear in the fabric of reality or because someone creates a tear. In the former case, the breach will eventually fix itself using the natural power of the universe. But the latter will need to be closed manually and usually requires a vast amount of energy. It would then close immediately. The behavior of this tear tells me it's natural."

"You mean, whoever is on the other side doesn't know about it?"

"There's a possibility they may not be aware of it. It also means we may be able to wedge open the tear for a little while. It will slow down the repair but not stop it completely."

"Do it."

"You must first understand the risk. The pressure from the universe will continue to exert itself on the wedge, and eventually the wedge will snap. The breach will close suddenly. This may create a shockwave throughout the court and destabilize the fabric further."

He's asking me to choose between giving my bond brother more time to find his way home and the stability of the fabric of our world.

I love Hrath. He's a part of me. But our people must always come first. We've lost one world. We can't risk another.

"Your Grace? What is your decision?"

A weight settles on my chest. "We stand down. We wait, watch, and hope that he finds his way home."

HRATH

"He's waking."

"Don't touch him, stay back."

My head throbs. Why does it...Someone hit me! I stay still with my eyes closed, taking a moment to gather my thoughts.

I'd gone through the breach. I'd gone through, and someone hit me.

"We know you're awake, djinn. We can hear it in your pulse. Open your eyes."

There are five faces peering at me. All female. All... maras? These are maras female. Moonlight kisses their silvery gray skin and runs through their dark blue hair. Their regard is sharp with curiosity and intelligence.

But there's one who stands out. Her skin tone is a deep indigo, and her eyes and hair are silver.

"What is your name?" she asks. "How did you get into our dreamscape?"

Dreamscape? "This...This is a dream?"

"It is more than a dream. This is our haven, a reality built from our will. We did not invite you."

The maras are owned by Umbrane, which means... "You're in the Court of Shadows, aren't you?"

She hisses, and her eyes narrow. "Who are you?"

"Hrath, from the Court of Flame. I mean you no harm."

"And yet you invade our haven?"

"How can this be?" one of the silver-skinned maras asks the indigo one. "How can he be here?"

"Did Umbrane send you?" Indigo demands.

They're hiding here from Umbrane? "No. I despise that male."

There must be enough vitriol in my tone to placate her because the lethal intent in her eyes ebbs.

I need to understand where, exactly, we are. "Where is this place?"

They all look to the indigo female. She's their leader.

"This is our escape from our prison."

"Prison?"

"Yes. Umbrane keeps us in a place with no windows and only a single door. He comes to visit from time to time. But mostly he sends others to take away our young. We are his breeders. This place is hidden from him and accessible only by us until..." Her eyes go wide. "Did *she* send you?"

"Who?"

"I'm not sure what she is, but her pain called to me. A tiny slip of a creature with dark hair and mournful eyes. I kept her safe until he came for her."

Wait...hadn't Umbrane taken Veena before the final trial? "I think I know who you're speaking of. Her name is Veena. But she didn't send me. There's a breach in the Court of Flame. I came through to investigate."

The maras begin whispering in alarm.

The indigo woman hushes them. "Let me think."

"Let me help. Explain how this place came to exist."

"It is a reality that we created for our dream selves to inhabit. Our astral selves roam free here, but our bodies remain in our prison. Even if there is a breach, as you claim, we cannot use it to escape, but it seems that creatures can get in."

"We must shut it down," one of the other maras says.

Panic spikes in the air. "It's all right. It's closing itself."

"Lilliana!" One of the women nudges the indigo female. "If it's closing, then that means..." She looks at me in alarm. "You must go. This place is not built to house flesh and bone. If you become trapped here, it *will* tear you to shreds."

"We'll take you back to the fairground where we found you," Lilliana says. "You can find your way back from there."

The world tilts, and when it rights itself, I'm standing by the carousel where they knocked me out. "How did you do that?"

"We willed it." Lilliana smiles. "We control the terrain and the travel."

Here in the buttery sunlight, her beauty shines brightly. Her features are sharp and chiseled, but there's a softness to her mouth and sadness in her eyes.

"Which way?" she asks.

I spot the golden pillar. "This way."

We head toward the structure.

"I did not want to say this with the others listening, but I have a favor to ask," Lilliana says.

I think I can guess. "You want freedom."

"We did not come here to be prisoners. We came as warriors. To work alongside the fallen, not to be abused and confined. You are the first outsider that we have come across, and I cannot help but feel your visit is a gift from fate."

I don't know about fate. But I'll be damned if I stand by

and let this injustice stand. "I swear to you, we will find a way to free you. We have a new Satan, and she won't stand for this injustice."

"Only destroying the contract that binds us to Umbrane can free us. Can your Satan do that?"

The air becomes charged, and my skin tingles. There is a light up ahead. The breach. But it's pulsing. Dimming.

Urgency grips me. The pure, unadulterated primal knowledge that I must leave. Now.

I take a step, but Lilliana grabs my arm. "You must find the contract. I saw it in Umbrane's mind before he learned to shut me out. It's hidden behind a green door. A green door with a golden handle. It must be destroyed."

The light begins to shrink.

"Now go!" She shoves me with surprising strength, and I tumble into the light.

IGNATIUS

"It's closing," Pelar says. "I'm so sorry, Your Grace."

He's gone. Lost to me. My brother...my friend. I can't watch. I won't. I make to turn away just as a figure flies out of the breach, arches through the air, and lands on the burning sand.

Hrath! My boots beat sand as I sprint toward him. "Hrath! Get off the sand!" His sylph nature can't withstand the heat. He'll burn. "Hrath!"

He shoots up into the air on a gust of icy air. It swirls around him, holding him aloft and bringing him to me.

A ragged laugh falls from my lips. "You made it."

His face appears through the swirling vortex of air. "Did you doubt me?"

My smile dims. "I never doubted you, Hrath. But I was worried. The breach—" I look back at the spot where the breach once tore our world. "It's gone. You made it out just in time."

"What did you see?" Pelar joins us. "Did you find the fawda?"

"No," Hrath says. "I found something entirely unexpected. Not a threat to us or our world, but...we must speak to Nyx immediately."

Agreed. "That can be arranged."

FORTY-THREE

NYX

I wasn't surprised to find Sin gone when I woke. The fact that he stayed until I fell asleep was surprising enough.

Something had shifted between us, and I wasn't sure what. Maybe the fact I was going to be crowned Satan. Maybe he saw me as an equal now. Although Sin had never treated me as lesser, not even when he demanded I surrender control during our acts of intimacy. Although... intimacy had never felt as real as last night.

Last night, Sin peeled back the layers between us in a way I didn't completely understand. But there was a heaviness in the pit of my belly, a fullness in my heart that didn't usually follow our sexfests.

We needed to talk. But not now. After the coronation. I was sick of his hot and cold bullshit. Sick of the secrets he was keeping from me.

If he wanted me vulnerable, if he wanted this kind of intimacy, then there couldn't be any lies between us.

There was a rap at the door, and Zinichi called out, "Nyx? Are you ready?"

Oh shit, the fitting. "Give me five minutes!"

Mallini and Chase tagged along to my dress fitting trip. Veena might have come too, but she was in the kitchens. Zinichi dropped us off at Chesra's personal workshop, telling us that the dressmaker would be with us soon.

Chesra had a magic touch when it came to clothes. It was a shame I'd missed out on seeing her put together Mallini's and Veena's dresses. Being here, surrounded by fabrics and lace, made me ache to see Tristeene.

She should be here with us, not trapped in a fancy prison in the abyss. Odette was supposed to take a sample of my blood to work on the blocker for Tristeene, but she hadn't asked about it yet. I'd forgotten to chase her. How could I forget?

"Nyx? Are you all right?" Mallini asked.

"I forgot about Tristeene."

Mallini frowned. "What do you mean?"

"I was supposed to give Odette a blood sample so she could work on a blocker for Tristeene, and I forgot."

She gave me half a smile. "I think you can be forgiven for that, considering everything that's happened since you got back."

My temples throbbed, warning of a headache. "It's not just that. There's so much to do. Sev, Loke, Zepar, the Accords, Tristeene, and this sentient sickness...I don't often get overwhelmed, but I'm feeling it."

"Stop," Mallini said. "I think you're forgetting you don't have to do this alone. You have us. We can all take on tasks and work together to get it all done. We'll have a meeting after the coronation, and we'll sort this out."

She was right. Of course she was right. I had my siblings. A council. I might wear the crown, but the Satan seat belonged to us all. I hugged her on impulse, and she relaxed against me.

"It's going to be okay," she said.

I let out a rough laugh. "You know, I'm usually the one doing the consoling."

"I know, but maybe it's time for someone to be your shoulder to lean on." She pulled back and looked me in the eye. "We're lucky. We have each other, several shoulders to lean on."

Chesra bustled into the workshop, ducking so that her gazelle horns didn't catch on the door frame. She was carrying a large roll of shimmery black fabric, which she set on the counter before parking her stocky frame on a stool with a satisfied sigh.

"Well, I was beginning to think we'd have to repurpose an old dress, and that would not do. But lucky for you, the delay meant this luscious fabric had time to arrive from Superbia." She fingered the star-speckled fabric. "It's perfect for what I have in mind." She looked at me. "If you'll give me creative control..."

I shrugged. "Sure. As long as I can walk in it and my tits and snatch aren't on display, I'm happy."

Her brows shot up. "I wouldn't dream of leaving you so exposed."

"Then we go for it. Make me look"—I wiggled my finger in the air—"Satany."

The next hour was spent taking measurements and tucking and pinning fabric until I was swathed in it.

The creation didn't look like a dress, and according to Chesra, it wouldn't be finished until just before the ball. Which was fine by me.

"You'll wear britches and a tunic for the official, closed coronation in the morning," she said. "You'll wear the dress for the ball in the evening."

"I thought the coronation had to happen on a full moon. How are we doing the official one in the morning?"

"It's still a full moon, child," she said. "Even if you can't see it till the sun sets. Your coronation outfit will be brought to you tomorrow morning."

Tomorrow.

The coronation was tomorrow. I took a breath to stem my nerves. "Thanks."

We left the workshop and took the narrow corridors back to the main part of the keep. Zinichi had offered to stay and escort us back to our quarters, but I was good with directions, only needing to take a journey once to learn the path.

"What are your plans for the rest of the day?" Mallini asked.

"I'm going to find Odette and give her my blood. Then check on Zepar. After that...I'm not sure."

"You want to have a sleepover?" She gave me a cheeky smile. "I'm sure Veena can provide the snacks now that she's friendly with the kitchen staff again."

"You mean like a midnight feast?"

"I mean exactly that."

This is what we did. We huddled and clustered before an event. It was like recharging. I couldn't explain it, but it felt right.

"Okay. I'm in."

"I'll organize everything. My room, eleven p.m. Bring blankets and pillows."

We climbed the steps to the floor that housed our quarters to find Odette coming toward us. Her emerald dress swept the floor behind her as she glided across marble. The woman had regal down pat.

"Nyx. I was looking for you. Sin asked me to collect a sample of your blood."

So he'd remembered after all. "I was planning to see you about that."

She gave me a terse smile that didn't reach her eyes. "Good. We can take the sample here. I don't need much." She pulled a vial and needle from her pocket. "Please roll up your sleeve."

What was with the snippy attitude? "You want to draw blood here, in the corridor?"

"It's as good a place as any," she said coolly.

Heck no. I wasn't having this. "I'll see you later, Mallini."

Mallini arched a brow and sidled away but mouthed, *Slap the bitch,* from over Odette's shoulder.

I waited until she'd rounded the corner. "What is your problem with me, Odette?"

Her eyes flinched. "Aside from the fact my son lost a wing because of you?"

Guilt formed a lump in my throat, but I swallowed it. Guilt wouldn't bring his wing back. It wouldn't heal him. True, my decision to go after the thief had led us to the alley, and I'd regret that for as long as I lived. But I wouldn't allow her to use this awful incident orchestrated by the faebloods to drive a wedge between me and Zep.

"Your son saved my life, and I'll be eternally grateful to him. If *he* wants to rage at me and blame me, then I will gladly listen, but you have no right."

"I'm his mother."

"And I'm your *Satan.*"

She blinked in surprise.

I gave her a moment to process before continuing. "You don't have to like me, Odette, but you will respect me and my position here. Are we clear?"

Her throat bobbed, and her eyes hardened. "Crystal."

I gave her a mirthless smile. "In turn, I'll respect you *and* your position, both as Superbia's head conji *and* as Zepar's mother."

Her ice chip eyes bore into me. "Do you have feelings for my son?"

"Yes."

She dropped her gaze for a long beat, and when she looked up, a little of the hostility was gone. "We can take the blood here or in my chambers."

Now that she was giving me a choice... "Here is fine. I'd like to see Zepar afterwards."

"He won't wake till tomorrow. The pain tincture along with the sleeping draught will keep him under."

My heart sank. "Will he heal?"

She considered my question for a moment. "His body will, but only time will tell how he'll cope psychologically without his wing."

That's what I was worried about. Flight was a part of who he was, and now that it had been taken from him, how would he cope?

One thing was for certain. He wouldn't be left to deal with it alone.

I held out my arm. "Take as much as you need, and if you don't mind, I'd like to help with the blocker, any way I can."

She nodded. "In that case, it might be easier to do this in my laboratory."

Maybe Odette and I would be able to find a middle ground after all.

FORTY-FOUR

SEV

Being back in the Court of Shadows evokes a cocktail of emotions. The air smells like home, but my heart sits heavy in my chest, aching to be in its new home with Nyx.

Our blood oath connection is broken, but there's a stronger connection between us now. One I never imagined I'd form with anyone. Loving her has changed me.

The imp screams as a brand is pressed into his skin, and the acrid scent of burning flesh fills the throne room.

The demon lords and ladies standing against the walls of the chamber don't dare take their eyes off the scene. This is a show of Umbrane's power. His swift justice on the imp who dared steal from the duke's kitchens. A loaf of bread to feed his family living in the dark, dank marshes of the Shadow Court. An area that the nobility prefers to forget exists.

The imp sobs, huge wracking cries of agony. His pain is sharp and poignant, but my hunger barely stirs. Pain no longer gives me the same thrill it once did. It no longer arouses me like it used to. Only one person can do that now.

Nyx is my aphrodisiac. Being with her, her scent, the silken soft feel of her skin against my fingertips and the vanilla taste of her in my mouth are the only things that make me hard.

"I'm glad to see you've not lost your taste for pain," Umbrane says.

I'm breathing fast and shallow, and when I follow Umbrane's gaze to my crotch, I find myself engorged.

He thinks I'm aroused by the imp's plight. This pleases him.

Fuck it, let him think what he wants. Let him believe I'm still his pet.

The imp begs for his life as the maras, a young male I've never met, approaches him with cold, detached eyes.

Umbrane sits back in his seat, a smug smile on his face. "Sev, this is Vix, your replacement in my court, and I have to say, he's coming along beautifully."

My chest tightens. So this is his new pet. His new project.

"Vix inflicts pain because I order him to," Umbrane continues. "He doesn't derive any joy from it. He simply follows my orders. My praise is the *only* thing that he craves."

Vix grabs the imp by the horns, forces his head back, and presses his dagger to the creature's throat before looking at Umbrane. He waits for instruction like the good puppet he is.

Umbrane takes a moment to sip from his goblet, sigh, and tap his fingers on his armrest. All the while the imp whimpers and pleads, but Vix stands like stone with the creature held firmly in his grip.

The knot in my chest tightens. This maras is barely a man. His features are still soft, his body slender and wiry, but his eyes...his eyes are dead.

Umbrane lifts a finger and gives the nod.

Vix slits the imp's throat, not in a quick slashing motion, but by slowly dragging the blade across his neck.

The sound the imp makes claws at the inside of my skull, and a frisson passes through me—the echoes and remnants of the male I once was.

Vix drops the imp and waits for further instructions like an automaton.

Umbrane's eyes are alight with fervor. I know that look. I've seen it before. "You and you." He points to two servers carrying trays of pastries. I catch the fear in their eyes before they cover it with a bow and hurry from the room. "Vix..."

Vix nods and follows. Umbrane takes a moment to finish his drink. "You won't be coming with me, Sev. Not this time. You'll have to earn your pleasure. Work for it. Prove to me that you're worthy of the pain I can provide for your consumption. Until then, you'll go hungry." He snorts. "The princes made me vow that no harm would come to you. That you wouldn't be confined, but little do they know that you thrive on pain. It's nectar to you. As to confinement, the terms they've set will do that just fine."

He stands and adjusts his cuffs. "Enjoy your return home, Sev. I'll enjoy watching you starve."

He climbs off the platform and crosses to the door Vix exited through. I know where he's going. What he'll have Vix do to the demons while he watches. Always watches, never participates. He thinks excluding me is a punishment, and if I'm going to succeed in finding the contract that binds my people to him, I'll have to play the part. Show stubborn resistance with flashes of craven need. He'll expect me to break and eventually beg for his favor. Beg for him to allow me to feed on pain.

I'll find the contract before it comes to that, and right now is the perfect time to begin my search.

Umbrane will be busy for hours.

And so will I.

FORTY-FIVE

NYX

Dhuma carried two mattresses into Mallini's room and dropped them by the bed. Keelan brought in two more. They almost collided but sidestepped one another as if they'd choreographed the move.

"They're so big, but they move like dancers," Veena said.

"It's the art of being a fighter," Mallini said. "You have to be light on your feet."

A pile of blankets and pillows entered the room with Gus's legs sticking out the bottom. He dumped the haul and then stood with his hands on his hips, eyes bright with satisfaction.

Keelan returned in his pj's—an undershirt and baggy pants—barefoot, hair loose around his shoulders.

Veena hurried over to the dresser and grabbed a brush. "Can I braid it? Please?" She gave him the big, pleading eyes.

He grunted his assent before dropping to the mattress pushed up against the bed. Veena climbed up behind him, ready to style his mane.

Dhuma returned carrying a tray laden with food. Zinichi followed, pushing a cart with even more treats to choose from.

"Don't stay up too late, will you?" Zinichi said. "You have an early start and a very busy day."

Butterflies fluttered in my belly. Tomorrow was the big day, after all.

"We'll leave you to it," Zinichi said.

"You can stay if you want," Mallini blurted out. She addressed them both, but her attention was on Dhuma.

Zinichi smiled. "Thank you, child, but unlike you young things, I need my sleep."

"Dhuma?" I smiled at him. "Want to join us?"

"Thank you, but no. I too need my sleep. But I will be close by if you should need me."

But not for long. Once tomorrow was done, Dhuma would be off to the abyss to act as my regent there.

After tomorrow, everything would change.

But not this.

The door closed behind them, and Gus let out a snort that sounded suspiciously like a laugh. I followed his gaze to Keelan, now sporting two cute braids that arched out of his head from behind his horns.

Veena's eyes were twinkling with mirth.

Mallini grinned at Keelan. "Looking good. Very intimidating."

Keelan frowned and reached up to touch his hair. "What? Veena? What have you done?"

"You don't like it?" She sounded disappointed, but Keelan had his back to her so couldn't see the smile on her face. "I thought you'd like it." She injected the threat of a sob into her voice.

"It's fine," he said quickly. "I love it."

"You do?" Her tone lifted with hope.

"Yes, yes. Now how about we eat?"

"You're going to keep your hair like that?" Mallini asked. "Seriously?"

Keelan gave her a warning look. "I love it."

Gus burst out laughing, and Mallini followed suit.

I shook my head with a smile. "She's messing with you, Keelan."

Veena put her arms around his neck and kissed his cheek. "Because I love you."

Keelan groaned. "Thank goodness. Now take them out quickly."

She pulled out the ties and ran her fingers through his hair. "There, all better." She hopped off the bed and crossed to the cart of food, returning with a plate of swirly pastry, capped with cream. "I made these specially for us."

The pastry was flaky and buttery, and the cream was thick and sweet. I detected a hint of cinnamon too. Delicious.

"Oh, my," Gus said. "Veena, this is wonderful."

"So good," Mallini said.

Keelan grunted in approval and popped another one in his mouth.

Veena beamed from ear to ear. "It's a recipe I created. And I'd like to create more." She looked at me. "I'm not good at the political things like Tristeene, and I'm not a fighter like Mallini and Keelan, or all knowledgeable like Gus. I'm not a leader like you, either, but I understand food. It makes me happy to create. So I was wondering if I could have charge of the kitchens here at Morningstar once you're crowned. The menu is so bland, and morale isn't great because of it. I know I can make it better."

"That's fine by me." I snagged another pastry and passed

it to Chase, who wolfed it down. "Gus can have the library, and you can have the kitchens."

"We should have a special meeting room," Mallini said. "One that has a training room attached."

"Better working hours for Minorax," Keelan said. His lip curled. "The Minorax in the Court of Flame are well treated, but outside of the court, we're treated like grunts."

"Access to education is scarce for imp younglings in most courts," Gus said. "I'd like to address that."

And once Tristeene was cured, she'd make an excellent emissary. This...Us...We were the perfect Satan. I might be the figurehead, but Satan was all of us.

For the first time since I'd been told I'd been chosen, I believed that this could work. Because together, we could fix, achieve, do anything.

Chase nudged me with his nose and chuffed, and I tuned back into the conversation.

"Imps are faster because we have lighter bones," Gus said.

"But zuni are lighter all around," Veena pointed out. "And we can run fast from when we used to be hunted."

"Zuni were hunted?" I stared at Veena in horror.

Gus rolled his eyes. "That was so long ago it's older than ancient history."

"Zuni were the rabbits of the demon world," Keelan said.

Gus beamed at him. "That's right."

Veena glared at Gus in annoyance. "We are not rabbits."

"Not anymore, you're not, but there was a time when..."

I settled back to enjoy a history lesson courtesy of Gus.

This. Right here. With them. Might just be my favorite place.

FORTY-SIX

Odette answered my knock on the door to Zepar's quarters with a roll of bandages in her hand. She blinked at me in surprise.

I didn't blame her. It was early, like *the sun is waking up early*.

"Odette, I was hoping to see Zepar before my coronation."

Emotions skipped across her face, too fast for me to catch and decipher. "Of course. I'm sure he'll like that." She stepped aside to let me in. "I forgot the salve. I'll be back in a few moments. His room is the last door on the left."

She stepped out and shut the door.

The sitting room was bathed in gray predawn rays. One of the sofas was set up as a bed. There was an open book face down on the side table. Beside it sat a small tray carrying pots of salve. Odette had slept here to watch over her son. She might be a bitch to me, but she knew what it meant to be a mother.

Zepar was a lucky guy.

Zepar's door was ajar, but no sound came from beyond. Had he fallen asleep? Maybe I shouldn't disturb him.

"Nyx? Is that you?" he called out.

"Yes." I pushed the door open a fraction. "Can I come in?"

"Of course."

The bedroom was relatively small compared to some I'd seen here, or maybe it was the huge bed taking up the space that made it seem that way. The heavy drapes were open, and the morning light gave Zepar's skin a slightly gray tinge.

He was on his front, bandaged back on display, head to one side so he could face me. "Mother said you'd come."

"She did?"

"She likes you."

"Oh? I didn't get that impression."

"She's not an easy woman to read," he said.

"Is that how you knew I was outside your door?" I snagged the dresser chair as I approached the bed. "Or did you hear my voice?" I set the chair down facing him and parked my ass.

"Neither. I could smell you. That sweet vanilla scent." He closed his eyes, a smile playing on his lips. "I dream of it sometimes, you know. Being surrounded by it." There was a wistful quality to his tone. "Last night, when I was riding a unicorn, I saw you by the lake."

Um... "A unicorn?"

He chuckled soft and sexy. "It had a golden horn."

My gaze flicked to the bottle of green stuff by his bed. Pain meds? Was he dosed up right now?

"I desperately wanted a cinnamon roll," he said. "The unicorn said he'd get me something much better, and he took me to you. And your scent...Much better than a cinnamon roll."

Oh boy. "Thank you."

"You and I...we're the same, you know," he said. "Left to find our own path by the people who should have been there to guide us. Different...unique." His gaze was like warm honey. "I'm so in love with you, Nyx."

My heart did a backflip, and my pulse fluttered. He was high on pain meds, and if he hadn't said it already, I'd have been inclined to believe he didn't mean it. But he did...he truly did.

I wanted to say it back, but not now. Not when he wasn't clearheaded. "Zepar, you should get some rest. We can talk later."

"You'll come back later?"

I dropped out of the chair and onto my knees by his bed so that we were eye to eye. "Yes. I promise. I'll come back later." I reached out and traced my index finger down his cheek.

He closed his eyes and swallowed hard as if my touch evoked too much emotion, and my fluttery heart swelled.

"I won't be able to come to the ball. Will you come see me before?" He opened his eyes, and his gaze was clear and unhazy. "I want to see you in your dress. The one chosen for your grand entrance."

I wanted him to see me in it too. "You know I hate dresses, right?"

"But they love you, Nyx. Every inch of you." His voice was like hot chocolate on a winter's night. Warm and satisfyingly good.

My cheeks warmed, and my gaze dropped to his luscious mouth. He was injured, incapacitated, and in pain, and I was thinking about jumping his bones.

I needed help.

The sound of footsteps told me Odette was back. "I should go."

"Yes," Zepar said with a proud smile. "Go get your crown."

ZINICHI FUSSED WITH MY HAIR, smoothing it back into a French braid that would work with the crown, that apparently, I'd only get to wear once for the ceremony and the ball. After that it'd be locked away until the power needed to be passed to the next Satan.

Chase sat by the dresser watching Zinichi work. He'd had his fair share of attention this morning too when he was groomed and brushed until his coat shone. Zinichi had somehow managed to tame his coarse coat into something sleek and shiny. And me?

I looked like a different person in fitted midnight blue britches and a tunic sewn with tiny glimmering stars at the cuffs. A ruffled white collar peeked out from the V in the tunic, and soft leather boots hugged my calves. I looked like a noble but the kick-ass version.

"Chesra did a beautiful job on your coronation outfit," Zinichi said with a sigh of contentment.

"She certainly did. Was it her idea to add the blade sheath to my boot?"

"Oh, Mallini suggested that."

"Of course she did." I smiled. "Mallini knows me too well."

I turned to the bed to ask Sev what he thought, but he wasn't there. Guilt raked its claws across my psyche. This bed was mine and Sev's, but I'd allowed Sin into it. I'd tainted our space.

"You miss him, don't you?" Zinichi said softly.

"Constantly." I touched my chest, the empty place where our bond had been. "But I'll get him back. I promise you." This was my last time in these chambers. When Sev returned, we'd be in royal quarters, and we'd pick a new bed, a new space, just for us.

"I'll go check on the others," Zinichi said. "Make sure they have everything they need."

"When do we leave for the throne room?"

"Half an hour. We're to take the hidden passages and—"

The door to the Court of Flame lit up.

Zinichi smiled knowingly. "Come, Chase, let's give Nyx a moment."

They hurried from the room as the door opened, and Ignatius stepped through.

FORTY-SEVEN

Ignatius carried the warmth of the sun with him. His spun gold hair was streaked with white strands from sun exposure, and the fiery tattoos on his golden skin shifted and moved eagerly as he crossed the room to gather me into his arms.

"*Qalbi...*" He kissed the top of my head and stroked down my back. "I've missed you."

"I missed you too." Our connection bloomed warm and solid, pulsing and anxious to be solidified. If only there was time now. I tipped my face up to his. "What happened? Why did you have to leave? Was it the breach?"

"Yes. Hrath, the crazy fool, went through."

"What!"

He smiled wryly. "Yes. The breach was closing, and he wanted information. For a moment, I thought he wouldn't make it back."

"But he did."

"Yes. Thank the stars. But, Nyx, the breach doesn't belong to the fawda."

"Then what? Where does it go?"

"Hrath found female maras there. It's a dreamscape. A reality created by the women to escape Umbrane's cruelty. In reality, they're locked away in a windowless place with only one exit that is barred. They told Hrath that Umbrane uses them to breed more maras, and the young are taken from them."

"I didn't think I could hate Umbrane any more than I already do. I'll need to tell Sev when I visit the Court of Shadows as Satan."

"There is a way to get him back," Ignatius said. "The maras female told Hrath there was a contract—"

"I know. It binds the maras to Umbrane. I found out recently from Ramiel. Sev knows too. He's going to find it."

"It's behind a green door with a golden handle. That's what Lilliana told Hrath."

"Then we need to let him know. We'll also need to draw Umbrane away from the court so Sev can have free rein to search."

"That won't be easy," Ignatius said. "Umbrane rarely leaves his court, and when he does, he rarely stays away longer than a day."

"I'll find a way."

He cupped my face. "We'll find a way. Together." He tipped my face up and pressed his lips softly to mine. "Now, shall we go and get that crown?"

I gripped his nape, pushed up on tiptoe, and claimed his mouth in a real kiss. He melted against me, fingers biting, pulling me tightly against this taut body. His hair slid between my fingers like silk, and his tongue lashed at mine with fiery, elemental need.

I wanted him here and now.

"Ahem. Nyx!" Mallini said from the doorway.

Ignatius stilled. "Fuck." He said the word against my lips.

I smiled against his mouth. "Later?"

"Mmmm..." He stole one final kiss. "I'll hold you to that."

We broke away from each other. I straightened my clothes and smoothed a hand over my hair. "How do I look?"

"Edible," he said.

"Groan," Mallini quipped. "Now come on, we've got to go. You can't be late to your own coronation."

"After you," Ignatius said.

It was showtime.

I WASN'T the only one dressed like nobility. My siblings wore the Morningstar colors of silver and black. Tunics and trousers for Mallini and Veena and fitted shirts and slacks for Gus and Keelan. But, whereas my clothes were heavily embroidered at the cuffs and collar, theirs were more subtle, setting me apart from them.

Nugen led us through the hidden passages. We came out at the elevator that opened on the throne room and piled in.

It was a tight squeeze but not unpleasant, considering I got to cozy up to Ignatius on the way up.

Shame the ride was so short.

We stepped into the throne room, onto the smooth obsidian floor speckled with starlight. Balconied seating rose on either side of us made up of silverwood and cushioned velvet seats. But the throne was the feature of this space. Set on a wide platform, the winged, obsidian chair dominated the room. Those carved wings curved so they'd bracket whoever sat in the seat, protecting them. The wintry dawn peeked in through several windows, providing a backdrop for this magnificent seat.

For a moment, all I saw was the room. The throne. My seat. But there were demons already here, figures dotted about in preparation for the ceremony. Like the demons occupying the seats to our left.

"Witnesses," Gus said. "Demons from each court."

Dhuma stood to one side, arms crossed, feet shoulder width apart. He smiled at me with his eyes and gave me a slight nod.

Artimus was positioned beside the throne, and two Erinyes sat at a table close by, quills hovering over parchment. The record keepers of this event, no doubt. The three princes were lined up on the other side of the throne. They'd dressed in Morningstar colors today—black pants and silver shirts that clung to their imposing frames. Merihem's tousled auburn locks were gone in favor of a buzz cut that left his features looking stark and bare. There were dark smudges beneath his eyes as if he hadn't slept well.

Where was Sin?

"Nyx, please join us," Ramiel said. "The rest of you can take a seat."

Nugen positioned himself to one side of the lift doors, and my siblings peeled away to join the noble witnesses on the padded seats to our right.

Here went nothing. I approached the throne, heart beating a little faster the closer I got. The air was charged with anticipation, which was to be expected, but a prickle of unease skipped up my spine regardless.

A door on the other side of the throne room opened, admitting Sin. With his larger-than-life presence, horns, and six-foot-six stature, Sin was a beast of a man, but I'd have thought dressing in black would somehow make him look smaller.

I was wrong.

His shirt was a midnight sky stretched across his shoulders. It hugged his biceps and powerful waist, all muscle from swinging the anvil at his smithy. He carried a wooden box in his hand.

"Apologies for the delay." He didn't explain why.

His gaze slipped past me to the throne, then skipped to the princes.

Was he avoiding my gaze?

Moths spawned in my belly. Something was wrong. The slight frown on Artimus's face told me he'd picked up on it too.

I'd been pushed around and used like a pawn on a chessboard too often not to pick up on another play. "What's going on here, Ramiel? I'm getting some seriously sketchy vibes, and I want to know what you're not telling me."

Ramiel pressed his lips together and looked across at Sin.

"Sin?" I turned to him. "What am I missing here?"

He set the box on the table by the Erinyes before looking at me directly. "I suppose it's time you knew the risks of claiming the seat."

"Risks? I thought the risks ended with the trials."

"Satan created the trials to test his spawn. Admittedly, I doubt he anticipated how many spawn there'd be. But the trials did their work, even though the actual events weren't what whittled down your numbers. Competition can do that to the best of us."

He had no idea, and I wasn't about to tell him.

"You were chosen based on your performance, not only in the trials but outside of it. Your connection with your siblings, their love and high regard for you, is what decided us, but there is still a final player who must cast its vote." He pointed to the throne. Was he saying the seat had to choose me too? "You'll take the seat. Slit your palm and press it to the armrest, and the seat will test you and decide whether you are indeed worthy."

This didn't make sense. "Wait, I've sat on the seat before. We all have."

"A baseline test only," Ramiel said. "Set out in the terms of the first contract."

Nugen, the weapons master, had been the one to bring us into this room all those weeks ago and ask us to test the seat, but he looked just as surprised as me.

Ramiel continued. "All those that didn't take the seat were rendered ineligible for the throne."

Veena...All this time, she'd been disqualified. If Umbrane had known, he would have left her alone. But... "Why make them go through the trials then?"

"Why not?" Sin said coldly.

Every time I thought we were getting close. That he was lowering his walls and letting me in, he shut me out again. I guess this was what it felt like to have the shoe on the other foot.

I lifted my chin. "Fine. Let it test me and be done with it. If I'm not worthy, there are several others here who may be. I'll watch them ascend with pride."

"Yes, there are others here the seat could test, but you won't be here to see them rise," Sin said.

Gooseflesh broke out over my skin. But it was Artimus that asked the question hovering on my lips.

"What do you mean? What happens if she's rejected?"

Sin kept his gaze locked with mine as he answered. "If she's rejected, then she burns."

Forty-Eight

It took a moment for me to process his words, then rage burgeoned inside me. "You're telling me this now? Why the fuck would you wait?"

Commotion broke out around me, my siblings, Artimus, the witnesses, all talking at once. It seemed that this was a shock to everyone. Everyone except the princes. Everyone except Sin—the male I'd trusted above everyone. Trusted before I'd ever known who he was. He'd never been an open book, but I'd always believed that he had my best interests at heart, but this...This was not in my best interests.

"No," Artimus said. "She's not doing it."

My siblings surrounded me. "Nothing is worth that risk," Mallini said. "You can keep your throne. We don't want it."

"We did your trials," Gus said. "We did them because if we didn't, we would have died."

Satan's blood bound us into completing the trials, but this... "This isn't part of his blood contract, is it? The trials were, but taking the throne..."

"No, it isn't," Sin said, almost reluctantly. "But someone

must. One of you. It must be one of you, or the power held inside this seat will be lost forever."

I was a high daimon. There was a chance I had one more death in me, but I wouldn't be able to come back without a body to return to. If the throne incinerated me, I was fucked.

Ignatius spoke for the first time since we'd entered the room. "Fire cannot kill an efreet. And it cannot kill the twin flame belonging to one." He locked gazes with me. "You will take that seat, Nyx. But only after we consummate our bond."

"No." Sin's voice was a boom that shook the room. "There can be no test without the real risk of failure. If you take that seat knowing that you can't be harmed, then it will undoubtedly reject you."

I didn't want to die, but if I didn't do this, one of the others might. They could get hurt. But if none of us did this, then the power would be lost, and if the fawda attacked, we'd be fucked.

"I believe in you," Dhuma said. "You are Knightwood. You are Beelzebub's spawn, and you are worthy."

"Maybe we were wrong about the reason you weren't raised in the demon realm," Artimus said softly.

He was referring to Satan sending me away to be hidden. To him asking Arty to watch over me. It was tempting to believe that my father had known I'd find my way back to the demon realm and to the throne. That he'd believed I'd be worthy, but it didn't matter what anyone else believed.

I had to believe in myself.

This had to happen. Deep breath. I took a seat on the throne.

Gasps filled the room.

I held out my hand to Sin. "Give me the damn blade."

There was tension in Sin's movements as he unlatched the box to reveal a sparkling silver crown and a silver needle blade. He plucked the blade from the velvet interior and handed it to me.

I barely felt the sting of the metal slicing into my palm. Blood thundered in my ears, and my pulse pounded in my throat as I passed it back to Sin. He caught my gaze, locked on for a moment, and I imagined there was regret in that look. But who was I kidding? Sin didn't do regrets or apologies.

My siblings watched me with a cocktail of mushy emotions that I was totally going to file away for later.

If there was a later.

Dhuma's gaze was steady, Arty and Ignatius looked as if they were holding their breath.

I gave them all a nod then slapped my palms to the armrests.

Seconds bled into one another.

Nothing happened. "Is something supposed to—"

Heat raced through my body and exploded outward. The room winked out, and when the lights came back on, everyone was gone.

FORTY-NINE

A RTIMUS

Nyx's body goes into a spasm, back arched, head thrown back, palms plastered to the armrests. Sin takes a step forward before checking himself, but that one step is all that's needed to show that he cares. His cool, detached demeanor is a farce. He fucking cares just as much as we do.

Nyx's head falls forward, and her eyes are milky white. The irises are gone.

"What's happening?" Veena demands. "What's wrong with her?"

"I don't know," Sin says. "But if she's not on fire, then I consider it a good sign." His tone gives nothing away, but the flex of his fingers as they oscillate between forming a fist or not reveal his disconcertion.

Nyx stares across the room, unseeing. Her body is stiff,

in the grip of the seat's power. What could be happening? Where is she right now? Because she isn't here with us.

"Come on, Nyx," Ignatius mutters. "Come back to us."

NYX

The throne room was empty. Where had everyone gone? I made to stand, but my body refused to cooperate.

"Hello, Nyx, it is so good to see you." The voice came from all around me, feminine and soothing. It was the same voice I'd heard when Nugen allowed us to try the throne on for size all those weeks ago. But no one else had mentioned hearing it.

I searched the room for the speaker, but even the shadows were empty. "Who are you? Why don't you show yourself?"

"My name is Theo. Your father named me when I was born."

"Born? Are you...Are you one of his children?"

Her laugh was a melody. "Oh no, child. I'm not flesh and bone. I am power made sentient."

Power? The seat's power was alive? "Where are you? Come out so I can see you."

"This *is* me," she said. "A voice. A presence. That is all I am. For now."

Did the princes know about this? About her? "Who else knows about you?"

"Beelzebub was the first, and now you."

"The princes don't know?"

"We decided that would be best," Theo said. "Bub wasn't sure how they'd react to my existence."

"Bub?"

"It's what I called Beelzebub. I believe you call it a nickname?"

She sounded suddenly unsure. Younger. "Theo, how old are you?"

She was silent for several beats, either considering the question or trying to find a way to sidestep it. When she finally responded, she sounded almost sad. "In some respects, I'm ancient. I feel as if I've existed forever. But I believe you want to know when I became...aware, right?"

"Yes. That's right."

"Fourteen years ago."

She was a teenager. Great.

"No, Nyx, I'm not a teenager."

Whoa. Had she just read my thoughts?

"Yes, Nyx. I can do that while you are here, on the seat, connected to my world, and to answer your question, no. I am not a teenager. I've been alive for eons. It's only the awareness of my existence that is new. My knowledge is vast because I'm an amalgamation of ancient powers. But this world, your world, is new to me. Bub educated me, and once you and I bind, if you allow it, I can learn more."

"Allow it?"

"I will not look through your eyes without your permission. You have my word on that. But I would like a window to the outside world once more. I've created my own keep to roam, built from what I saw through Bub's eyes, but it's lonely here."

This place was a replica of the real world, and it was Theo's home. She was trapped here.

She sighed. "Not trapped. This is my world. I can make it

as I wish it to be. I'm as trapped as you are in your world, but being aware is lonely without someone to share it with."

My mind whirred. She'd seen through Satan's eyes for fourteen years—did that mean... "Do you know who my mother is? Did you see her through his eyes?"

"I'm afraid not. Bub had already sired his offspring by the time I was born. He had no female companions that I saw. He would have told me if he had. He was my only friend." Her voice is thick with emotion. "My only connection to the wonders of the world, and then he was taken from me."

My pulse quickened. "Wait...Theo...Were you there when he was killed? Did you see who did it?"

Theo was silent for several beats. "Yes. But I was powerless to help him. I couldn't heal the wound. I tried and tried, and then I was here. Alone. Cut off from him, and I knew...I knew he was gone."

"Who was it? Theo, who killed Bub?" No one at any time had explained how Satan had died, and none of us had thought to ask. Everything had become about the trials and surviving them. But someone had killed Satan, and that someone was still out there. "Who killed him and how?"

"I don't know the killer's name, but his face is seared in my memory. The dead look in his eyes as he plunged the glowing blade into Bub's chest. Bub burned so bright. Then he was gone, and I...I was back here. Trapped. Alone and waiting."

The rush of blood in my head drowned out her words. Theo knew the killer. Together we could find him and finally get answers as to why? Why kill Satan? Was the killer linked to the fawda? There had to be a bigger plot here. Who was the mastermind?

"Theo, if you saw the killer again, would you recognize him?"

"Oh, yes, Nyx. I would. I'd recognize him." There was a hard, bitter edge to her voice now.

"Then let's do this. I'll let you see through my eyes if you respect my privacy."

"Agreed. But you must promise not to tell the princes of my existence. Bub always said they would try to own me. Use me. I don't want to be used."

"I won't let you be. But I need something from you too. I need you to tell me if you see the killer."

There was a smile in her voice when she spoke next. "Oh yes. I'll tell you, and together we'll find a way to make him pay." I liked the sound of that. "I knew you were the one as soon as I felt you in the seat. His presence is strongest in you, and that is why I choose you. Will you bind with me, Nyx?"

"Heck yes!"

FIFTY

Afizzing sensation raced through my veins, and a pressure settled at the back of my mind.

I had a rider in my head. And even though part of me said I should be panicking, my senses were calm, as if they knew this was meant to be. That this was right.

"Thank you," Theo said. "Shall we wake now?"

"Yeah, Theo, let's do it. Let's wake up."

Theo's world winked out. I was back in the real world, in the throne room with everyone's attention on me. Theo was a comforting presence in the back of my mind, her power seated in my veins, ready for me to use if need be. My eyes heated. She was looking out at the people in the room. Knots of tension formed in my belly because if the killer was in this room...

The heat ebbed and died.

We were clear.

"Nyx?" Sin moved closer. "What happened?"

But he wasn't the one I needed to speak to. He hadn't been here when my father was killed, so I focused on Ramiel.

"How did my father die? Who killed him, and how did they kill him?"

The room went silent.

Ramiel looked across the room to where the witnesses and my siblings were sitting. "Everyone. Out. Now."

"No!" I stood slowly. "My siblings will stay. Get the witnesses to sign whatever needs to be signed, give me my damn crown, then we talk."

Sin smiled thinly. "You heard your Satan, now get to it."

WE GATHERED in the opulent chambers behind the throne room—special quarters for Satan to entertain guests.

I pulled Artimus close. "Do you know how he died?"

"He was burned. Charred. But there was no evidence of a fire."

"Because the fire came from within," Ramiel said. "Caused by the weapon with which he was killed."

Levistus and Merihem exchanged glances.

"A celestial blade," Sin said.

I looked to Levistus. "Like the one you were going to kill me with?"

"That particular blade was repurposed to kill daimons," Levistus said. "A pure celestial blade only kills celestials. It is, in fact, the only thing that *can* kill an original fallen, and it is for that reason that they were locked away."

"So you're saying one's missing?"

"No," Merihem said. "We counted. There are none missing from our vaults. Which means there is another blade out there somewhere."

"You're telling me there's an assassin running around who has a weapon that can kill you guys?"

"Being vulnerable heightens the experience of living," Merihem said. "It makes every moment precious to know that it could be your last."

Whatever.

"A little maudlin, don't you think?" Sin said. Then to me, "Why ask about Beelzebub's death now?"

Theo stirred in my mind, warning me to keep her secret. "Seems like as good a time as any. I'm just annoyed I didn't ask sooner."

"None of us did," Mallini said. "We were all focused on the trials."

"There's a killer out there with a weapon that can wipe you out," Gus pointed out. "A killer who has an agenda we don't understand."

"He could be working with the fawda," Ignatius added. "Or have an altogether different plan."

"Or he may simply have had a grudge against Beelzebub," Levistus said. "I wanted to kill him plenty of times."

"And maybe you did," Ignatius said. "Any of you could have. You have the weapons."

"True," Ramiel said. "But we did not do this. We would not kill our own, when there are so few of us left."

"I believe you," Artimus said. "Beelzebub spoke about the brotherhood of the fallen, how after being forced to slay your own kind in the heaven's war, you vowed never to slay your kind again."

"But we did," Ramiel said bitterly. "During the Chaos War, many original fallen were infected, and they killed their brethren using the blades."

"It was why we gathered every blade and locked them away," Merihem said.

"But you either missed one, or someone managed to

make one," Gus said. "Could someone have forged one? What material are the blades made from?"

Sin looked at him in surprise. "Irridiam, but it's only available in heaven."

"If you fell, other things could have too, right?"

"It's a possibility," Ramiel said. "Which is why we've taken precautions against attack using special sigils hidden on our bodies to warn us of the presence of irridiam."

"What matters now is establishing your position as Satan," Levistus said. "Because once we do find the mastermind behind the assassination or the fawda finally reveal themselves, we'll need the power of the seat at our backs to defend our realms."

Theo stirred again, listening, watching.

"What do you mean, you'll need the power?"

The princes looked to Sin, which was strange, because he'd been absent during this whole setup.

"The seat holds a little power from every realm," Sin said. "Even the ones that fell during the Chaos War."

Whoa, wait a minute. "How is that possible if those fallen are dead?"

It was Ramiel who answered me. "When we came to this world, we, the nine most powerful originals, siphoned a little of our power into a crystal which we sealed away. After the Chaos War, after many fell and dissent erupted, we decided to form Morningstar, named after Lucifer, our fallen brother. We channeled the power from the crystal into the throne. We chose Beelzebub as the peacemaker because of his relationship to us all. His ability for democracy, his sharp mind and passion for knowledge made him the perfect candidate. It helped that he was also Lucifer's closest ally."

"Helped your story," Ignatius said.

Lucifer had freed the infection and caused the abyss to fall, but all they'd focused on was him closing the breach. They'd left out the daimon queen's part. Left out her sacrifice and woven a tale that made the fallen the saviors.

Ramiel sighed. "Yes, well, stories bind people, and this one helped us create peace."

Sin's jaw ticked, his attention on a point over my head. Did the part of him that was Lucifer feel remorse for his actions?

"We chose Beelzebub to bind to the crystal's power and to the throne. The power now belongs to his bloodline, to you. And it is your duty to use it to defend this world and its creatures in any way that you can."

"Morningstar is a haven," Merihem said. "The courts are connected to it for a reason, and now, so are you."

I wanted to ask more. To ask how the seat's power would defend us, but there was a knock on the door, and a silver-skinned conji wearing a dark-blue hooded robe entered.

"Your Grace, your summons has arrived."

He was looking at me. "Summons?"

"The source has sent a doorway."

My questions would have to wait. I was off to the afterlife.

FIFTY-ONE

Ramiel whisked me through a door at the back of the guest chambers and into a small entranceway that housed an elevator with a golden door. A smooth glass panel was built into the wall beside it.

"You need to press your palm to the panel there," Ramiel said. "This is a doorway to the source, but only when she opens it."

"How did the conji know the door was ready?"

"Morningstar is one huge machine made with many cogs, and it functions because each cog knows its place and plays its part."

He was trying to be subtle, but I didn't have time for pussyfooting around. "If this is your way of telling me not to ask questions, then save it. You know as well as I do that knowledge is power."

"Yes, I suppose it is." He smiled tightly. "I'm beginning to believe that telling you *not* to do anything is pointless. You'll do what you want regardless."

He made it sound like I made flippant decisions, as if I

didn't weigh up the pros and cons, which was bullshit. "I do what's best for myself and the people I care about."

His whiskey eyes hardened. "Maybe so. But now that you're Satan, you'll need to do what's best for *all* your people, even the ones you've never met..." He leaned in slightly. "Even the ones you hate."

Until coming to Morningstar, I'd always looked out for myself and my small circle of loved ones. But my small world grew when I met my siblings, and now the whole of Morningstar was my responsibility.

Acknowledging that invited a weight to settle on my shoulders.

But I'd be damned if I let him see it. "I'll do my job just fine. Why don't *you* focus on doing yours and find the bastard who killed my father?" I pressed my palm to the panel, and the elevator door slid open.

It was only when I was standing inside the small space with the doors closing on Ramiel's stupidly gorgeous face that I realized I hadn't brought an emissary with me.

The doors closed.

Too late now.

The inside of the elevator was a four-by-four golden box, but before claustrophobia could set in, the space lit up so bright I had to cover my eyes. For a moment there was nothing. No body. No breath. No pressure at the back of my head. Zilch.

When the light died, I could no longer sense Theo in my mind. Maybe the afterlife was somewhere she couldn't travel, even when bonded to me.

The doors opened into a small stone courtyard. The gray walls hung with flowering plants, and moss made patterns across the flagstones. There was a fountain in the center of the yard, and a woman with long golden hair stood peering into the water. Her back was to me, so I couldn't see her face, and I wasn't sure she'd sensed my presence until she spoke.

"Do come in, dear," she said. "I won't be a moment."

I stepped into the courtyard. "I'm assuming you're the source."

"You assume correctly. And you must be the new Satan."

"That's right." What now? Should I wait here or go over to her?

"Come over here, child. I need your opinion."

She didn't look up at me when I joined her at the fountain. Her attention was on the water's surface, where a scene was being magically projected. People sat around a large table drinking from mugs. They looked like they were a family, a woman and four...no, five males, but the image focused on one male in particular.

"Does he look happy to you?" she asked.

He was smiling, eyes bright with mirth. "Sure. He looks happy enough."

She sighed. "I thought as much." She waved a hand and the image rippled then vanished. "Shall we get down to business?" She finally turned her face up to mine and smiled.

This was the source? She looked too young to be the ruler of the afterlife, but then looks could be deceiving in my world, and when I looked past her sweet, heart-shaped face and into her somber gray eyes, there was eons of wisdom staring back at me.

"I can see why Loke was so taken with you," she said.

Good, she'd brought him up. "And you punished him for helping me."

"Is that what you think?" She arched a fine brow. "That I punished him?"

"Didn't you?"

"No. I did *not* punish him." She looked sad about that. "There would have been little point in it."

"What's that supposed to mean?" She walked away from the fountain, leaving me no choice but to follow her. "Why did you make him leave Morningstar?"

"It was time for him to return," she said. "He'd played his part."

"Played his part? Life isn't a theater production."

"Of course it is," she snapped. "And we all have a part to play."

She was beginning to get on my nerves. "And what was his part, hmmm? To watch over me? Why?"

Her eyes narrowed, and her face sharpened. "I think you're under the misconception that I owe you answers." Was her voice deeper? "Watch your tone when you speak to me."

Some primitive part of me warned me to back off, reminding me that this creature was no ordinary being. That the sweet face and doe eyes were merely a façade. I had no idea what I was truly dealing with. Yet. Best to err on the side of caution. For now.

I dipped my head. "I apologize. I just need to know he's all right."

That seemed to placate her because her features softened once more. "I can tell you that he's home. He's safe. And he's happy."

Happy? He was happy without me...

"You mustn't worry about him, Nyx. You have more important things to concern yourself with. You have a realm to run. You have threats to root out. People you need to save, people like your nightmare and your sibling."

"How do you know all of this?"

"I know many things," she said almost wearily. "Too

many things. I've seen worlds born and die. Warriors and champions walk their paths and rise to glory or become immortalized in death as heroes. There's nothing I haven't seen."

I didn't care about what she'd seen or done. "I want to see Loke."

Her expression hardened once more. "No."

Dammit. Backing down here wasn't an option. "Why not?"

"Because I said so!" Her face contorted into a gray mask with dark pits for eyes, and her voice invaded my head, rattling my brain. But it was over in a flash, and her sweet visage was back. She smoothed down her skirts and gave me a close-lipped smile. "I do apologize; I'm a little sensitive today. How about we get down to business?"

I wanted to argue with her, but once again, alarm bells in my head warned me to back off. Getting to Loke meant staying on her good side. Maybe I could win her over in a visit or two, and if not, then I'd find a way to bypass her altogether.

I returned her smile and forced my shoulders to relax. "You're right. We should get down to business." Whatever that was.

"Good. I have something for you. Something that Beelzebub agreed he and his blood would carry for me." She held up a hand, and an amulet appeared on her palm, a red stone surrounded by precious metal.

I'd seen it before. In a painting of Beelzebub. He'd been wearing it. "What is it for?"

"Nothing you need worry about. Your only obligation is to wear it."

Ominous. "All the time?"

She smiled again. "You won't have a choice in that

matter. Once you place it around your neck, it will be bonded to you, its connection to you maintained by the strength of your life force. If you die, it will be returned here to me, ready to be handed to the next Satan."

Yeah, that sounded sketchy to me. "Listen, if you want me to carry something for life, you need to tell me what it does."

She studied me speculatively for a moment. "I don't *need* to tell you anything. Information is not part of the contract Satan signed with me. But I'm feeling generous, so I'll tell you that this amulet is one element of an intricate lock."

More locks. Great. "A lock to where?"

"A prison keeping something terrifying at bay."

What was this? Load Nyx with responsibilities week? "Why can't you keep it here?"

"It's safer elsewhere, and it was decided by us all that Morningstar should house it."

"Who decided? The princes?"

"Enough with the questions. Your time here runs short. Take the amulet, put it on, and be gone."

"And if I don't?"

"Then you die." She shrugged. "I can show you the contract if you like, sealed and signed in Satan's blood, binding his progeny for all eternity."

I fucking hated this contract business. "Fine." I snatched up the amulet and slid it on. The sensation of a noose tightened around my throat before melting away, leaving the amulet hanging neatly between my breasts.

I tucked it under my tunic. "We good then?"

She studied me for a moment, a small smile playing on her lips. "Yes, Nyx. We're good. You may go."

"Can I come back to visit?"

She looked momentarily thrown as if no one had ever

asked to come back and see her before, and her next question confirmed my assessment. "Why?"

I shrugged. "I get the feeling I could learn a lot from you."

She didn't look convinced. "We'll see. Maybe. Soon."

I wanted to ask how soon was soon, but it was best to leave it there, on good terms. "I'll see you later then."

I headed back to the elevator, the amulet a solid weight between my breasts. Another responsibility, and no real news on Loke. I had to trust he was safe like she'd said, and not hurting somewhere.

Until I could see him and confirm it for myself, that's what I'd believe, because the alternative would drive me nuts.

The elevator doors closed, and bright light flared.

I was headed home.

FIFTY-TWO

Satan's quarters took up a whole wing that somehow backed onto the throne room. It came with its own secret passages and special guest rooms. There was a study, a library, a conference room, a balcony garden, and private kitchens where several zuni lived and prepared meals for Satan and his guests. I also had my own maids.

I'd thought we'd been spoiled in the spawn quarters, but this...This was on another level of pampering, and there was no way my siblings were missing out. With so much room to spare, it would be stupid for them to remain in the spawn quarters.

Minorax trooped in and out of the wing with boxes and cases, and my siblings directed them to the relevant rooms.

Artimus and Dhuma were busy greeting the dignitaries that were already arriving for tonight's ball, and Sin had gone off with the princes to do whatever they needed to do. The bastard hadn't bothered to take me aside and make sure I was okay or speak to me at all when I got back from seeing the source, but Ignatius was here with me.

He'd taken a tour with me, his hand in mine. Fuck Sin. Who needed him anyway?

Chase padded at my heels, chuffing now and then when we stopped to look at a painting or study the view outside one of the many windows.

My chambers were on the floor above my siblings', but we had a communal sitting area that I could get to via a separate staircase.

We did a sweep of the wing and ended back in the communal lounge—a spacious room with a hearth that you could roast a boar in, clusters of seating spots, and tiny tables to rest cups and trays on. Books and more books were neatly slotted into bookcases built into the wall, and beautifully embroidered rugs that I'd have to take my boots off to walk on covered hickory floors. Satan had taste, and it matched mine. This place could be home.

Theo was back, watching, taking it all in. But she'd been here before, so she retreated. I'd have to ask her if it was all right to share her existence with my siblings and the males I loved, but not now. Not today.

My hand went to the amulet hidden beneath my tunic.

"What is it?" Ignatius asked. "Are you hurt? You keep touching your chest."

I tugged the chain to reveal the amulet. "Getting used to this. The source said I had to wear it."

"Satan wore one exactly the same."

"It is the same." I tucked it back under my tunic. "I can't take it off. It's bound to me, and it ends up back in Tarrifel if I die."

"So when Satan died, it went back there?"

"Yep."

"Did she tell you what it was?"

"It's part of a larger lock to keep something bad at bay."

"Perfect," he said dryly.

"That's what I thought." I tipped my face up to his, and he kissed my smile. His amber eyes darkened in desire as he pulled me close, and my breath hitched in anticipation for a deeper kiss.

But the echo of boots broke the spell. He squeezed my shoulders, his gaze promising a rain check.

Nugen and Zinichi entered the room.

Zinichi carried a clothes bag slung over her shoulder, and Nugen held the box with the crown in it.

"Here you go, Nyx." He handed it to me. "Prince Ramiel said they'll crown you at the ball, since we didn't get a chance earlier."

"And your dress, love," Zinichi held out the clothes bag. "Chesra had it delivered a little while ago. There are shoes to match inside. She said to tell you you're welcome."

I took the bag, butterflies forming in my belly. "Thank you."

"Well," Nugen said. "That's all from us. It's been a pleasure and an honor working with you and—"

"We've loved every moment of it," Zinichi said, eyes misty. "You'll let me know how Sev is, won't you? When you go to visit and—"

"Wait a second...are you leaving?"

They exchanged glances.

"Well...yes," Nugen said. "We were tasked with taking care of the spawn through the trials. The trials are over. We have our Satan, so—"

"So you just go?" Veena joined us with Mallini close behind her.

Nugen scratched the back of his neck. "I was due to retire anyway."

"Do you *want* to retire?" Mallini asked.

He pushed out his bottom lip. "Pah, and sit on my ass all day?"

I looked to Zinichi. "What about you? Where will you go?"

"I'd be back managing the maids, I suppose."

Keelan and Gus entered the room and wandered over.

We were all here, just as it should be. Just as we needed it to be. "You can't go. We need you." I crossed my arms. "There are plenty of rooms here. Pick one each and move your stuff in. We have kitchens here and staff that need someone to manage them. Someone I can trust." Her mouth trembled. "Please stay. Both of you."

"We need to be sharp when it comes to combat," Keelan added. "We need you, Nugen."

Nugen sniffed, almost angrily. "Fine. There are some new blades and lightweight arrows being delivered this week. We can try those out." He rubbed his chin in thought. "Maybe we can repurpose one of conference rooms into a training room."

"I'll help," Keelan said.

I relaxed, smiling as my family made plans for our new home.

Maybe being Satan wouldn't be all work and no play. We'd start with the ball tonight.

A ball and a fancy dress. My stomach fluttered again. Crap, I was getting excited about a dance. A fucking dance. I needed to go punch something STAT. Or maybe...I slipped my hand into Ignatius's and squeezed.

He met my gaze with an inquiring one that shifted to understanding when he caught my expression.

"If you'll excuse us," Ignatius said. "I believe our new Satan needs a nap before all the festivities."

He led me away from the others and their knowing smirks, his hand a warm brand on the small of my back.

"Enjoy your nap," Mallini called out.

Cheeky bitch.

We took the stairs to my private chambers two at a time and shut the doors behind us, before turning toward each other.

"Hello, *Qalbi*," Ignatius said softly, brushing a tendril of hair off my cheek.

I gently gripped his wrist, turning my head to kiss his palm. "Will you stay the night with me tonight?"

He cupped my face and turned it up to his. "Yes. I'll stay." He kissed me softly. "I'll stay as long as you want me."

"I always want you." My breath came shallow as he trailed kisses from my mouth to just below my ear then down my neck. "I want you, Ignatius. I want us to consummate our twin flame bond. Now. Here."

He wrapped an arm around my waist and lifted me off my feet, mouth dabbing kisses up the column of my throat and leaving tingles in their wake. I wound my arms around his neck and let him take my weight. He carried me easily across the room to the stately four-poster bed hung with thick midnight-blue drapes.

This was a bed made for fun, and there was another just like it in the adjoining room. The room I'd picked out for Sev and me. But this bed...this one was for now. For Ignatius and me.

He lifted me onto the mattress, and we fell back onto the sheets, hands roaming, mouths colliding in kisses that grew in heat and desperation. The air thrummed with intention, and the bond that had existed between us from the start bloomed and tightened, drawing us closer.

I wanted to feel his skin. I wanted to taste every golden,

gorgeous inch of his body. We shucked off our clothes between kisses. Fingers glided across taut naked flesh, tracing the planes of hard-packed muscle and powerful sinew. His body was peach-soft but steely hard. The combination excited me, heightening the throb between my thighs. I hooked a leg around his hip and rolled us so that I was on top of his epic body. I slid down his torso, inch by inch, kneading his flesh and dropping soft, suckling kisses here and there. He tasted like a cinnamon roll dusted with sugar.

His fingers sank into my hair and made a fist. He looked down the hard planes of his torso, watching me through thick dark lashes, his golden gaze molten lava as it roamed over my face. "Whatever you want, *Qalbi.*"

His hand flexed and let go, surrendering his body to me. The in-control male who had instilled fear into the hearts of his people was letting me sit in the driver's seat. My stomach flipped hard. I wanted him all. I wanted him inside me, beneath me while I rode him, but I wanted to taste him first. He sucked in a sharp breath when I gripped his cock.

"Mine." I licked the head, and he groaned. "This is mine." I lapped at the slit, tasting him, salty and ready.

"Nyx..." His chest heaved.

I locked gazes with him while I took him into my mouth.

He lifted his hips, offering himself to me, hands clutching the sheets. When he moaned, heat flooded my pussy, leaving me slick and wet.

I worked him, taking him as deep as I could until he was pulsing and ready.

"No." He reached for my head, fisting my hair. "Not like this. I need to be inside you for the bond to take hold."

I released him with a pop and a final lick, then straddled his hips. His golden skin was flushed, tendrils of hair stuck to his cheeks, and his pupils were blown. He looked undone, but I wasn't finished with him yet.

I sank onto him, and this time, my groan matched his. He filled me just right, every inch of his arousal rubbing me perfectly. One roll of my hips and I knew it wouldn't be long before I came. I was swollen and ready. I needed this; I wanted this. I began to move, riding him, head thrown back while he held me tightly and thrust up to meet me. The familiar sensation of a pending orgasm tightened my body at the same time as a hollow pit opened in my chest.

He needed to fill this void. "Give it to me." My voice was a guttural demand. "Ignatius...please...Fuck. I need it. I need it now."

IGNATIUS

"Please, Ignatius. Now. I need it now."

The seed inside me, the one made for her, aches to be free. To find root inside her where it belongs. I held it at bay the last time, but it won't be cheated this time. I take control and flip her so she's beneath me and I'm driving into her, taking her with such force that her cries remain trapped in her throat. Her neck arches, and her mouth opens in a silent scream.

Mine. She's mine. My twin flame. My *qalbi*. I release the seed that will bind us.

She lets out a sob of relief then comes around me. The connection takes root. Flames fill my vision. I come so hard that I'm momentarily outside my body, watching myself take her, watching us connect in a way that transcends the physical.

I sink back into my body as the waves wash over us. Patterns bloom across my skin, snake down my arms, and slide onto her flesh, painting it with swirls and whorls to match mine.

Mine.

I press my body to hers and claim her mouth. She's mine.

FIFTY-THREE

NYX

The dress Chesra had made for me took my breath away. The fabric was black but shimmered with every movement. It had a fitted bodice with a sweetheart neckline and was cut to caress my hips and then fall in a waterfall flow to stop mere millimeters above the ground. The shoes were comfortable ballet flats the same color as the dress. Zinichi and I had decided to leave my hair loose tonight, and it fell down my back in silken, artfully teased waves. A lick of mascara, a sweep of kohl, and a smudge of blush, and I looked regally hot.

Ha. Me. This was me.

I reached up to adjust the amulet. There was no hiding it in this dress.

Zinichi watched me, hands clasped to her breast, looking every inch the proud mama. She sniffed and blinked back tears. "You look...Oh, Nyx. I'm so proud of you."

I arched a brow at Chase. "I know what Zinichi thinks, but what about you?"

He chuffed his approval with a twinkle in his warm brown eyes.

Ignatius had bowed out to let Zinichi dress me, saying he needed to join the other dukes in preparation for my official entrance at the ball, and I hadn't seen Arty or Sin since the throne room. Zepar was still healing so wouldn't be attending tonight; still, I had time to pop over and see him before the ball started. But there was one person who wouldn't see this, a person that should be here with me now.

I fingered the material, mood dipping slightly. "Sev should be here."

"You'll get him back," she said with certainty. "This is just one day. You'll have the rest of your lives together."

She was right, of course. Our separation was temporary. It didn't make it sting any less, though.

"Carriages have been drawing up all day," Zinichi said. "Dignitaries from the other realms coming through the monoports."

"Has Orina arrived yet?" I'd sent a carriage to wait for her at the station. The demon had a description of her and a sign with her name on it.

"Not yet. But I'm sure she'll be here soon," Zinichi said. "I'll take good care of her and make sure she finds a spot with your siblings until the official parts are over."

I gave her a hug. "Thank you, Zinichi. I don't know what I'd do without you."

"Any time, child. Any time."

I straightened at the knock on my door. "Come in!"

Mallini popped her head in. "Oh...Wow, Nyx..."

She entered, crimson plumes spilling down her back

and contrasting beautifully with the midnight-blue sheath dress Chesra had made for her. It was shimmery material too, and it made her eyes pop.

I let out a low wolf whistle. "You look hot."

She gave me a little twirl. "Thank you. But have you seen yourself?"

I grinned. "Chesra came through."

"I'd best check on Veena." Zinichi ducked from the room.

"Are you ready to be the center of attention for the evening?" Mallini asked.

"Not really, but it won't be so bad once the whole crowning part is over."

"Don't bet on it. Everyone will want Satan's ear; you'll be swamped. But not if you spend the night on the dance floor with me." She gave me a kitten grin and reached for my hands.

We stood face to face. This stubborn, prickly female who'd started out as my nemesis now held a special place in my heart. "I love you, Mallini."

Her grin softened to a smile. "I love you too."

"Once the pomp is over, I'll speak to the princes about releasing your mother and whatever official stuff needs to happen to make it so."

She blinked up at me in surprise. "This is your night. You shouldn't be thinking about—"

"It's been in the back of my mind all day. I want to pardon her."

"What?" She stared at me in shock. "She conspired against you. Nyx, if you pardon her, you'll give the wrong impression. People will think you're weak. You need to punish her."

I allowed my lips to curve in a wicked smile. "Oh, I think having to work for and take orders from me will be enough punishment, don't you think?" She opened her mouth to protest, but I cut her off. "Erinea has been the heart of Morningstar for decades. She knows this place, the people, and their secrets. It would be foolish to let her go. Umbrane knows how dangerous she is too. Framing her was probably his way of getting rid of her without getting his hands dirty. So we keep her close." I shrugged. "And we offer her a second chance."

Mallini's jaw tensed, her eyes glittering with emotion. "If she betrays us again, I'll kill her myself."

I believed it. "Listen, I promised Zepar I'd see him before the ball, but I'll be back in time for the escort to the ballroom."

"I'll let the others know."

Chase made to follow. "Chase, stay with the others." I crouched and rubbed my cheek against his face. "I'll be back soon."

A secret passageway got me to the guest wing. Nugen had given me a quick tour of the passages earlier, pointing out the symbols for the various wings. I came out in the southern guest wing where Zepar was housed. The corridors were empty as I hurried to his quarters. I had forty minutes tops before the ball, so thirty if I wanted to get back in time for the escort. But I'd promised I'd come see him, and I wasn't one to break a promise.

Besides, I *wanted* to see him.

I wanted him to see me in this dress.

I knocked on the main doors, and after a moment they opened.

Zepar was on his feet, a black T-shirt pulled over his bandaged torso. He'd tugged on his jeans too, but his feet were bare. He had color in his cheeks now, and his lips, which had been pale before, were now pink and rosy.

"You came." Relief etched his face.

"You doubted me?"

He stepped back to let me in and closed the door. "That dress..." His gaze dropped to the amulet, then back up to my face. "Nyx...you look..." His throat bobbed, and his eyes darkened. "I wish..."

"What?" I moved closer to him and tipped my face up to his. "What do you wish?"

He dropped his forehead to mine, and I caught a whiff of aniseed. "I wish I could be with you at the ball. Stand by you and hold your hand."

Butterflies beat their wings in my belly. "You can. You could come for a little while."

He smiled, but it was more a smile of regret than anything. "I can't. Not this time. But there will be a time when we stand side by side while the world watches. I promise you." His lips hovered above mine. "A time when you'll be mine." His hand slid up my neck to cup my cheek. "For the first time in my existence, I'm in love." He brushed my nose with his, then he kissed me. It was a soft kiss, a gentle pressure that had heat spiraling in my chest. I gripped his biceps, leaning into him, opening for him. The sharp, distinct taste of aniseed rippled over my tongue, leaving a strange numbness in its wake.

The back of my head tightened.

Something was wrong.

He broke the kiss and looked down at me with sorrow. "You'll understand one day soon. I promise."

"Wha...wh..." My mouth refused to work, and then my knees gave way. He caught me, holding me against him as my body gave out and my head fell back.

His lips...The kiss...The aniseed smell.

No... "You, pois...yuh..."

"You'll be okay," he said. "I just need your heart to slow down enough." The back of his hand brushed my breastbone, taking the weight of the amulet.

Pressure bloomed in the back of my mind.

Theo.

Theo, help me.

But she couldn't read my thoughts; she could only watch.

"It'll be like falling asleep," Zepar said. "When you wake, I'll be gone." He laid me down on the soft carpet, his hand still wrapped around my amulet. "The toxin is temporary. It won't do lasting damage." He sounded like he was trying to convince himself.

My eyes wanted to close, but I forced them to stay open, to ask him: why? Why do this? How could he protect me one moment, sacrifice his wing for me, and then do this now?

He began to whisper strange words.

What was he saying?

The room darkened. I was slipping away, each thud of my heart taking longer and longer.

Theo was a stark pressure now, a writhing warning in the back of my mind as she tried to fight off the darkness that was pulling me under, but my power and hers were locked behind a wall, held at bay by whatever drug he'd poisoned me with.

I couldn't fight it any longer.

"It'll all make sense soon," Zepar said. "I promise you."

Theo's voice sliced through my mind just before darkness swallowed me whole.

He's the one. He killed Beelzebub.

Nyx's story concludes in Demon Wrath, the final book in the Demons of Morningstar.

Other Books by Debbie Cassidy

Debbie has a large backlist of books which you can check out on her Amazon Author page or on her website, debbiecassidyauthor.com.

About the Author

Debbie Cassidy lives in England, Bedfordshire, with her three kids and very supportive husband. Coffee and chocolate biscuits are her writing fuels of choice, and she is still working on getting that perfect tower of solitude built in her back garden. Obsessed with building new worlds and reading about them, she spends her spare time daydreaming and conversing with the characters in her head. She writes Urban Fantasy Romance and Paranormal Reverse Harem Romance with kick-ass female leads and swoon-worthy heroes.

STAY IN TOUCH WITH DEBBIE CASSIDY

Join her <u>Newsletter</u>
Hang out in her <u>Facebook Reader Group</u>
Or
Follow her on <u>Bookbub</u>